NOTHING

LEFT

TO BURN

HEATHER EZELL

RAZORBILL®

RAZORBILL®

An Imprint of Penguin Random House LLC
Penguin.com

RAZORBILL & colophon is a registered trademark
of Penguin Random House LLC.

First published in the United States of America by Razorbill,
an imprint of Penguin Random House LLC, 2018

LIBRARY OF CONGRESS CATALOGING-IN-PUBLICATION DATA IS AVAILABLE

ISBN: 9780448494265

Printed in the United States of America

1 3 5 7 9 10 8 6 4 2

Book design by Corina Lupp

For Amber, Madeline, and Grant

1

5:22 A.M.

The Sunday morning after I lose my virginity, I wake to knocking. My mom and dad's alarm clock reads 5:22 A.M. More pounding from downstairs—loud and rapid—and I wonder if it's Brooks. *No.* He's probably still at the party, passed out on a couch, or better yet, on the floor where I left him. This thought enables me to move.

I jump from the bed, Mom's caramel afghan around my shoulders. The room sways. My hips ache, and there's a raw throbbing between my legs. I might still be drunk. I might only be hungover. I need to shower. Need to go back to bed.

I pull aside the curtains. It's still dark, but porch lights and streetlights and brake lights and red and blue lights illuminate the dense smoke that hazes the street. Our pepper tree whips in the October wind, spraying leaves on the police car idling at our mailbox. A man shouts. The lashing gale takes his words. The doorbell rings—once, twice, three times.

Move. I need to move.

I drop the afghan, run downstairs, and yank the front door open to smoke and two firefighters. My dad's old In-N-Out shirt sticks to my back. I'm not wearing a bra, and rum laces the spit beneath my tongue.

"Mandatory evacuation," the older man says, his gray hair a crown of ash. "The fire is approaching the ridge."

I peer across the street for evidence—flames, a spark—but the scrubby bank's top is concealed by white smoke.

The younger firefighter lowers his chin, shifts. If he were a friend, I'd think he's about to hug me, but instead he coughs with a wheeze and says, "Miss—"

"Brooks said it'd be okay," I say, because he did. But the words are mud in my throat and I know it's not true, I know it's not okay.

"Can we talk to your parents?" The older firefighter studies me, and I wonder if he knows Brooks. "You have twenty minutes before you have to go."

The blister on my palm throbs against the door, and I'm about to say *fine, goodbye* when I see a deer at the base of the hill that leads up to the Cleveland National Forest, where the fire burns. The deer is looking up toward the pluming smoke, as if she can see the flames. Where will the deer go?

I step back. "I'll wake my parents," I lie. "We'll be out."

The potential hugger says, "Twenty minutes."

I slam the door—*evacuated*—and scramble to the kitchen. The hardwood floor slips beneath my feet. I spin to the kitchen phone, the landline Dad insists we keep specifically for emergencies. *Mom, pick up, pick up, please.* "Hi, this is Alison. I can't answer my—" I slam the phone down, imagining her and Maya nestled in their air-conditioned room at the Hilton. Maya has her eye-mask on, socks with Vaseline on her toes. Her audition doesn't start for another five hours.

The oven clock reads 5:32 A.M. My backyard is an eerie gold. Is the light from the fire or the soon-to-rise sun? I call my mom once more, watching the door of Maya's old plastic cottage swing open and shut. An olive tree branch floats in the pool. Mom's phone rings out again.

I call Dad. He's in Colorado for a work conference. It's an hour ahead there, and he's an early riser. He has to be awake.

"Audrey?"

"The fire—"

"Go back to bed," he says. "It's fine."

"Firefighters came to the door! They said we have to leave."

"What? When?"

"Now, Dad, just now."

I clutch the porcelain edge of the kitchen sink and hang my head down, phone still pressed to my ear. My cereal bowl from yesterday morning is crusted, a trail of ants line the rim. I think of last night, and I think I might puke. Brooks's lips on my stomach. *Now? You're really ready now?* I spit into the sink, aching to be empty, to erase every curve of my body.

"Listen," Dad says. "Grab some clothes. Your schoolwork, whatever you need." If he were home he'd be acting in fine precision—checking tasks off his mental evacuation to-do list by the minute. "The metal safe in the office, that's *extremely* important. And the photo tub! Don't forget the photo tub in the family room. Pack all that up and go and meet Mom or head to the school or somewhere. I've got to get to a meeting, but I'll call you after, okay?"

I want to crawl into Maya's faded plastic cottage and chain the pink door shut. At thirteen, she hasn't been inside for years—surely the grass has grown high and dry inside. Warm hay. It'll make a nice bed. The phone is slick in my grasp. I think of last night and how I slept in my parents' bed. How I

3

burrowed beneath the duvet like I used to as a kid when I was sick, nuzzling my mom's pillow.

Dad's still talking, still listing.

It's 5:36. I've wasted four minutes.

"Don't forget the safe. Crap, the desktop too," he says.

The oven clock twitches. 5:37.

"Dad." I'm done spitting at the ants in the sink. "I need to go."

"You can do this," he says. "Call me when you're out."

The phone is glued to my hand, and my tongue is glued to the roof of my mouth.

"I love you," he says.

It's too late for me to respond, to say *I love you too*, because I've already peeled the phone from my ear, my thumb is on the End button, I'm already running upstairs. I throw my gym shorts and the In-N-Out shirt onto my bedroom floor, then snap on a bra, pull on a blouse, zip up my jeans. I yank on a hoodie and grab my cell, its charger too. My hands shake. I shove shirts and underwear and sweats into a duffle bag. My backpack is untouched from school on Friday. I push in my laptop, and it's ready to go.

For half a beat, I stare at the pillow Brooks gave me on Thursday for our three-month anniversary. It's embroidered with a list of epic couples: *Romeo & Juliet, Lancelot & Guinevere, Antony & Cleopatra, Odysseus & Penelope,* and in the middle, in red: *Brooks & Audrey.*

I take my crocheted green baby blanket instead.

The small metal safe and my backpack go into my truck first, followed by Dad's computer. Outside, the dry wind is hot. The dark sky is still tinted gold, and the two firefighters are only a few houses away. They'll be back.

I cough on the smoke. Above, a helicopter fights the wind, its red light blurred. I wish the sun would rise and the smoke would clear.

5:49. *Another twelve minutes gone.* I run back inside.

The giant tub of photos is impossible to move. I was supposed to scan them all onto a hard drive this summer, but I was too busy making out with Brooks. I yank out the mass of plastic grocery bags from underneath the kitchen sink, cram them full of images of my youth, and lug them to the truck. I keep the doors open for the cab's light, and embers drift in the glare. Back inside. Back outside. A bag rips open and pictures scatter across the driveway, snapshots of a vacation to Big Sur spinning in the wind.

"No!" I chase the photos. "Stop!"

Beyond our yards' dividing hedge, Mr. Peterson is carrying a crate to his SUV. "Crazy, isn't it?" he calls over. He's known me since I was in Pull-Ups. "You need any help? Your parents home?"

"We're good," I say. "Thanks."

I pull a photo from the rosemary needles—a picture of all of us, my family, sitting on a collapsed sequoia. Dad's wearing the goofy voyager hat he still has and Mom still hates. Mom's holding toddler Maya, mid-wail, on her lap. And then there's pigtailed seven-year-old me, showing off my newly braced teeth, red-faced and grinning as if I won a trip to Disneyland.

A second helicopter roars above.

Another minute gone.

I search for the photos in the rosemary bushes, but it's too dark, too windy, and I can't stop coughing. I'll have to give up on them. Another fire truck flashes into view and parks at the base of the bank. Did Brooks's cell finally ring? Are his boots laced tight, is he somewhere nearby, finally living his dream, fighting the fight? A cop car crawls, its headlights blinding and intercom booming: "Mandatory evacuation. Evacuate immediately. Mandatory evacuation. Evacuate immediately."

But I'm still not done.

I run inside one last time, up to Maya's room. It doesn't smell like fire in here, but instead like snickerdoodles and vanilla, as if she's stashed cookies in the walls. Her bed is made, zebra comforter smoothed down, stiff sequined pillows properly placed, like always.

Donny, the ratty stuffed elephant I gave to Maya on her sixth birthday, hides behind her therapeutic memory foam pillow. I picked him out myself at Target. Maya toted Donny around for years, to the doctor appointments and the hospital visits, and—when she was declared lymphoma-free—to the studio. He'd sleep in the car, and then in her dance bag, snuggled with her street shoes and jeans. But then Maya sprouted four inches, and Mom redecorated her room to look like a college dorm, and suddenly Maya was too classy for the old elephant.

But Maya is big on beauty sleep, and I drink caffeine and can be sneaky, so I know she still dozes off with the stuffed elephant tucked beneath her cheek.

I snatch Donny and scan the rest of the room. Her walk-in closet is a mess—piles of clothes that somehow smell, though Maya never smells. I'd take her journal from her sock drawer too, but then she'd know I've known its hiding place. I choose her first pointe shoes instead.

Donny and shoes in hand, I rush into my parents' room and grab Mom's afghan from where I dropped it on the floor. She brought it home from her and Dad's fifteenth-anniversary trip to Italy years ago. I ignore their closet—they each have a suitcase full of clothes with them—and charge down the stairs and out of the house. I lock the dead bolt. Dad will be pleased.

6:01.

I'm late. The whole street is late.

I back out of the driveway and accelerate away, past my neighbors shoving their lives into their cars, past the waving firefighters and cops and the evacuation boundary, and into the still-sleeping, still-dreaming land where families are tucked into their beds—families that won't wake for their pancake breakfasts and church gatherings and golf club visits until the sun rises over the flames.

I drive out of Coto de Caza's gates not knowing if I'll still have a home when the day is over. The burn on my hand is tender and hot, and I think about Thursday night, when the sparklers blew, and last night, and what I did and did not say.

2

FRIDAY

The fire broke out Friday morning in the neighboring canyons of the Cleveland National Forest, crawling southwest into Caspers Wilderness Park.

Ash swirled down onto my high school, but according to the *Orange County Register*, Caspers Fire was calmly blazing southwest through the government-protected valleys of cacti and oak and flax. Coto de Caza residents were safe to remain in their air-conditioned homes. Windows locked. Lawns watered. Patio furniture cushions moved inside. We were safe.

That night at Celinda's Deli, Brooks licked salsa from his fingers and said, "I'd be out there now if it was really that bad. It's in my battalion, you know."

His overgrown hair was still damp from his shower at the gym, after his supposedly essential daily lifting with his crew—or, really, three of the other Level 2 Reserve volunteers who assist the Trabuco Canyon careers. He looked vulnerable like that, fresh from the shower, his hair flat and sticking to his forehead.

My quesadilla sat untouched. It hurt to use my right hand because of the blister on my palm. My lips still tingled from my afternoon with Hayden. And across the table, Brooks watched me in breaths.

"Audie," he said.

He reached to me, and I smelled his sweat and his soap. He rubbed his thumb across my cheek. Just a brush, and I leaned in, as I always do, inhaling his skin. Under the table, my knees were still pressed together—because my body hadn't yet received the message that this was him, Brooks, *my* Brooks. He felt like he always did, warm and somehow safe.

"I lost my Zippo." He dropped a white lighter on the table. "Cameron gave me that Zippo for my seventeenth birthday, and now it's God knows where."

I clenched and unclenched my hands. He'd never told me that before, that the Zippo was a birthday gift from his older brother.

"It'll show up," I said. "When did you last have it?"

He barely flinched. "Yesterday, probably."

I stared at my quesadilla, the cheese oozing onto the plate. "I don't think I'm going tomorrow," I said. "To Maya's audition."

"What?" He crunched down on a chip. "You've been planning on it since July. She's been working for it for even longer. I thought it was a big deal."

"It *is* a big deal, but Derek's party is still on." I glanced up. "I want to go. See my friends."

He squinted. "You'd rather go to a miserable party than support your sister?" He even laughed. "What have you done with my Audrey?"

I broke a chip in two. "I'd only drag Maya down."

Brooks finished his taco and sat back against the sunset-pink plastic of the booth. He looked up at the hanging light, and I chewed on my water straw, bracing myself for what he might say.

"Audie," he said. "If this is about last night—"

"So our anniversary was kind of a bust." I shrugged. "Big deal."

He reached for me again, but this time I didn't let his hand touch my skin.

"Hey," he said.

"Don't." I forked my quesadilla.

"This isn't you."

I let him put his hand on my knee under the table, because that's something I would do. Friday night, me not eating Mexican food, me feeling nothing and my body feeling everything, I wanted to scratch his skin until he bled. I wanted to lower myself into his arms and let him kiss my head. I wanted to let the entire restaurant know that my heart was beating the fuck out of my chest, and I wanted to scream at Brooks, *Look at me look at me look at what you've made me.* I wanted the naive summer back, so sweet it hurts your teeth. Not this, not October.

Brooks's lopsided left eye was acting up, tears slipping out—a faulty tear duct courtesy of a childhood rottweiler attack. He kept one hand on my knee and, with the other, snagged another chip and asked, "You actually want to go to that party?" Brooks has always hated parties.

"I do," I said, because maybe if I said it enough, it'd be the truth. "It'll have a good view of the fire."

"Let's hope it's out by then." But his hand came off my leg, and he gave himself away. He propped his elbows on the table and toyed with the lighter.

Stared at the flame. Brooks wanted the fire to burn long enough for him to be needed.

His cell phone had been at his side all summer long, his station-specific ringtone wailing for fender benders on Antonio Parkway, fatal teenage drag races down in the canyons, and a few structure fires due to poor wiring or sleepy smokers, but no real-deal wild land fires. And Friday night, the air spiked with a peppering of ash, a fire hissing just fifteen miles south, Brooks's cell still hadn't rung. The San Juan Capistrano and Coto de Caza crews were handling it. Caspers Fire was 80 percent contained and the trenches were dug.

Everything was normal. No danger lurking under the table. It was Friday night, the first week of October, and Brooks and I were simply eating Mexican food after a somewhat turbulent Thursday, a somewhat turbulent three-month anniversary.

Brooks peeled my quesadilla off my plate and finished it in five bites. I chewed a tortilla chip, slow, careful, the salt sparking on my tongue, while he wiped his mouth with a napkin and shook his head.

"This won't be it," he said. "This isn't my fire."

3

6:21 A.M.

When he calls, I'm retching into a Starbucks bathroom toilet. His name on the screen is a flying arrow. There's no time to duck, to reconsider. I wipe my mouth with the back of my hand and answer. I can't say hi, can only say his name. "Brooks."

"I'm headed to the station." His voice whooshes, because he has me on speakerphone and his window is down, letting in the new day, the smoke. "They'll be calling us within the hour. I can feel it." I picture him easily: sunglasses on, sleep-manic hair, lips split into a grin. "All local responders are on it. Audrey, it blew up."

"I know," I say. "I was evacuated."

He doesn't respond to this because he's not listening to me. "I wanted to tell you, *need* to tell you before I go out there, I love you," he says, and my chest compresses, a rock in my throat. He loves me. The words melt like ice in my hands. "We've got this handled," he says. "It'll be out in no time." He says this as if he's chief commander, not a volunteer. Not just a boy who likes to play with fire. I've never heard him so euphoric. He pauses before asking, "Where are you? Are you safe?"

I guess he is kind of listening to me.

"Starbucks. Puking the night out," I say. "Maybe homeless." I meant it as a joke—making light of a dire situation—but my voice cracks on the word. *Homeless.*

I ache for Maya and my mom and dad, ache so bad to be home on an easy Sunday morning. Dad making scrambled eggs with too much salsa, Maya stretching across the living room floor, me arguing with Mom that I'm old enough to drink coffee—doing nothing, doing everything.

"Oh, Audie," Brooks says.

I close my eyes. "Stop."

There is a click in the line, and suddenly his breath is closer, a phone held to his ear. "Hey," he says. "I need to take this call, but you be safe today. Okay?"

"*You* be safe," I say.

"You're kidding. I was trained for this." He laughs. He actually laughs. "I'll call you as soon as I can. We'll get this figured out. I'll see you soon."

As if it's a normal Sunday, just like any other day.

I want it to be okay. I need it to be okay, so I say, "Yeah."

"I have a fire to fight," he says. "I guess it is mine."

He says, "I love you," and hangs up before I can respond, before he can hear me say, "Mine."

Though I'm not sure why I say that. I never wanted a fire to claim.

4

SATURDAY

The party was at Derek Sanders's place—the first weekend of October paired with his parents being out of town apparently the perfect excuse to throw "the season's greatest Halloween rager."

Early afternoon, when the sky was yellow, Derek posted online:

Feel the heat? See those flames? Yeah, gonna be an epic night, girls and boys, so don't let the smoke scare you away. Come to my place, take swigs on the pirate ship, and embrace the rage. BYOB, witches and bitches!

I wasn't planning on going to the party. Grace's Saturday was booked with babysitting and preparing for her girlfriend's birthday on Sunday. (Quinn had yet to see the Redwoods, and that needed to be remedied ASAP via a camping trip up the central coast.) And if Grace wasn't going to the party, I wasn't going to the party. She's the spine of my social life.

More importantly, Mom had planned a girls' night in Newport Beach for Maya's audition. The Orange County Institute of Ballet isn't even forty minutes away, but Mom's convinced that treating an audition extravagantly results in dancing extravagantly. I wasn't interested in the girls' night or the glitzy hotel—I only cared about being there for Maya. My little sister was doing it, her *thing,* pursuing her dream.

I had every intention to go to the audition with her and my mom.

But Friday afternoon, as the fire grew, I was wavering and making party plans with Brooks, and by Saturday morning, I knew I absolutely needed to stay home. The fire's containment had dropped to 50 percent overnight: far too close to out of control. I had to stay. I had to keep watch, though I couldn't explain it—my need to stay close to the fire.

I broke the news to my mom at the last possible moment, when she was polishing herself for their departure in the cave of her walk-in closet.

"You don't want to support Maya?" she asked.

I sat on the edge of her porcelain bathtub. "I can support her from home," I said, running my toes across the cool travertine tile. "The oh-so-distant half hour south."

"This is a big deal, Audrey." A slam of a drawer. "How far she's come."

"Of course it's a big deal," I said. Because it is—three years ago we didn't know if Maya would still be alive, let alone auditioning for her dream academy.

"Well." The soft scratch of clothing hangers. "I'm not exactly comfortable with leaving you alone for the night with your boyfriend so nearby."

"*Mom,*" I said. "I'm sixteen."

A drawer rolled closed. "Yes, exactly."

"Brooks will probably be working anyway," I said, "and I have to start my psychology project—it'll take the entire weekend." Lie. "I'm meeting with Hayden."

Not a lie, though Hayden and I wouldn't be starting until Sunday night, so I guess kind of a lie. "I *want* to go, I do, for Maya, but it'd be irresponsible."

Mom emerged from the closet, a chiffon scarf around her neck. "Is this about you, sweetie? It's understandable if you're jealous." She touched my head, as if checking for a fever, as if a fever would expose my secrets. "It's okay if this is triggering some regrets."

I pushed off from the tub's edge. "Now I'm *definitely* not going," I said, heading for the hall. Two years ago, I quit ballet—walked out of the same audition Maya will rock today, and my parents are still convinced that this was a mistake.

"Run it by Maya!" Mom called.

I knocked on my sister's door, turned the knob. Pop music played loudly from her laptop. She was sprawled out in the splits, her stomach hollow and elbows down on the carpet, texting.

I coughed at the thick scent of vanilla cookie spray. "Hey."

"I heard you and Mom," she said.

I leaned against her mirrored dresser. "You mad?"

Maya looked up. "I thought you were excited," she said. "Like for-real excited."

My heart ached. "I *am* for-real excited," I said. "I'm beyond excited."

"But you'd rather get drunk and kissy-kissy with Brooks?"

"I don't get drunk," I said. "It gives me hiccups."

She laughed at that and asked, "Can you keep a secret?"

"What? Why?" I stilled at my response, at my lack of a simple *yes*.

Maya looked at her hands, her white skin flushing pink. "I need to tell Mom something, but she's gonna flip—"

Mom jumped through the doorway. "Flip about what?"

"Maya would really love to get a pedicure after the audition," I said, because sometimes—rarely—I can think fast. "And have a glass of champagne if she so desires. But only a glass. She's prone to hiccups."

"Not true!" Maya demanded over her laughter.

Mom beamed at Maya. "Of course, hon! A mani-pedi will be in order. And *maybe* some bubbles." She clapped her hands. "Five minutes and we're on the road, come on, come on, get moving!"

Mom swung back to her room, and Maya gathered her bags.

"You can tell me on Sunday," I said, assuming that her secret was a crush or maybe the arrival of her delayed period. "The secret."

She smiled small. "Yeah, okay." And then, "You're really not coming?"

"If you need me there—"

"No, whatever," she said. "I'll get a bed to myself if you stay home."

"See, win-win."

"I agree with Mom though."

"On?"

"You're totally jealous."

"Well, you're a snot." A tease—a sister ritual necessary from time immemorial. I pulled her into a hug. "*And* you're going to knock the judges dead with your cancer-perfected pirouettes."

She laughed into my shoulder. "My pirouettes have indeed been proven to be potentially lethal to both me and observers," she said.

I held her tighter. "You're dynamite, sis."

So Mom and Maya left for Newport Beach, for their girls' night before the audition, and I sat glued to the TV in the family room, where flames mere miles away danced on the screen—inching closer to my community. Legs tucked beneath me, I stayed there until Brooks let himself in through the front door. My calves were numb. The sun had set.

Brooks kissed my head and ran a thumb over the wrapped blister on my hand. He said I needed to get my mind off of it. He said the station hadn't called him in yet, so obviously the fire was under control. He said that I was going to make myself sick. He said Derek's party would help—hadn't I said I wanted to go to the party?

"You hate parties," I said.

"Not if the party makes you happy," he said. "And it will, because . . . distraction, you know?"

So Brooks and I went to the party.

5

Starry Night

To her credit, Mom isn't like the other studio moms, or at least she didn't start out as one. She isn't reliving her glory toe shoe days through Maya, nor did she gush over my solos out of nostalgia. Mom has never worn a ballet slipper. And unless you count a rather tacky seventies Halloween costume, as far as I know she's never worn a leotard.

I was five when she asked, "What do you want to do?"

I guess I said be a fairy or a dancer or something, and I guess Mom listened, because it seemed to become her mission to help me live out my ballerina dream. But dancing never felt like a dream—rather it became something required, like school. Ballet was my decision, but I don't remember making the choice.

Me, a toddler in a tutu and tiara. The works: ballet, modern, jazz, tap, theatrical dance. Maya followed close behind. By fifth grade, I was dancing six days

19

a week and growing bored. That was also the year Maya passed out at recess, and three specialists later, a CT scan revealed tumors in her throat and chest.

A high rate of division—up close, the bad cells look like a starry night, Mom explained.

Burkitt lymphoma, stage 3, Dad said.

Will you dance for me? Maya asked, after chemo. *Right now, please?*

I was ten, and all I understood was that our world was shattering. I would have yanked off my ears if she'd asked. I liked ballet most then—when it wasn't simply something I did because it was on the schedule taped to the fridge. I loved ballet when every plié was in my sister's name.

So I didn't question the next steps, the next class. Autopilot. Me, obsessive, one-track mind, all-or-nothing attitude—that's what Grace says anyway. Maya was in and out of the hospital, on and off chemo for almost two years. My dancing was the levity. I was the healthy daughter, the strength. It was essential that I succeed. If Maya couldn't dance, I would dance for her.

Ballet was never my thing. It was *hers.* My thing was being her light when she was sick. And then she was no longer sick, and I guess, in a sense, I dimmed.

Ultimately, obviously, it wasn't my dancing that saved the day. Modern medicine kicked ass and Maya kicked ass and she was dancing again by the time she was nine, and then we were dancing at the same time, and it was good, she was happy, it was her passion, her urgency.

The way she smiled after class. That glow. I wanted to feel passion like that too, but I didn't feel a thing. Actually, no, that's a lie: I was sad, miserable, wrung out.

I was thirteen—it was the summer before freshman year—and I was still prepping for my Big Deal academy audition, but I wanted to tell Mom that

I didn't want to dance anymore. And I almost did it, I almost quit, but then Maya relapsed and they took out her spleen, and it hurt so much, and *Dance for me, Audrey, spin for me*, and I couldn't quit, not when my dancing made Maya so happy, when it gave my parents something good to hold on to.

Fouetté, fouetté, fouetté, show me your mastered fouetté, she'd giggled from her hospital bed as I attempted to jump in the small room, laughing as I landed in the most ungraceful position, and Maya cheered, proclaiming, *One day I'm so gonna out-fouetté you, just you wait.*

So I kept at it. I pushed and I pushed, empty at the barre, empty all summer long.

Don't get me wrong. I'm a fantastic dancer. My form is enviable, my ease with patterns nearly mechanic. My stubbornness kept me in the studio until I got the choreography *down*. The structure and discipline made sense to me. I was a machine.

But see, I didn't have the spark, the passion. Ballet never belonged to me.

And then it was autumn, and my family didn't need me anymore: Maya was recovering so fast, already dancing again, slowly at first and then full speed ahead. So fourteen and two months old, in the middle of my Big Deal audition, I quit ballet.

Whoop-de-do.

What matters is this: Maya's thirteen now, three years cancer-free, and today she is pursuing her dream. And now that Brooks has his fire, I'm back to looking for my own thing.

6

―――

6:29 A.M.

I'm still in the bathroom at Starbucks. Someone is pounding on the door. I have to leave.

"Sorry," I say, moving past a woman with frizzy bed hair, a little boy tugging at his Buzz Lightyear pajama pants. I step aside—straight into Brooks.

He's dressed for the fire, in his turnout gear and boots. All that's missing is the jacket and helmet. He showcases tousled bedhead that could easily be mistaken for a hard night's work. I lose my breath. He's beautiful. He's making heads turn. He's blocking my path, and I can't run away.

"I had to see you," Brooks says, drawing me into his arms. "I had to say goodbye."

7

June Gloom

I met Brooks last June, the Monday night of my final week of my sophomore year.

I'd followed Grace and Quinn, and some of their older friends, to the staging of the senior prank. It was midnight, and the campus was cloaked in June fog. Students tossed caution tape around the one-story stucco buildings and haloed light poles and sycamore trees. Ketchup and sandy gray dirt were thrown, old newspapers and toilet paper flung: a lousy attempt at a fake murder scene.

Grace was eager to lend a hand to the upperclassmen, the majority of whom were drunk, roaming, loud, and sloppy, littering the quad with Budweiser cans and cigarette butts. Watching from a bench, I was content to enjoy the show.

I was mid-yawn when Brooks sat beside me, nearly spinning me into space. He was ready for a bank heist—black jeans, a navy pullover, and a gray beanie framing his thick eyebrows. Something was off with his left eye. It was lopsided, ever so slightly drooping, the green somehow sharper than the right.

That night, damp from June Gloom that teased rain that never came, Brooks sat beside me and said, "I don't know you."

My knees shook. "Nope."

I didn't know him either, not really, but that's also not totally true. We all knew Brooks. He'd been the talk of the semester. The mystery troubled kid dropped in from somewhere north after being booted out of his old school, that's the story we made for him. The older guy with both tentative charm and outbursts in the classrooms to his name, who never showed his face beyond school, keeping wholly to himself in a manner that only elicited more attention. From me included.

I recognized him from around campus. I was even familiar with his scarred eye from the whispers in the halls. It was suspected it was the reason he'd been kicked out of his previous school—maybe something as terrible as a knife fight. But a few of my friends had been in classes with him, Grace's brother included, and they had used words like *chill* and *intense* to describe him. "He's way too into chem and entirely checked out." Every description a contradiction.

I sometimes saw him at lunch whenever he sat beneath the sycamore tree in the middle of the quad, dust jackets always stripped from whatever book he was reading. I'd wanted to talk to him. Of course I wanted to talk to him. Everyone did.

Yet the night of the senior prank, he sat next to me—*me*—on that bench. And he was looking at me, a flush in *his* cheeks.

"You're not a senior," he said. He smiled so steady, but his hands were shaking, and he must have noticed that I noticed, because he stuffed them into his pockets. He leaned away and, exaggerating his gaze, looked me up and down. "You should be more excited right now—a youngster in on a senior prank. Huge deal," he said. "You look ready for bed."

"Hey," I said, my voice a squeak. "I'm *not* a youngster."

I was a sophomore in pajama pants and an old *Nutcracker* tee. My face was bare beyond sugary lip-gloss, and I hadn't touched my hair since that morning. I was totally a youngster.

"I'm guessing fourteen?" Brooks asked.

I laughed naive, fourteen-year-old-like giggles. I felt tipsy on the sparkling wine Grace likes to snatch from her mom. "I'm nearly sixteen, thank you very much," I said.

He grinned. "Hate to break it to you, but fourteen and fifteen are pretty much the same thing."

"Maybe for you," I said, "but not for me."

He toyed with a silver Zippo, striking the flame up only to let it breathe out and die, and I remembered the silver glint in his hands while he'd read at lunch. The way he would quickly pass the metal back and forth between hands, letting it catch on the sun for a glance. Toying with campus contraband so carefully but with urgency.

"You should know I'm not a creep," he said. "I'm recently acquainted with Quinn and Grace. They directed me over. Quinn said she'd pay me a buck if I made you smile."

This was disappointing. I'd rather him have been a creep who'd simply wanted to talk to me than a friend-provided escort. I turned around and spotted the two of them watching, snickering. I rolled my eyes and turned back to Brooks.

"I guess Quinn better pay up," I said.

A guy with a buzz cut and steroid-induced biceps squirted ketchup onto the sidewalk. Our campus looked like the aftermath of a fast food battle, not a murder scene.

"I have to say, as a fellow senior, I'm embarrassed." Brooks drew in a breath. "Weak, weak, *weak* prank."

"It's not that bad," I said, and I wondered why he was there at all, why he'd ever voluntarily choose to come to the social gathering of a prank. I let myself imagine he'd come just to meet me.

"We're clearly not needed here," he said. "Want to go for a drive?"

"I don't even know your name." Lie.

Still sitting, he bowed. "My apologies, mademoiselle. I'm Brooks Vanacore." He clutched my hand and pressed it to his lips. I was horrified— my palms had been sweating since he'd sat down—but I was electrified, smiling, unable to stop. "May I have the pleasure to know your name?" he asked.

"Grace didn't tell you?"

"She did." His green eyes soaked me. "But I'd rather our meeting be, well, traditional and shit."

"Right." I looked at our hands, still clutched together—his so warm and heavy, calloused and firm, my hand too small. "I'm Audrey."

"Audrey?" Brooks ran his thumb along the inside of my palm. I was as bright as the sun, so light I could have swum to the sky. Time slowed, and he wasn't letting go, was looking at me as if I were already his everything.

I breathed. "Audrey Harper," I said.

His smile hitched my breath—a small smile, but so sweet and genuine and only for me. He pulled his car keys from his back pocket and dangled them in the air. "Well, Miss Harper. I'm bored and you're bored and I have gas in my tank, so let's go."

My jaw ached, and yet it felt so good. Talking to him felt so good.

So, I went.

8

_____

6:31 A.M.

Brooks is here. He's kissing my head and touching my cheeks, and everyone in the café is watching. He's whispering those words again—*I had to see you one last time*—because I keep asking, *Why, why, why.* He's holding my hand and ordering a latte and a blueberry crumble muffin, buying me a cappuccino and a chocolate croissant that I don't want. Well, he's not actually *buying* anything because the woman behind the register is blinking at his uniform—everyone is blinking at his uniform—and she's smiling so wide with these misty hazel eyes.

"We got you covered," she says. "Thank you so much for your service."

Brooks bows his head. "My pleasure," he says.

I want to add that it really is, that it really is his fucking pleasure. But I don't because I'm getting sucked into this too, because it's *him*: Brooks in his fire-resistant pants and boots, a metal canteen hooked to a belt loop. Brooks standing tall, ready to fight what's forced all of us out of our homes. He's going to save the day. Brooks, *my* Brooks. He's a hero. He has to be. He is. I still believe in him and—

My mouth tastes like puke.

"Don't you have somewhere to be?" I ask into his arm.

He kisses my ear. "I had to see you."

"Excuse me." An older man approaches us. He shakes Brooks's hand. "Thank you. I wanted to shake your hand properly and say thank you."

And then another. "So, what do you think?" A dad with a kid hiding behind his legs. "You think this will be beat soon?"

And Brooks nods, because he knows what he's talking about, this is fire after all, and he's been waiting to talk about fire his entire life. "In time," he says, and it's strange because his voice doesn't shake like it normally does—the fire has cured his perpetual shyness. "We'll get this in time."

And the dad asks, "Would you mind? Would you mind taking a photo with my son?"

You have got to be kidding me.

But Brooks doesn't even consider it. He's kneeling beside the boy, his face serious but with the slightest of smiles, one arm slung around those small shoulders shaking beneath a thin blue shirt.

Brooks can't wipe the dazed smile off his face. I wonder if anyone has noticed that he's not dirty and ashen, that he's in a freaking Starbucks waiting for an extra-hot latte and warmed muffin and not out, you know, *firefighting*.

"You're already a legend," I say, after we get our drinks and food and go outside, where the patio is vacated and the wind rips ash and leaves across the parking lot. "I guess dreams do come true."

He doesn't catch my tone—he must not—because he smiles. "Maybe." He's nervous now; he's never been so nervous. He chews a hunk from his muffin and says, "I wanted, you know, I needed to see you."

His smile bites my heart.

I hope my words bite back. "You need to get into your car and go."

Brooks sets his breakfast on the patio table. "Please, Audie, please do me a favor and don't freak out. You have to treat it like it's a normal day."

"How is this possibly a normal day? How can you even ask me that after—"

"After what?" He levels my gaze. If anyone is observing us from inside they're thinking he's dazzling. He's charming. What a brilliantly awkward smile. What wide, sad eyes. None of that is incorrect; it's just not the whole story. His green eyes narrow just the slightest, and he says, "After last night?"

"No," I say. "After my being evacuated, after so many families being evacuated." I can't find the words I need to say, the words I want to say. The wind tangles my hair and it hurts to breathe and it hurts even more to speak so I stare at him instead, until I don't want to stare anymore, and I say, "My house could burn down."

A family passes us as they go into Starbucks. They're in pajamas. They're an upheaved mess. They're smiling at Brooks and he's nodding back.

"*Many* families' homes *are* going to burn down," I add.

Brooks finishes his muffin in a single bite. He looks at me. "Do you really have so little faith in your local firefighters?" He tries to laugh but it's dry. "We got this."

Something spurs in me deeper. It must be the caffeine. "You have nothing," I say, a crack in my throat. "You're a liar at Starbucks consuming copious amounts of sugar."

I've never talked to him like this before, and I know he's thinking the same thing: that we're pushing beyond repair. Our hearts are already broken.

"A liar, eh?" His voice is hushed. "Don't forget it takes two."

I step back. He's no longer smiling. A beat passes. His jaw pulses. "Why are you so convinced that I'm the beast here?" It's so soft, like how he says *I love you* late at night, in the car, over the phone, after a din of silence.

I don't answer. I can't answer. Because if he isn't the beast, what does that make me?

But he tugs me into him, embraces me so tight that for a moment I forget where we are, what day it is, what we've become.

"I didn't mean to start a fight," he says. "I only came to say goodbye."

And as angry as I am right now, after the final words of last night, I can't let go. There's a part of me that still wants to tuck him in and keep him safe. *Mine.* My everything. He's not ready to fight any fires. He's doesn't need to fight fires.

I press my lips into his shirt. "Stop acting like you're going to die out there," I say.

He holds me tighter. "Trust me, please?" He's grasping my chin, letting his left eye drip tears on my cheek. "You have to stay quiet, stay low."

"And what if I don't?"

On cue, his phone lets out a low wail. The station is calling him. It's happening. He talks fast now. "You're risking my life, Audie. *Our* lives," he says.

"The sooner we—"

But he ignores me. "Thank you for last night." He raises my hand to kiss it, like our first night together, almost bowing, a knight heading off to battle. "Just—" He presses a finger firmly against my lips. "*Shhhhhhh.*"

The morning spins and he kisses me deep and I kiss him soft because maybe we aren't beyond repair. But then he's leaving, walking backward into the wind, hair blowing, keys and wailing phone in his hand. It's his time to fight.

"Trust me," he says.

9

Quaking

Brooks drives a black Audi—a sleek two-door that reeks of old coffee. That first June night I met him, after we'd escaped the senior prank, he drummed on the steering wheel and announced my first and only nickname.

"Audie," he said. "It's brilliant. Audrey. *Audi. Audie.*" He didn't pronounce it like the car, but rather just my name without the *r*, like what Maya called me when she was four. "I'm a genius!"

I stared at him. "You're naming me after your car? Seriously? *Your car?*"

"Nicknaming you," he said. "And Audie with an *e* so—"

"Is there a difference?"

"*Is there a difference?*" He scoffed, giving me a side smile. We abandoned the parking spot, zipping past the condiment-dousing seniors, up the bank, away from the school. "Really, you should be honored. This car is my pride, worth three summers of pizza and espresso slinging. I must really like you."

I was too flustered to acknowledge the last statement, too flushed and exhilarated. So I texted Grace, letting her know I'd left.

"*Audie*," I said, trying it on, my tongue slipping.

"You hate it. Shit. I am an ass." His voice cracked. "Really though, seriously, it's a compliment—this is my glory. Did I mention the espresso slinging?"

I shook my head. "There's no way you bought this from minimum wage."

And then Brooks grinned, revealing an extra-pointy back tooth, an oddity of his otherwise braces-straight smile. "Impressed yet?"

But I was already far past impressed. I was enthralled.

I'd never had a nickname before. I'd never had a boy so eager to talk to me. And this was *Brooks*, the guy I'd ogled all semester, the boy everyone wanted to know, who everyone thought was dark and creepy. He wasn't. I could see it, feel it already. He was striking—his tough exterior and half smiles and scarred eye—but he was also more than that. He was vulnerable, passionate, springing with excitement. Smiling at me. He was beautiful and sweet. And he'd chosen me, *me*, as a companion for his drive. I couldn't make myself care that his car partly inspired his name for me—the name already felt like mine, like a secret between him and me.

"You can call me Audie," I said.

We sped through Trabuco Canyon, and he asked me whether or not I liked Orange County and if I had a favorite tree. His is the quaking aspen, a tree speckled through his native Washington state and nowhere to be found in the dry Southern California terrain.

"Quaking," I said. "Like earthquakes." Like a dimwit not knowing how to hold a conversation about trees.

Brooks smiled. "Sure, like earthquakes." He shifted, rounding a dark curve. "The leaves—" He lifted a hand from the steering wheel, waved his fingers down, demonstrating. "The leaves kind of do a tremble deal in the wind, like quaking, you know, or something. You can't find them here. Up in Washington though, in the fall—shit, they're gorgeous. Have you ever seen a fall outside of Orange County?"

"No. I'm born and raised." A tizzy in my throat—I knew his state, his home.

"In Washington, my older brother used to take me camping in autumn—we'd go east and backpack and pitch this sad sheet of a tent. We had to share a sleeping bag to keep warm. It'd be freezing, but so worth it. We never went summer camping. Why bother building a fire if you don't really need it to survive?" He shrugged. "Cameron said summer camping was too easy. Autumn a doable struggle."

"How old were you?" I asked.

"I don't know, probably ten the first time?" Brooks said. "And then, there on out, it was a tradition."

I could see it: a thirteen-year-old leading his younger brother into the forest, dirt-smudged cheeks and fallen branches for walking sticks.

He stared ahead. "Cameron went out east for school though, two years ago. And now I'm here." With one hand, Brooks flicked his Zippo against the steering wheel. "Cameron said the trees were the only reason to backpack. The reward. I'll find photos for you. You'll see. When October hits, the quaking aspen groves, they look like fire."

This is how it was between Brooks and me. How it started, and how it remained. We are defined by his stories. I would have listened to him talk all night long if he'd let me. I wanted to swallow every sentence. Wanted to catch his fervor in my hand, store it in my gut and let it fill me up.

And that night in June, beyond the headlights, the canyon road was black. Oak trees hunched over the road, their spindly branches bridging the roadsides above, cloaking any light from the sky or homes nestled among the foothills.

"Tell me," Brooks said, his eyes so briefly meeting mine. "What do you love?"

My response was immediate. "Maya. My little sister. She—"

He waved his hand. "Not *who*. What."

I stilled, thinking I didn't love anything worthy of mention. "*Having* a sister then," I said. "I love that. And baths, showers, water. I miss the rain."

He smiled. "Keep going."

I pulled at the drawstring of my pajamas. "Grace. I love her, and I love that she's my best friend, that she isn't afraid to share with the world who she is—her full self—and that she talked to me first, insisted we be friends." Because I guess I can be off-putting sometimes. My silent discomfort translates into bitchy intimidation. "And I love school." I went on. "The sense of control when I've finished my homework. Like, when I understand something new, when I *know* I've learned something after trial and error," I said. "I love that."

"Yeah." He was nodding. "Me too."

"What about you?" I asked. "What do you love?"

He squinted at this. "I love that you love those things." Which felt like a cop out, but I was too entranced to call him out on it.

When he wasn't messing with the Zippo and pretending his fingers were quaking aspen leaves, Brooks gripped the wheel with both hands. His gaze rarely diverged from the road ahead. I could stare at him freely. Stare at the stubble on his face, at his heavy eyebrows that crept from the beanie he tugged at, stare at the edge of his cheek. I wanted to get closer, closer until I found every last scar on his skin, every secret tucked away.

"When did you move to California?" I asked, though I mostly knew the answer.

Brooks nodded at the street, as if nodding north. "This past winter. My dad was offered a position at a firm down here." He held his Zippo in his right hand, against the wheel, pressing it into his palm. His smile faltered. "He and my mom were on rocky grounds already—finalizing their divorce—and my mom and me, we're not on the best terms, so he took the leap."

"And you jumped too," I said.

"Yeah." He flicked up his flame but had nothing to burn. "I did."

I was in a car with a boy talking about his favorite tree and his brother's camping trips and his old home, and we were still zooming away, away from my home, into Silverado Canyon, and my breath felt short in a way I'd never felt before. I'd never felt any of this before.

"You know," he said, "I would have talked to you regardless of what Grace and Quinn said. If anything, their intrusion made me hesitant to sit on that bench—the dare-like quality of it. And I wanted to sit next to you, because, you know, you're beautiful, and I was intrigued."

I looped my fingers through the drawstrings of my pajama pants. "Yeah?" I asked, never knowing how to say thank you.

"Yeah, Audie," he said. "One hundred percent yeah."

My pulse skidded when Brooks pulled over beneath a canopy of live oaks.

I thought he might kiss me. It dawned on me that some rumors claimed he was dangerous, that I didn't truly know him, not yet, and that he'd just driven me through a maze of ridges and valleys. But it also dawned on me that perhaps I wouldn't mind if Brooks kissed me, which felt so foreign—for so long I was afraid of being touched, never comfortable with my own body. But I trusted Brooks even then. My first real kiss, me only fifteen, him eighteen, nearly a high school graduate.

Kiss me. Ignore the squirrels on my pajama pants and kiss me.

But Brooks only turned in his seat so that he faced me and—just as he had back when we were sitting on the bench at school—he grasped my hand again and lifted my knuckles to his lips.

"This has been a fantastic night," he said.

"Fantastic," I said, my habit of echoing him already ingrained. "Yeah."

Brooks didn't kiss me that night. He didn't even try.

We were almost out of the canyon and to the bridge that climbs to suburbia, to our waiting homes in Coto de Caza, when Brooks turned into a small parking lot of a terra-cotta-roofed building. It was dark, and I couldn't make out the words on the sign, but I recognized the large garages. The simple design.

"What are we doing here?" I asked.

Brooks cut the engine. "Until I get back up north, this place is my home."

"A fire station?"

"I'm a reserve," he said, grinning so wide I could see his sharp tooth. "Or, I will be, officially, in a few weeks."

"A what?"

"A firefighter." He grinned. "Joining forces with good old Smokey."

I watched Brooks. His smile. The passion. Fireflies swooped in my chest, behind my ribs. They tingled in my hands and toes. It was then that I decided I wanted to join forces with him.

10

7:02 A.M.

I'm right where Brooks left me. The abandoned ashy patio of Starbucks. I've been standing here for too long, because if I don't move maybe I can pretend that Brooks was never here, that there isn't a fire burning so near, because if I acknowledge any of it—*anything* that's happened this past week—I'll break.

And I need to be able to put myself back together.

I chuck the croissant in the trash. My brain is fried, my lips peeling, my hands electrified. I failed at evacuating and forgot my toiletries, and I need to brush my teeth. I cross the street to Pavilions Grocery. The smoke has thickened with the morning light, and the air tastes like burnt toast. The sun is a blood-red smear. It's just 7 A.M., but the grocery store parking lot is packed with cars dusted with ash, like it's Thanksgiving Eve. An anthill inside. A hushed mob of evacuees.

Tense smiles, slow tears, the shuffling of slippers and whispers. The commotion buffets me. I'm the only solo grocery store wanderer. I never realized my corner of Orange County was so interwoven with families, so many families—

It is so quiet.

I want to scream.

I pick up face wash, a toothbrush, toothpaste, face lotion, lip balm, ibu-profen, peppermint gum, and Vaseline for my palm. The metal handle of my basket digs into my arm. The main checkout lines snake through the aisles—yoga pants, workout shorts, pajamas—carts filled with cases of water bottles and fruit and boxes of cereal.

Should I be buying water too?

Thank the smoky sky for self-checkout. Only eight people waiting. A woman with matted hair and a baby on her hip disrupts the peace, breathing sorrow onto a ghost of a checkout boy.

"You're out of surgical masks?" she says. "There's a *fire*, and you're out of surgical masks?"

He blinks. "CVS should—"

"I already went to CVS." The baby cries against her shoulder, and the woman bounces from side to side. "Is no one in this town prepared?"

Checkout Boy rubs his eyeliner-smeared eyes.

I want to tell her it's okay. Brooks said it'll be okay. I want to say I'm so sorry for what she might lose. I want to apologize to every last patron in this store. I want to hug her, but she's already rushing away.

I head back to the allure of coffee.

I should call Grace, but it's still early. She's definitely not awake. And there's a small part of me petrified by the possibility of seeing Hayden after what he witnessed last night. Starbucks is booming now. I'm not the only refugee who sought comfort in overstuffed chairs, caffeine, and mellow lights versus the fluorescents at Mission Viejo High School, the current evacuation center. Classmates. Neighbors. Total strangers.

So many. There are so many people uprooted.

I clean up in the bathroom—wash my face and brush my teeth.

Mom still hasn't called me back. It's 7:34 A.M. She has to be awake, the audition is in nearly two hours, but Mom likes silent mornings. She believes TV and cell phones trigger a cluttered mind, and a cluttered mind is not good for pirouettes. No TV or cell phones in the morning, *especially* mornings before dancing. The morning of my OCIB audition, she snagged my cell phone before I even woke up.

Maya will be wrecked when she hears we've been evacuated. One good thing has come from my mom's cell phone–free obsession: Maya might not know yet; she surely doesn't know yet.

Across from me, a woman braids a girl's red hair. So small and pale, the girl can't be older than seven. Bruises spot her shins, and I wonder if she's sick. *Seven.* That's when Maya first got *sick*-sick, when she dropped twenty pounds and bruised like a September peach.

I need to stop thinking and step into Mom's deluxe washing machine. Option: *whitest whites*, the hottest of water, a dunking of bleach. Burn my body until my thoughts bleed clean.

I need to drive to OCIB.

But if I see my mom, she'll smell the smoke on my skin, and I'll have to tell her about the evacuation, and that'll crack Maya's calm morning zone. If I don't go, there's a chance Maya won't learn about the evacuation until after the audition, if Mom's careful. There's a chance I won't sabotage her big day, and maybe this will all actually end up okay and—

"*Audrey!* You were evacuated?"

The high squeal pitches in my head. It's Sam, Maya's friend from a few streets over. She's in hot-pink pajamas, and her hair is pulled up in a messy bun. She looks younger than ever, her white skin sweaty, eyes glossy.

"Yeah," I say. "You too?"

"It sucks." She slurps on a Frappuccino. "It's Maya's audition day, isn't it? Is she okay? Is she still auditioning?"

"She and our mom stayed up in Newport last night, so hopefully she doesn't know," I say, and then, just in case Maya manages to grab hold of her phone, I add, "So don't text her or anything about it, okay? At least not until later—you know how she gets."

Sam nods. "Oh yeah. I won't text her." And then she jumps. "*Wait*. Wait a minute. Did you get Shadow?"

I stare at her. "Shadow?"

"Maya's cat."

"Her what?"

"Oh my God. She hasn't told you." Her eyes tear up. "Poor Shadow."

The room is starting to blur, and Sam's voice is too high, so I pull her down beside me and I hold her hand, and I speak very slowly. "Sam, I need you to be honest and totally clear. Who is Shadow? Where is Shadow now? Why does Maya have a Shadow?"

Tears run down Sam's face. "She found her, this kitten. She followed Maya home one night from my house a week or so ago, like a shadow, *so*," Sam explains. "It was sick. Really skinny. Maya snuck her into your house and has been keeping her in her closet. I let her borrow my old cat stuff. She was going to tell you, but she said you've been super busy and—"

"There's no way." This is some sick dream. "I would know if Maya had a cat in her room."

But I remember yesterday, her secret, and my stomach knots up.

"Your house is big." Sam sniffles. "It's easy to keep things secret."

Maya's smile when she was going to tell me her secret—so excited, such love. I thought it was a crush, womanhood. But a cat, I never imagined a cat. Our house might burn with a cat inside. *He used to burn cats alive.* I close my eyes. I need to get Maya's cat.

"Do you want to sit with my family?" Sam asks.

"I have to go."

She stands, but before turning away she asks, "Do you think Shadow will be okay?"

"I hope so," I say.

My little sister's kitten is trapped in my house, and I refuse to let this cat burn alive.

11

Idolization of Roots

That first night in June, after the senior prank and the drive in the canyons—after Brooks asked for my number and I tapped it into his phone, after I said bye and he said goodnight and I tripped up Grace's driveway—after all of that, I snuck into her foyer and was blindsided.

Hayden sat on the staircase, a textbook in his lap. He swung his gaze at me. A blast of light, the shock to my eyes, I stumbled back against the door. He wore a camping headlamp, like a child with a comic under a bed, because turning on a light apparently wouldn't have been sufficient for his reading. The shadows cast his pale skin into a ghoulish shade.

"You're back," he said, looking me over, the jolt in my expression. He paused and asked, "Did something happen?"

I shielded my face. "You burned my eyes—that's what happened."

"Oh. Sorry." Hayden yanked the headlamp off and held it so the light shone at the steps. "Grace asked if I wouldn't mind waiting up for you. To lock up after, you know."

I leaned against the bottom of the banister. "Waiting up for me required camping out on the staircase?"

His cheeks colored. "It's a nice place to read. New settings help the mind retain information, and I can only spend so much time at my desk, so." He gripped the edge of his book, peering up at me. "Grace said you were out with Brooks. Did you—" His words were clumsy. "Where did you go?"

Last June, Grace's older brother was still just that to me: Grace's older brother. He was Hayden, who—for the most part—seemingly avoided me around the house. He smiled when we passed each other at school, but otherwise he remained aloof. Like I was an allergen that he couldn't fully avoid. Grace said it wasn't me, that he was weird with everyone, but I was unconvinced. Everyone at school adores Hayden.

"Yeah, Brooks," I said. "We drove around in the canyons. Not a big deal."

"Oh. Cool," Hayden said. "That sounds cool."

I walked up a step past him. "Thanks for waiting for me," I said. "Happy reading."

He fastened the headlamp back over his dark curls and returned to his book. "Anytime."

After the blast of Hayden's headlamp, I was too wired to sleep, so I sprawled out on Grace's bedroom floor and typed to the rhythm of her soft snores. I googled Brooks's beloved tree, his quaking aspen. He was right: It's a beautiful tree. You'd never find it in Orange County.

I typed too loud, fingers clacking across the keys. Grace rolled over, mumbled an obscenity. I typed some more. She chucked a pillow at me.

"Dude," she said. "You writing a novel or something?"

"Tree research."

She sat up, her hair sticking up in spikes. "You woke me up for tree research?"

I clicked on a government link. "Not my fault you're a light sleeper."

She turned on her bedside lamp and climbed out of bed, splat herself on the carpet beside me. "Might this tree research have anything to do with Brooks?"

I nodded. "He's kind of fascinating."

"I *knew* you two weirdos would hit it off. He a good kisser?"

"No idea." I squinted at the screen. "How do you know Brooks anyway?"

"I don't," she said. "He was in Hayden's stats class. They had some group thing." She bit her thumbnail, and I thought over my conversation with Hayden on the staircase, his tentativeness to ask questions or offer commentary. "Brooks came over once so they could prepare beforehand, and I *maybe* hovered. He wasn't what I expected. Weird, but probably because he's a fellow loner like you."

"Did Hayden like him?" I glanced at the door that led to their Jack and Jill bathroom.

"Uh, he liked him enough," Grace said. "But Hayden likes everyone. You know that."

"He doesn't like me," I said.

"Oh hell no," Grace said. "I am not playing that game with you. He likes you fine."

I looked back at the screen. Native Americans and early Pilgrims extracted a quinine substitute from quaking aspen bark. Quinine—a substance used to treat malaria in the seventeenth century.

"Are the stories true?" Grace asked.

I opened a new tab and typed *Brooks Vanacore* into the blank space. I stared at the blinking cursor, only to hold my breath as I deleted his name, letter by letter. It felt too invasive. I wanted to learn who he was through him, not whatever the internet had to say.

"Audrey," Grace said.

"I don't know," I said, clicking back on the tree web pages.

"Well, he's graduating," Grace said. "Perfect end-of-the-year hookup. He's sexy, yeah?"

"I don't do hookups."

"Correction: You've never had a hookup."

"Because I don't do them," I said.

She thought on that. "Well, Brooks probably doesn't do hookups either."

"He seemed like a charmer to me," I said.

"Because he likes you!"

Quaking aspens make poor fire fuel. They dry slowly and rot quickly. Despite their yellow—sometimes red—leaves, they give off minimal heat. Nonetheless, the wood is frequently used in campfires. It's supposedly cheap.

But here's the thing about quaking aspens: They rely on fire for survival. By wiping out interfering brush, fire gives the trees the space they need to grow. So, Brooks's quaking aspen can't withstand fire, and yet without fire, it'd go extinct.

I'd find my own tree to idolize.

Grace chucked another pillow in my direction. "Are you even listening to me?"

"Not really," I said.

"Right. Okay. I'm going back to bed."

"Sleep soundly," I said.

"Search softly."

I cracked my knuckles. "I'll try my best."

12

7:56 A.M.

I'm walking to the truck when I call Grace.

"This is insane," she says. "Bonkers-crazy insane. Your house—my dad said your area is screwed. Crap. *Sorry.*" She jumps over her words. "Is Brooks out there yet?"

"Yeah."

"Shit."

"I need your help," I say. "And I also need to shower."

"Dude, what are you waiting for?" she asks. "*Mi casa es su casa.*"

13

SATURDAY

Derek's house, last night's party house, is an aspiring European villa—complete with ivy-blanketed terraces and lush rugs, a backyard flanked by towering palm trees, and rock waterfalls feeding into the massive pool. He wasn't exaggerating on Facebook: An actual pirate ship borders the water's end.

"My parents had the ship design based on the one at that resort in Cabo," he explained, tossing Brooks and me beers from the pirate bar. "What's it called? *La Playa* or something?" He nodded at me. "You know what I'm talking about."

I cracked my can. "I've never been to Mexico." The cool aluminum felt good in my hand.

"Dude." Derek swigged from his beer, nodding at Brooks. "You need to take your girl south of the border. You're depriving her! Need to treat the lady right, am I right?"

Brooks kissed my cheek. "I am depriving you, aren't I?"

"Oh, absolutely." I sounded breezy, but I was thinking of Thursday night, of Brooks's brother, the fire. Leaning into his arms, grateful my insides weren't open for public viewing, I sounded fine. "I'm *totally* deprived."

A crowd of seniors emerged from the house, a roaring huddle of banter, escalating to a fight. Derek nodded at us, walking backward toward the hustle. "Make yourself at home, *mi casa es*—you know!"

Brooks's arms encircled my waist. Ash drifted down like *Nutcracker* snow on closing night—deceptively white from the theater seats, but in reality dirty, almost brown, hot from the stage lights.

"How about we leave," Brooks said. "Watch a movie at my place, you know, hang out."

"I don't want to go." The party made it easier to ignore the raining ash. "Have you ever been to Mexico?"

"Are you kidding?" Brooks laughed, swigging from his beer. "I can barely tolerate Orange County's fiesta bullshit. If I were going to spoil you, I'd take you somewhere quiet. The mountains, Alaska, or something."

"Alaska," I echoed, and the words tasted like butter, thin slivers melting on hot toast. "Okay. Let's go."

Brooks squeezed my hand. "Inside first? This air quality is shit."

"Yeah," I said. "Baby steps."

Brooks and I played a round of beer pong against Rich and Mikey. We lost but still cheered them on as they attempted a celebratory break-dance in the foyer. I hugged Rich four times because I was kind of tipsy and I've missed Rich and I guess Grace isn't my only friend.

"You're *here*," he said, his light-brown skin gleaming with sweat. "And you've been here for over an hour! What a miracle."

I glanced at Brooks, who was smiling, talking to a guy I didn't know.

"It really is," I said.

Rich grinned. "Will you watch my new move—offer your thoughts on it?" And he started spinning his ass across the marble floor, only to pull me down with him, collapsing in laughter.

"It's perfect." I grinned.

Brooks was wearing an Orange County Fire Authority crew shirt. Word spread that he's a firefighter. Word did not spread that he's a volunteer. He answered questions about the fire, explained that the greatest hope was digging trenches, creating a strong fire line. He managed to slip in the woes of his oh-so-breezy pack test—a three-mile hike carrying a forty-five-pound pack in forty-five minutes or less. He completed the test back in June, yet still in October, he tosses it into conversations. *You ever heard of a pack test? Fighting fires—it's nothing compared to that.*

His smile grew and grew. After a summer of resisting, he was finally enjoying a party—his social anxiety waning with his new respected popularity. It was his night. He didn't know it yet, but his fire was gaining momentum outside.

"You must be so strong," Anela—a volleyball player, tall with a perfect spray tan—said, her glossy hair pulled back in a ponytail. I sit next to her in English. She gawked at him, looked down at me. "Audrey, what's it like to have a boyfriend who saves lives?"

He held my hand, his skin—his callouses, new and old—against my own. His palm can cover my closed fist like a sheet. Over six feet, built from manual labor and bouts at the gym, he is twice my size. Brooks makes it easy to hide. I love him for this.

But as far as I know, he hasn't saved a single life.

A few hours into the party, Brooks snagged a bottle of rum from the liquor cabinet and led me up the stairs. He opened the double doors to the master suite. I was surprised it hadn't already been claimed.

"Don't think I can handle much more of that shit," he said. "Is this okay?"

The room was dark and cold. Plum drapes partially concealed the balcony doors. The air conditioner wheezed from the overhead vent. It didn't smell like smoke. It smelled like Chanel perfume and clean sheets. I wished Grace had bailed on babysitting. The roar below rang in my ears, and the hot night was sticky on my skin.

Brooks was watching me. His left eye dropped a single tear. He rested his head on my shoulder, his hair tickling my neck. "Felt like I was drowning," he said. "I only want to be with you, alone with you."

We were standing just inside the room, the light from the hall a broken stream. Every cell of my body was lit. I closed the door.

We drank spiced Captain Morgan on the balcony. Two beers alone would have rocked me into a breeze, but I went past that. As I pushed beyond tipsy, we watched ash blow in the wind—the day and night already spiraling beyond familiarity.

From the top tower of the pirate ship, a stone slide whipped down to the glittering pool. Girls in miniskirts and Daisy Dukes unbuttoned their blouses and howled the entire way down, emerging from the water with eyeliner raccoon eyes.

"Maybe I'll go down later," I said.

"You'd never have the guts." Brooks wrapped his arms around me from behind and brushed my hair to one side, fixing the clip that held back my bangs. He was seeping back into his summer ways. He was familiar. He was safe. He was nothing like he was on Thursday.

"The guts to climb a fake pirate ship and go down a slide?"

"The guts to strip for all of the school to see." He nudged me around so that I faced him. "But that's why I love you. Your shyness means you're all mine."

I've never thought of myself as shy. I just like alone time. There's a difference, right?

On the bed. His hands slick and fast. The silk duvet was cold on my back. I tingled from the beer and rum, and my ears hummed from the bass downstairs.

Fingers under the edge of my jeans. In the backyard, a girl screamed. A splash in the pool. Cheering, more shrieking. The ceiling chandelier glinted from the torchlights and pool lights and back porch lights outside. He kissed me and I kissed him and the fire grew fast and, last night, everything was fine.

14

8:12 A.M.

Dad calls when I'm crossing Antonio Parkway, approaching the gates. Grace also lives in Coto—more than half of our school does—but the white picket fence horse-haven gated community is large enough to be its own town. Her house is a fifteen-minute drive away from mine.

"Audrey, honey." Dad's voice is piped fast. "How's it going?"

How does he think it's going?

SUVs stream out of Coto's gates, abandoning the dark sky. There isn't a line to get inside. The gate detects the pager stuck to my windshield, and the prong rises. I drive through, past flashing lights, my phone nudged between my ear and shoulder.

"I only have a few minutes," Dad says. "Communicate, please."

Foot on the gas, I say, "The fire is still doing its thing. The sky is disgusting. I drank too much coffee. Mom never called me back. I think everything is going fine."

A cop is on my tail. Talking on your cell while driving is a major no-no. My head has been cocked to the side for a suspiciously long time. I drop the phone and pull over by a brass fence, a fence sheltering a colonial estate with a sprawling green lawn—the size of two football fields, I swear, and *always* green, even now when land beyond the sprinkler lines is cracked and shriveled. Even now, when California is in a record-breaking drought, and a fire burns just miles away.

The cop drives on by. I nod as he passes. Nothing to see here; please don't let me waste your time. He doesn't even glance my way. I pick up my phone. Hold it to my ear.

"So," Dad says. "Really still no word from Mom?"

"I think it's for the better," I tell him. "Maya—it'd freak her out."

Dad ultimately agrees Mom's annoying phone habits are for the best. No reason to raise alarm. I gathered the important items when I evacuated—all crucial documents are safe in my truck. I'm safe in my truck. Dad explains that he's already booked a room at the Ayres Hotel & Spa in Foothill Ranch, closer to home than where Maya and Mom stayed, yet far enough away that there's no threat of being evacuated again. So it's all good. *It's all dandy.* He flies into Orange County later this evening, and soon we'll be reunited as a family. Maya is very sensitive to emotions, Dad and I both agree, so we can hold off sharing the news a tad longer. My legs are shaking because he won't stop talking, and I don't think this ten-minute call is necessary, especially when I have a cat to save.

We're about to say goodbye, and I'm about to click on my blinker, but then Dad asks, "Is Brooks out there?"

I drop my head. Dad is Brooks's number-one fan. Brooks is a solid boy, such a passionate worker. A volunteer? A volunteer *firefighter?* Saving lives.

Working his way into college, hoping to go into forestry law or whatever. If only he was better in social situations, probably should work on his networking charm, so Dad says, but otherwise: yay, Brooks!

I'm not being sarcastic. I promise. Dad thinks I should try to learn a thing or two about commitment from Brooks. Dad is probably right.

"Yeah, he's out there," I say. "As of this morning."

When I was fourteen, newly ballet-free, Mom and Dad sat me down at the kitchen table, because they'd called me when I was sleeping over at Grace's house and heard boys in the background, and, *boys,* when did Audrey start hanging out with boys?

Really, I'd only started hanging out with boys that night.

It wasn't the birds and the bees talk. We were way beyond that. No, this was a bumbling reminder chat. Dad slurped his wine and Mom tried to meet my eyes, but I was rather perplexed with the view outside.

"Audrey, we want you to be happy, to be safe, okay?"

They said hormones make boys wild.

They said to present myself like the beautiful young lady I am.

They said, *Don't be stupid.*

And me, fourteen, never been kissed, never so much as hugged by a boy, scared of so much as having my skin accidentally brushed by a boy, I nodded, only understanding one clear message: don't have sex. And if you have sex, whisper-caution-whisper.

"We trust you on this, sweetie," they said. "You understand, right?"

Understood: yes. *No sex.* Because sex would break Mom's heart, and sex would raise Dad's blood pressure high.

And now Dad asks, "Is Brooks excited?"

"Excited?" I repeat. Excited, yes, of course, Brook is excited, because he had sex with your little girl, because your not-so-perfect little ex-ballerina didn't use the magic chastity word. "Dad," I say. "He's probably choking on smoke."

And not even a year after that bumbling reminder, he and Mom met Brooks for the first time. That night, Dad said, *He's a good kid, respectful— nervous, understandably—a good kid would be nervous.* And Dad said, he actually said, despite Brooks being eighteen, *I'm not concerned.*

"I bet he's excited," Dad says now. "Finally the chance to show he's up for the job. Use the skills he's trained for."

"He's spraying water on a fire," I say.

"You sound upset."

"Well, I'm kind of worried about the house. You know, the *evacuation.*"

"I'd think you'd know from Brooks," he says. "Evacuations, even mandatory, they're just a precaution. I think it'll all be fine."

Dad sounded concerned this morning—when our computer was at risk, the photos, the file box. He sounded convinced our house would burn. It was okay to be dramatic then. I want to remind him of this. I want to tell my dad a lot of things, but I don't know how to say what I don't yet understand.

"Yeah," I say instead. "I know."

"Unnecessary dramatics are the last thing we need," he says.

Because I am always so goddamn dramatic.

"You're not here," I say. "I'm just—" I inhale. When I exhale I will be calm. I will not be on the edge of Mt. Sobbing Dramatics. I will be calm, an adult safe in the Valley of Maturity. I exhale and say, "I am just kind of afraid."

"I know," he says. "I'll be there soon." He thanks me for being such a champ, tells me that, by the way, it's okay to feel sad if I'm having some ballet regrets, *Mom and I understand.* "Don't worry," he says, and then, "I love you."

59

"Love you too," I say.

But he doesn't ask, *Are you okay?*

But even if he had, I don't think I would have been able to say it.

I don't think I would have been able to lie and say yes.

15

SATURDAY

And last night, still last night, I pushed through the sweaty mosh of the party to the front door. Outside, the dirty sky glowed. Through the swaying palm leaves and sycamore limbs, music ricocheted from the backyard.

I held my bare arm to my mouth and bit my skin. I tasted like salt. I passed Brooks's Audi. I listed the cars in my head. A Mercedes-Benz, BMW Z, lifted Avalanche, convertible Mini Cooper, Land Rover with silver rims, an orange Eclipse. Ash dusted each one. The muffled party noise, the acrid air, the wind spiraling beer cans down the street.

I looked at my phone. Maybe Grace was home from babysitting. Maybe she could steal her mom's car and come get me. I sent her a text. It was past one. My house was at least an hour's walk away. I ducked my head against the hot wind and considered collapsing on the white jasmine bordering the driveway, but I ached for my mom's bed, where I could pretend to still be six.

"Audrey!"

Hayden jogged from the house. He smiled when he reached me. I tried to smile back but failed. I didn't know how to stand in a way that didn't hurt. He wore a black shirt with thick white letters spelling RIDE—broadcasting his being a volunteer for Safe Ride, a student group with the sole purpose of lurking weekend parties and driving drunk teens home.

Of course he was working last night.

In the past month we'd gone from little sister's friend/best friend's brother to two bumbling desk partners in AP psychology. We talk in class and sometimes study together after school, much to Grace's chagrin. And sometimes he makes me laugh, and sometimes I make him laugh. So I think he's now my friend too.

A friend I maybe kissed on Friday.

And last night, after I left Brooks in Derek Sanders's parents' bedroom, after Hayden's sprint down the driveway, all I could say to him was, "Hi."

"You okay?" he asked. "Saw you bolt back there."

I stared at his shirt. Focusing on the letters. The *R* and the *I* and the *D* and the *E*.

"Is Brooks here?" he asked. When I didn't answer, Hayden pushed his wire-rimmed glasses up his nose—glasses that have been lopsided and loose since I've known him—and he asked, "You need a ride?" And it was like we were back in class. We weren't breathing ash. We were clumsy and tongue-tied, only he had the upper hand. He was sober and I wasn't, and I nodded what must have been a confusing nod because he laughed and said, "Affirmative, yeah?"

"If you don't mind."

He looked over his glasses, smiled, and said, "Anything for my Round Table Lady."

A recycled joke from September—from the second day of psych, a random math pun I didn't get at first, which inevitably fell flat. *So, let's say our desk is a round table, and you're, uh, the lady of the round table, who would be your, um, most well-rounded knight?* He'd had to explain it to me, had to backtrack and explain, *I just had trig, was on my mind, dumb, I know, do not repeat that to Grace,* and then I'd smiled. *Oh, no, I get it.* I'd said, *No, it'll be our thing.*

And last night on Derek Sanders's driveway, though I didn't laugh, I felt myself smile, remembering the simplicity of that September morning. And somehow, right then, a warm inhuman instant, the leaves stopped flying and the trees stood still and the ache behind my ribs eased, and in that moment, that single entity of a second, I was okay.

"Well, Sir Cumference," I said. "Lead the way."

He beamed. "It shall be my honor."

Grace would have puked if she'd heard us.

Hayden drives an Accord. He turned and reached to the backseat, to a case of water bottles. His hair brushed my cheek. I leaned against the passenger door. Breathed deep. He handed me a bottle. It was Kirkland brand, an environmentally friendly plastic bottle—if such a thing can exist—less plastic, more flimsy. I clasped and twisted, and water gushed out onto my jeans.

"Thanks for this," I said.

He shrugged, pulling out onto the street. "It's the only reason I go to parties."

"What?"

"The Safe Ride thing," he said.

The pick-up-sloshed-idiots thing. "Right."

"Water," he said. "Seriously. Drink it." I finished the bottle, the plastic crinkling.

He coughed. "Would this be a bad time to ask you about yesterday?"

"Did you tell Grace?" I asked.

"Did *you*?"

"I haven't been telling her a lot of things these days," I admitted.

My arms tight against my stomach, I dug my fingers into my waist. I stared out the window at the cracking leaves in the dry gutters. I breathed through my nose, breathed in the stringent lemon and the lingering scent of peppermint. It calmed my nerves, made me think of when I was a kid and couldn't sleep and Dad would make me Sleepytime tea and I'd lower my nose into the mug and breathe in the scent.

Hayden didn't turn on the music, and he didn't ask questions. Grace would have asked me what happened, why I was leaving the party early, why I was leaving without Brooks—insist that talking would help. Hayden didn't. I adored him for this.

"You know," Hayden started, "they say dancing helps prevent Alzheimer's."

I thought of my grandma at Leisure World, her own history unraveling. Did Grandma ever dance? "Are you suggesting I have a memory problem?" I asked.

"I'm just saying," Hayden said, "maybe you can show me your moves sometime."

I bit my tongue. "I thought you only went to parties to drive the drunks home."

"I was thinking more along the lines of swing dancing, for our project."

He cleared his throat. "Ms. Bracket would love it if we did something like that. Real live research. We're still on for tomorrow, right?"

"Of course." And I was about to ask him where he wanted to meet, confirm the time, but I was cut off, jolted, when Hayden slammed on the brakes.

We were at the final crest before the turn into the slope that runs down into my subdivision. Far out in a back valley—but not too far, not that far at all—flames glowered, a violent pool of light. I thought of Brooks's cell phone on Derek Sanders's parents' floor. Silent. Not yet wailing. Was he still lying there, his face in the rug?

"Man," Hayden said.

"Yeah."

"What do you think started it?"

"Lunatics," I answered. "Or the wind."

"Whatever happened—" A beat passed. "You can talk to me."

"Hayden."

"I at least deserve that," he said. "Your trust."

It hit me in throat, how Hayden's never asked anything of me. He's never demanded my attention. He's simply been there, accepting my growing proximity, letting me do as I please—as if he always knew it would happen on my own terms.

Until I made a mistake yesterday—pushing too fast, too hard, in the totally wrong way.

And he does deserve to know I trust him, because I do.

But I didn't respond, didn't react, didn't speak. My heart broke. I bit into my tongue, and he focused on driving. Five minutes down the street and the fire was hidden. Only the brown smoke that veiled the night sky was evidence that something wasn't right.

"How about we go back to my house?" Hayden stared at my dark house, at the pepper trees bending in the wind, the black of the high foyer windows. "Grace would be elated to find you when she gets home."

"It's fine. I'm okay." I pushed open the door and stepped out. "Thanks again for the ride."

He tossed me another water bottle. "Drink it."

I raised the bottle in salute, kicked back the door, and turned up the drive.

Hayden rolled down the passenger window, and so normal, so everyday, like nothing had happened, he yelled out, "See you tomorrow, my Round Table Lady."

16

8:37 A.M.

Grace meets me on her doorstep, squinting in the smoke and twisting her hemp bracelets around her wrist. I can't stop coughing. Ever since Dad's call: cough, cough, cough.

"This is insane," she says. "Are you okay?"

"Yeah," I say. "Fantastic."

I think of the framed photos on the living room bookshelf and my grandma's paintings in the office. I think of my favorite hoodie in my dirty-clothes hamper—a maroon zip-up I bought from the Berkeley Shakespeare Festival when Mom took us up for a girls' trip last year while Dad was abroad for work. I think of the pillow Brooks gave me, and my heart hurts. I think of a kitten meowing in Maya's closet. I follow Grace into her air-conditioned, tiled foyer, shivering.

The grandfather clock chimes the quarter hour.

My eyes swell. It feels so nice, so pathetically nice to be here. With Grace.

Safe. The familiar. My best friend. I'm okay. It's okay. Her house is clean, all in order, even the smell of burnt eggs normal. Her parents' and Hayden's voices echo from the kitchen, where coffee always drips and newspaper pages crinkle and flip like clockwork. The TV is on too, a low hum, a reporter listing the devastation only a few miles away at my front door. But here, in this house, it's a normal Sunday—close to the disaster, yet blissfully far enough away.

I bound for the stairs and Grace's room before Hayden can see me.

"So, what happened?" Grace asks.

"Some firefighters knocked on my door and said I had to go."

I collapse on her bedroom floor. Grace has the best carpeting—purple, plush, put in specifically for her. It matches the hemp bracelet she gave me on my birthday.

"I meant what happened last night."

"Last night?" I yank my bracelet around my wrist.

"You sent me a text at one in the morning. *Mayday, mayday, mayday.*" She throws me her phone, our stream of messages on the screen.

I swallow back a knot. "I just drank too much," I say.

"I'd assumed it was about Brooks," she says. "That summer is finally ending for you two. As it probably should."

I roll over on my stomach and pick up a novel I loaned to Grace back in September. I ignore her comment and fan through the pages.

"FYI," Grace picks at the ends of her bleached hair. "When I set you guys up, I never thought it'd go beyond a weekend fling."

"You didn't set us up."

"I told him to go talk to you!"

I move onto my back and stare up at the ceiling, at a photo of Grace and me, freshman year, dressed up like malicious fairies for Halloween, adorned in red tutus. Not even a full month after walking offstage, I'm perfectly posed in an arabesque. But Grace is the focus of the photo. A hand on her hip, the other held above her head, eyelids painted black against her perpetually tanned skin, courtesy of track. She is two steps forward, towering over me, loose and confident with a filled-out body, while I'm rigid in the back with little girl bones—too pale from primarily existing in the dance studio.

"Quinn was the one who dared him to make me smile," I say. "So if anyone gets the credit, it should be her."

"Oh hell no. I initiated the whole relationship!" She points a finger. "Just like I initiated me and you—you always forget that I approached your skinny ass."

I burst into laughter. I'm so tired and raw and now so idiotically giddy. An almost drunk happiness. Shock. Something like shock. It must be shock, because how else can I be laughing after this morning, after last night? But then Grace has always been the balance to my melancholy—usually breaking through even my lowest of moods.

I laugh until I hiccup, and it makes me ache for Maya, wonder how she's doing, how she's feeling. It's 8:58 A.M., and in two hours she'll be at the audition barre. Will she be thinking of Shadow? And now I laugh harder, because it's all so absurd, and I hiccup and Grace throws me her water bottle, just like Hayden did last night. And, honestly, per the norm, she's right about her initiating our friendship, way back in the fourth grade.

"You okay?" Grace asks. "I expected sobbing, not laughter."

"This day. This fucking day," I say with a hiccup, coughing on a mouthful of water.

Grace and I met in tap class. Back then she was *all* about tap, a tap diva queen with a loud stage presence paired with a horrific inability to master patterns. But together, we made it work. I'm prime with beat and rhythm, the meticulous necessities of dance, but I lacked—and still lack—the voice and courage to move with alluring bravado.

We taught each other our strengths, practicing at recess, after school, after class. We went on to the intermediate course in middle school and—in our minds—all the other girls envied us for our perfect friendship, our dancing partnership. But then she left tap in the seventh grade, when she discovered her true love of track—her speed, her own pace, her own rhythm, similar to her zest for cooking and abandoning recipes with ease.

And I left tap to focus on ballet, only to ultimately leave that too.

I wish I liked running. I wish I liked something that adequately filled my life.

And, last year, when Grace came out as bisexual and joined the Gay-Straight Alliance, I was even more jealous. She *knew* herself. And then, last December, she asked Quinn to be her girlfriend. And I initially didn't know what that meant for me: how I would fit into the equation.

But it's no different from when Grace dated James. She has a girlfriend who sometimes takes priority, whom she loves in a different way. It barely changed a thing. And now it's no different from my dating Brooks—except Quinn actually likes hanging out with me, makes an effort to include me, and Brooks can't handle more than ten minutes around my friends.

So regardless of our communal breakup with tap—the thing that initially bonded us—and Grace having Quinn and me having Brooks, she's still my best friend and I'm hers.

"Did you see Hayden last night?" Grace asks. "I think he was covering Safe Ride."

"He was around. Doing the Hayden thing." I hide my face in the carpet. "Brooks said I was too afraid to go down the pirate-ship slide."

"He's right."

I practice it in my head: *Grace, there is a cat in my house, and we need to go on a rescue mission to save it.* She'll think I'm losing it, that I'm making the cat up. She thinks I made up the last one. I play with my phone. It's almost 9:06. I'm wasting time. I need to get to Shadow, to my house.

"When are you and Quinn leaving?"

"Around one," Grace says. "I think I even convinced her to let me drive, so I officially have a blindfold at the ready."

"You're going to *blindfold* your girlfriend on her birthday for seven hours?"

She stares at me. "It's five hours to Big Sur."

"Oh gosh," I say. "It is not." All Quinn knows is that Grace is taking her somewhere *cool*, and she needed to have an alibi for her parents, as she won't be back until late tomorrow evening. "It's a seven-hour drive, if you're lucky," I say.

Grace picks at her bottom lip. "*Shit.* Are there any closer redwoods?"

"Um."

"Maybe we'll stay until Tuesday—"

"You two are so getting busted," I say. "Especially considering that my being evacuated is going to screw up your story."

"Whatever." She huffs. "Hayden will cover me, and if not, it'll be worth it."

"You're definitely rocking the surprise element," I say. "Quinn texted me yesterday. She has an appointment at the salon this morning for an epic ball-worthy hairdo."

Grace grins. "That's my beauty."

"Hopefully she hasn't bought a gown for your camping trip," I tease.

"Hey, a gown would contrast fabulously against the beach and trees," she says. And then, so unexpected, Grace asks, "Think your house burned down yet?"

"Grace!" My pulse jumps. *Shadow.* We're actually going to save Shadow.

"Wanna shower and go check?"

Still, I hesitate. "Don't you need to get ready for the trip?"

"It's still early." She shrugs. "And I want to go with my BFF to see if her house is on fire." She raises a brow. "You game?"

And this is why Grace is my best friend.

17

Rubber Band

B ack in June, when Brooks called two weeks after we met, he didn't say *hey* or *hi* or *hello* or *what's up* or *it's Brooks, you know, from senior prank night*. He skipped all pleasantries, as if we were old friends, and he responded to my *hello* with, "You figure out your favorite tree yet?"

I was at the kitchen table, spoon in my abandoned oatmeal, phone clutched to my ear. I was wearing dance shorts and a tank top, my hair up in the bun I'd slept in, bare feet on the cool wood floor. The air conditioning hummed, but I was hot, suddenly so horrifically hot. His name on the screen of my cell phone. *His* name on the screen of *my* cell phone at 9:21 A.M. *Brooks*.

"Um," I said.

"Because when you didn't offer to share your favorite, I assumed you didn't have one yet, that you hadn't even thought about it before." His voice sounded different on the phone. Lighter, slightly higher. "I didn't want to embarrass you, so I didn't push it."

I laughed. "Should I be embarrassed that I don't have a favorite tree?"

Maya stretched on the floor. She looked up at the tease in my throat. "Is that a *boy*?" she sang in a whisper. "A *booooooooooooy*!"

I stuck out my tongue and motioned for her to go away, but instead she started a swan arm variation with her middle fingers up in response. I turned toward the window, my cheeks hot.

Brooks continued. "And now I'm assuming that you've spent the past two weeks in tree contemplation. Every minute dedicated to the pursuit of your beloved species."

"Beloved species," I said. "You really just said that."

"It's why I waited so long to call." There was a lift in his words, the ever-so-slightly higher pitch that comes through whenever he's talking through a jaw break of a smile. "To give you time."

I switched my phone to my other ear. "Time to research my favorite tree?"

"And?"

Okay, so I *had* wasted an hour or so in the attempt to find my tree. I scoured through pages of oaks and sycamores and pines, weeding through nursery and forestry websites. But there was no way I was going to tell Brooks that.

"Well, my mom's pepper trees are nice," I said.

He laughed. "You're so not off the hook," he said. "Make note, you're a bad liar, even over the phone."

"*Fine*," I said. "But take note that you're mean."

"Second question." He didn't even skip a beat. "Did you lose a hair tie in my car?"

"A what?"

"A hair tie. The thing chicks use to keep their hair up."

"You mean a rubber band?"

"Yeah," Brooks said. "That."

"You're asking me if I lost a rubber band in your car two weeks ago?" I glanced over my shoulder. Maya was still in the splits, middle-finger swan arming, giggling—having too much fun with her newly invented profane move. "That's even more ridiculous than the favorite-tree question."

"Hey, the tree question was a valid inquiry," he said. When I didn't say anything—I couldn't say anything, I was smiling too wide—he added, "Well, did you lose it, the supposedly rubber hair tie band thing?"

I grinned with a confidence I'd thought only existed in girls like Grace, this chatty banter, the sustained conversation. Usually my words fall flat. But there I was, at the kitchen table, my reflection bright in the window and my little sister listening behind. A somewhat gorgeous high school graduate soon to be firefighting boy had called me to ask if I'd lost my rubber band in his car two weeks ago.

"Yeah, it's mine," I said. "The rubber band." And maybe because of the endorphins, or the honey in my oatmeal, or the caffeine of my coffee, or maybe because quite simply I liked Brooks, I said, "I'm free today. Want to hang out?"

"Damn, Audie," he said. "I thought you'd never ask."

Brooks picked me up three hours later. We didn't talk as he sped up the I-5 but instead listened to whiny hip-hop. He rapped under his breath, and I tried not to laugh. It was past noon, but gray fog still gripped the coast, thickening as we merged onto the 55 West.

Brooks looked different in daylight. Tamer. His dirty blond hair was ruffled, as if he'd let it dry in high winds. He wasn't really prepped for a day at the beach—black pants and a fitted gray tee—so I was surprised when he asked, "You've been to Balboa Island, right?"

"Uh, no."

"How is it that I've lived here for a only a few months and Audrey Harper—a *lifetime* resident—is needing the tour?"

Audrey Harper. He'd remembered my last name. The way he said it made me dizzy, like he was recalling a memory, or naming a tree.

I bit my pinky nail, watching oaks give way to palm trees as we flew toward the sea, thinking of the studio mirrors and wood floors, how it's easy to blame my childhood dancing for all of my deficiencies, but the truth is that it's always been me. Beaches typically mean swimsuits, and swimsuits mean being seen. I miss the water, being submerged, floating, clean, but I hadn't shed my clothes in public since I was thirteen.

"I don't get out much," I said.

"What did I tell you?" Brooks forced a frown. "You lie for shit. Your voice gets all wheezy."

It was an asshole thing of him to say, but he was smiling, green eyes looking straight ahead, his voice somehow kind, presenting the sentence as if it were a compliment. No one had ever noticed my wheezy bullshit voice before. It felt good that he'd paid enough attention to notice.

"Are you afraid?" he asked.

I pushed my hair behind my ears, still wet from my shower. How could I explain that I didn't like stripping down to a bathing suit? "No, it's not—I love the ocean, water, but—"

"Exposing your psyche isn't second-date material, eh?"

A shot of euphoria. "This is a date?" I asked.

He didn't respond right away. I glanced at him and he glanced at me and I swear I maybe didn't breathe and Brooks said, "Would you like this to be a date, Audrey?"

I'd never been on a date before. I'd never had a boy talk so easily to me, pick me up, drive me to the coast, use my name directly. Even with the spotlight on me, a tiara on my head, my costume cinched in, even then, I'd never felt so significant. I'd never wanted to feel so significant.

"Yeah," I said, smiling so hard, feeling bright. "I think I would."

18

9:51 A.M.

Hair rinsed, my face rubbed raw, I'm still not clean and I'm far from content.

"I love you," Grace says, pulling on a pair of denim shorts. "But you look like hell."

I double knot my shoelaces. "I feel like hell."

"You should eat some bacon."

I force a laugh. "Bacon isn't going to fix this."

"What if I do your makeup?" Her eyes are lined neon blue to match her hair. A natural disaster is as good an excuse as any to rock a dramatic Sephora-inspired look.

"We don't have time for makeup," I say.

"You sure?" she asks. "A fresh face always helps my hangovers."

"I'll just sweat it off," I say. "Come on, let's go."

"Okay, okay, didn't realize we're running on a clock here," she says. But then, her hand light on my arm, "Are you sure you're up to this?"

"Of course."

"*Audrey*," she says. "Be honest."

People who don't know Grace think she's a bitch. They're wrong. She's resilient—has adapted to our venom-tongued culture—her skin spiky thick for protection. I was there when she cried for the four months of her parents' short-lived separation, when Marshall cheated on her freshman year, and when she held Quinn's hand in the halls, only to have her name scribbled in red ink on the bathroom stall with *cow* and *whore* and *dyke* acting as the prefixes.

And she was there for me the night before my audition, and the night after, and when my curves grew in and I wanted to take a knife to my skin but couldn't find the words to articulate it. She's here. For years, Grace has urged me to talk louder and cry harder. She puts up a front, but she cares.

"I'm *fine*. Let's go." The words are slippery cool, like limeade on a triple-digit day. "Fire doesn't wait."

My skin prickles. *Fire doesn't wait.* That's Brooks's line. That's what he said on the trail Thursday night.

19

Taffy

When the sun broke through the fog that late-June Tuesday in Balboa—Brooks's and my second date—he bought me a hat from a harbor boutique. It was a giant, frumpy thing, black with eyelet lace and flowers pinned to the bow. I posed on the pier, laughing, one hand on the hat and the other on my hip. Brooks took a photo on his phone, saying that only a classic beauty like me could pull off such an atrocious look. I didn't even roll my eyes at that line. I couldn't. My heart was too busy rising with the seagulls.

I wore the hat on the Ferris wheel, where Brooks held my hand and I was afraid that he'd kiss me—I didn't know how to kiss—but he didn't try. We only lurched up into the air over the harbor and then back down again. At the very top of the wheel, the bench rocked, our legs hanging in the warm breeze. I stared at our hands, my chipped green nail polish and his long fingers marked with the occasional scar. I thought of what everyone had said at school about his temper, his backstory, his markings. It all felt like fantasy.

"I've heard a lot of stories," I said.

"You mean about me?"

"Any of them true?"

He looked out at the water of the bay with a weird smirk, this quiet sigh. And as we swung up the wheel a second time, he answered, "One of them must be, right?"

"How about your eye," I said. "What happened?"

He touched his brow, as if needing a reminder. "Dog attack," he said.

"A dog did that?"

"I was seven," he said, so careful, "out on some bike trail with my brother when this rottweiler ran up." He rubbed his cheek with the back of his hand. "I got off my bike like a dumbass, wanted to pet it or something. Then I was down. Cameron tried to beat it off me with a branch."

"He beat a dog off you with a *stick*?"

"That's your takeaway from my traumatic memory?" He laughed. "Cameron and a stick?"

"It's an intense image."

"Yeah, well." He picked at his nails. "He deserves the glory—but the dog—" He showed me the inside of his arms, more pale scars, long jagged threads, some thick, like marks of a boil. "It bit at my legs too. Got a nice chunk of skin and then barely missed my eye. I could have died."

We were sitting so close, our limbs touching. I'd been afraid to meet his gaze, only letting myself glance up as far as his nose. But, as he shifted closer, I finally looked up and met his eyes, the swampy green, the pale dense snag of a scar beside his left eye.

"Thanks," he said. "For asking. No one ever asks."

"Were you afraid?"

He smiled. "I was a tad too preoccupied to be scared."

"But what happened? Was Cameron able to get it off you?"

"Was a ten-year-old able to beat a rottweiler?" He laughed again, a hand in his hair, talking fast now. "No, he tried though. Hell, I remember him screaming and the owners running up, this younger couple. Some blond chick crying. I went to the emergency room. My dad sued and his partner negotiated a sweet settlement—made the whole ordeal worth it. Best eighteenth-birthday present ever."

"How much does a sweet settlement entail?"

"Well, it bought the Audi." Brooks nodded down to the bay, as if to the path of the ferry where we'd crossed over the waves.

"Wait." I shook my head. "I thought being a pizza-coffee boy bought the Audi."

His lips pressed into a thin smile. "Well, those jobs helped too."

"Helped?"

"What?" He raised his hands in defense. "Minimum wage is high in Seattle."

I clicked my tongue. "And to think that you made me feel bad about my wheezy voice, when all along you're the liar." I brimmed with a hot energy—the relief of having something easy to say, a reason to tease him, rather than him teasing me. "So sad," I said. "Our entire friendship is built on lies."

"It was *not* a lie!" His voice pitched, and the Ferris wheel swung to a stop at the bottom, the ride over. He helped me down the platform, nodded at the gate attendant, all the while saying, "I brewed, like, a thousand cups of coffee." But his excuses were inane. We were both laughing, breathless fools tumbling down the boardwalk. "Cut me a break! I was nervous and didn't want you to think I was some trust-fund baby."

"A settlement isn't a trust fund," I said.

"I freaked out because I thought you were cute," he said. "It's a compliment!"

I whirled around to face him, unable to stop smiling. "You thought?"

"Think." He grabbed my hand. "Obviously *think*."

"Surviving a dog attack is far more impressive than being a pizza-espresso boy."

"I'll keep that in mind." He glanced around the boardwalk, hands in his pockets, suddenly antsy, and asked, "How do you feel about scoping out a frozen-banana stand?"

After the Ferris wheel and the chocolate-dipped frozen banana we shared but he mostly ate, Brooks and I headed from the harbor to the beach. The waves were wicked and the tide was high. I took off my Vans, held them and my new hat as we walked.

With my jeans rolled up, the sand sticking to my feet, my heart was so high, so entranced by the possibilities this boy offered. "So, what made you want to volunteer?" I said. "Want to fight fires?"

Brooks smiled, head tilted back. "It was never really a question." His thrill was contagious. "Isn't there something you're compelled by but can't explain why?"

A breeze tugged us down to the sand. We sat with an inch between us. I dug out broken seashells with my toes and tried to think of what I was drawn to, what I couldn't explain. Brooks sat with his legs crossed, shoes still on, his silver Zippo in hand.

"Can I?" I asked.

He passed it over. It was heavier than I expected, the silver cool in my hand. I ran my pinky over the Space Needle sketched into the base. And I thought how I could answer his question, that yes, there is something I was compelled by but couldn't explain: him. But otherwise, no, not unless you count pointless researching, straight-A grades in school, occasionally thinking about college. I don't have a *thing*. I've never had one, not really. Ballet never even felt wholly mine. At its peak, it was for Maya and Maya only.

Brooks was watching me with an attentiveness I could feel in my ankles. I flicked the Zippo open, fumbled to bring up the flame, and when I did, heat licked my finger. I dropped it with a sharp breath.

"Hey now," he said. "You okay?"

When I nodded, he took back the Zippo, striking a bright, high flame—blue, orange, yellow, red. I looked down at my finger. There wasn't a burn or scar or a mark, but the pain still numbly pulsed. It'd felt good—the scorch—why had it felt good?

"You haven't really answered my question," I said.

"When I was six," Brooks said, "my family took a road trip down to Oregon, and there was this crazy wildfire. That's my first memory of fire, it must be. I remember smelling it. Tasting it even. And then seeing what had already burned, on both sides of the highway, a forest of black matchstick trees. All those trees."

"That must have left an impression."

He rubbed his hands together. "Cameron wanted to stop and help; he was nine, around nine, and I think that's when I knew. After that trip, I knew I needed to get my hands on fire."

"Man," I said. "Career path decided at six."

"I really just wanted to be like Cameron," Brooks said. "That's what it was, what it *is*, if I'm being honest—but it stuck, the firefighting dream." He flicked the Zippo's flame into the sand. "When we caught up to the fire, it was like driving through a war. The flames nearly consumed us."

"They didn't close the road?"

He kicked at the sand, and, his voice clipped, he said, "Cameron said we almost got caught in it. That we almost died. I remember him begging Dad to stop the car—he wanted to help the firefighters." He shook his head and looked at me. "But can you even imagine? A family in an SUV burning alive?"

"No," I said. "I can't."

A pause—enough time for a wave to crash into the shore—and then Brooks asked, "How's your Latin?"

"Nonexistent."

He flicked the Zippo again, this time cupping his hand around the flame, letting it breathe and stay lit. "Fire—the word—it's derived from the Latin term *fascinare*. Meaning to enchant, to bewitch." The flame swayed bright and steady, and I *was* enchanted, but by him. "Fire is seriously, *literally*, fascinating."

I leaned back on my elbows. "I still don't understand," I said, though I did. I just wanted him to keep talking.

Brooks closed the Zippo. He looked at me, his expression so soft, hesitant, and then—in a breath—he ran a pinky down the side of my jaw. His touch was better than the almost-burn.

"Don't you know your clichés?" The skin he'd touched hummed. "Humanity wants to control beauty, control the impossible: fire. It's, I don't know, the human condition."

I looked down. "*Beautiful,*" I said. "That's not fire." The lace on my new hat was already torn. "It kills, destroys homes—" I remembered when I was a kid, watching a wildfire in the foothills from the lake. And I remembered when I was even younger, howling through an evacuation, flames thrashing the hills past my home.

"They're misunderstood." Brooks reached for my hand. "Yeah, they're horrendous when they hit civilization, which is why I want to fight them, to *help* save lives. But wildfires—they're part of the ecosystem." He released my hand, and my palm went numb. "Nature needs to burn. It's not a fire's fault people keep building houses in its path."

"Oh."

He frowned. "You don't seem convinced."

"Well." I spoke carefully. "You're talking as if fire were a person."

Brooks laughed. "Well, if it were a person I'd say it's a fickle bitch."

I tried to laugh too. "Is this—is this what you want to do forever? Like, a career?"

"Why, Miss Harper, are you asking me about my *future?* On our *second* date?"

"You just graduated high school," I said. "It's fair game to ask."

"Not necessarily out in the field. Maybe fire forensics—investigation— the science of it. I'm doing a year or so of reserve work down here and then going back to Washington or up to Interior Alaska for a degree in fire science."

"That's a thing? Fire science?"

"It is absolutely a *thing.*" Brooks smiled. "I'm not the only one who wants to understand the uncontrollable."

"You mean you're not the only pyromaniac?"

He ignored me. "There's going to be a big one this summer," he said. "I feel it. This place is prime for a blowup." Brooks tossed his Zippo in his hands, shaking his head. "It'll be huge. National coverage, maybe international. I bet we'll have a fire that at *least* makes national news."

I watched the tide, wishing it'd come closer, close enough to wet my toes. "Don't say that," I said. "How can you even say that? Just thinking about it—I can't even think about it."

He studied me, his euphoria draining. "I'm only hypothesizing. It won't—" He touched my hand, unable to meet my eyes. "I'm sorry. I didn't mean to scare you."

"I'm not afraid," I said. "I simply don't want my home to burn down, even if the land is prime for it. It's my *home*."

He blinked, dropped his head, as if only realizing then the implications of what he'd been saying. "Of course I don't want that either."

Brooks was so near. I couldn't move. I didn't want to move. He tugged me close, wrapped his arm around me and held me to his chest. I was in bloom, my skin licking with light. He leaned his cheek against my head.

"Hey." He talked into my hair. "I promise to protect you, always. As long as you'll have me." His voice swam down my spine.

Warmth consumed me. "Okay," I whispered, nervous, too nervous. "I'll have you."

Brooks was holding me, his lips near my skin. I'd never been so physically close to a person besides Maya, nor had I ever wanted to be. And I didn't need his protection. But my face felt hot, words stuck to the roof of my mouth: I was happy. His skin was so warm against mine, and he was stiller than he'd ever been, as if holding me was a balm to his frenetic energy. If I could have swallowed him up right then, I would have.

20

_____

10:17 A.M.

Grace and I are stopped several neighborhoods before mine. NO ENTRY. NO EXCEPTIONS. That's what the sign says. Two police cars block the road. The officers shout to the residents of this not-yet-vacated street, the residents of these expansive designer homes. They shout, *Voluntary evacuation, prepare for the worst, please comply.*

The wind is far stronger than it was this morning, the sky blacker, and it feels thirty degrees hotter than Grace's neighborhood fifteen minutes northwest. The fire isn't visible—all I can see is the tar-like smoke billowing across the sky, masking the mountains and hills and homes planted on higher slopes. The sun is concealed. It could be twilight. Or the apocalypse. That's what it looks like—the end of the world.

I expected a line of SUVs, residents waiting for answers. I expected to see some of my neighbors. But, for the most part, my little corner of the community has vacated the vicinity. My little corner, tucked away, closest to what grows wild and dry—does it even exist anymore?

I park and we stand by the truck, not yet daring to move closer.

"Oh, Audrey," Grace says. "This is terrifying."

I've always loved the contrast of it: wild against suburbia. Always loved looking down at my home from the trail—finding patterns in the varying houses and manicured lawns against the roughness of the high desert land, cacti and oaks and hills sweeping out in various shades of gold and brown and gray and pastel green. I always thought I was so lucky.

And I was, I *am* so lucky, privileged, to have grown up here. But I never considered the implications of a home built on the edge of the wild, a home shared with mountain lions and deer, and the possibility of floods and fires.

"You okay?" Grace asks.

We haven't yet moved from my truck.

"It's devastating," I say.

She squeezes my hand. "It is more than devastating."

We walk toward the barricade. Aside from the wind and the helicopters above, it's near silent. And my heart stops, I swear it does, because as we turn a corner, from this new vantage, the blaze is visible on a hillside to the west of my home—bright and beastly against the calm organization of suburbia. It looks so close. Is it as close as it looks? Several pitch-black narrow plumes spin up. Structure fire. Houses on fire.

Homeowners move slowly now, as if the fire has cast a spell. Ash swirls down, sticking to the palm trees, dirtying gurgling fountains. These families not yet evacuated—probably soon to be evacuated—stand at the end of their driveways, as if by doing so, they'll stop the fire from displacing their lives.

They watch the bruising sky, the blockade sign and the cops, the black clouds that flush up above my neighborhood to the south and spiral to the east.

They take pictures and murmur to one another. Others, perhaps the smarter few, lug suitcases and dog crates and framed paintings into their cars. A man with a thick beard rubs his eyes. A girl my age, in a faded sundress, cries beside him. I recognize her from the halls at school. She holds a cat against her chest.

Shadow. I need to find Shadow.

I hold Grace's hand, and we walk closer.

Breaking the spell, a middle-aged man runs into the street several houses beyond. Grace and I freeze. He's wearing hiking boots, cargo shorts, and a red T-shirt. He looks at his neighbors and waves his arms.

"We got to get out, everyone needs to get out!" He motions toward the hills, motions in every direction. "The fire is surrounding us—why are you all just standing around? *We got to get out!*" He stares at the two policemen. "What are you people doing? Do something for our homes!"

A flurry of whispers start up. People move. Turn back to their cars. Rush into their homes. Are they listening or are they hiding? One of the officers moves from the barricade, moving toward the man, telling him to settle down. But the man—he continues to yell. His fear and anger are more stifling than the heat. And then he's in his Cadillac, a family already buckled up, backing out of his driveway and speeding away, waving a hand out the window.

"What the hell," Grace says.

I glance at her. "I agree with him. They're on borrowed time."

A young couple now stands at the barricade. They both cry, hands to their mouths. They look past the police cars, and I know. I know they live near me—that they too woke at 5 A.M. to pounding on the door. The woman is in white yoga pants and a pink baseball cap, the man in hiking shorts and a wide-brimmed hat. Both wear surgical masks. A golden retriever pants on its leash. The woman points her phone up at the molten sky, the column of black smoke against the brown smolder. The man talks to the cop still guarding the barricade, arms folded, nodding.

I've never seen them before, but I see it: Their souls are battered too. Maybe the woman is also thinking about her mother's forgotten portraits in the guest bedroom, wondering if the paint is already peeling, burning, melting.

Grace and I move forward. The day is hot in my mouth. The man shakes the cop's hand, and the couple retreats. People watch Grace and me from the safety of their yards. My neighbor in pink nods at me. Between the cap and the mask, I can only see her eyes. Red. Weary. I smile at her, not with my teeth. A hug of a smile. I hope so, at least.

Grace rubs my shoulder. "Audrey?"

A stray ember lands on my skin. A small, hot shock. I keep my feet moving forward. "I just—" I sound far away, even to me. "I was hoping to grab some of the crap I forgot."

"Well, at least it was only crap."

"Thanks for the sensitivity."

"Just trying to diffuse the tension!"

Both of the cops are clean-shaven but shiny and red-faced. One is about to speak, shout an order, shoo us away, but I beat him to the stage.

"Any structure loss yet?" I ask.

He blinks at me, and then at Grace. "Excuse me?" he asks.

"Structure loss," I say. "Have any houses burned yet?"

"The evacuation center is at Mission Viejo High School—updates are being announced there." He glances at his watch, as if the hands will reveal the answers. I follow suit and glance at my phone. Only eleven minutes have passed since I parked.

"She's a resident of Falconridge Drive *and* her boyfriend is a firefighter." Grace coughs into her hands, wheezing until she is able to add, "She has the right to know."

Exhaustion settles in the lines of his face. His radio crackles, and he lifts it to his ear. "No official counts have been made."

"So some houses have burned?" I ask.

"Where are your parents?" He's stepping forward now, and we're shuffling back. "You need to clear the area."

"Can't you just tell me?" I'm sounding younger by the word. A toddler ready to throw a fit, my voice flooding with tears. "It's my home."

His radio croaks static-cloaked codes. "Again, updates are being released at the evacuation center—Mission Viejo High School."

"Can I just run by my house?" I ask. "I need to—"

"I'm sorry."

"But—"

"You can get more information at the evacuation center." He steps off the curb and waves his arms pointing at a car trying to get past the barricade too, motions for them to make a U-turn. I stare at his digital watch, at the small seconds racing forward. He looks so tired, so beat. Where does he live? Is he worried for his home too?

Grace huffs. "Are you legally bound to be a jackass?" With a swift turn, she rushes back to my truck, coughing the entire way—always happy to throw in dramatics.

"Sorry," I tell him.

The cop tries to smile, a weak, sympathetic *your house will be gone soon* smile, and wipes the sweat off his head with the back of his hand. His radio crackles again, and I hear what it says, a code of numbers, a name, and "Clear it." He closes his eyes. He shouts to his partner, who is now talking to a family a house over, "Code 43."

"You want to help your house?" he asks. "Let us do our job."

As I walk away, I hear it: He's speaking into megaphone. "This neighborhood is officially under mandatory evacuation."

21

Necessary

On the first day of July, Maya was invited to the October auditions at the Orange County Institute of Ballet. She celebrated with an hour of Pilates on the living room rug and a request of spinach omelets and bacon for dinner.

I wanted to spin with Maya to the moon, wanted to throw roses at the crazy universe, in gratitude that she was no longer sick but was now in full throttle to achieving her dream. But still, there was a cold thump in my chest. Maya was going places without me. She's my little sister, and I'm five thousand miles behind.

"We've worked out an intensive training schedule with Clarisse, on top of the core classes," Mom said to Dad. "It's going to be a busy, busy summer."

"The best kind of summer," Dad said.

"Just don't let it stop you from dancing like no one's watching," I said, cutting a rogue spinach leaf into threads. "What would be the fun in that?"

"Oh, I dunno," Maya said. "Dancing for applause is rather awesome."

"Speaking of summer plans"—Dad waved his fork at me—"have you started scanning the photos, or making a list for potential jobs?"

"Um," I said. "I intend to do both of those things tomorrow."

Maya smiled. "Key word being *intend*."

I faked disgust. "Excuse me. I've already mentally started the job list! I'm going to apply to that bookstore in Aliso Viejo, maybe at some café, or that new chocolate shop at the Spectrum—"

"Oh no you're not," Mom said, nodding at Maya. "I'm going to be driving this lady back and forth for her training. There won't be time for me to shuttle you all over Orange County to work."

Maya pulled a bobby pin from her bun, twisting it straight, and said, "I can carpool with other girls to the studio."

I sighed. "Not with your unique schedule."

"It would be a lot of gas money," Dad said, "if you worked that far out. Why don't you stick to only applying in Rancho Santa Margarita? And no farther out than Ladera Ranch."

"Really honey, it'd be best if you found a job within walking distance," Mom said.

Maya spun her water glass in circles. "If only we had real public transportation." And she sadly sang, "Forever stuck out in the suburbs." Which is what it feels like sometimes—the nearest bus station is outside of Coto de Caza's gates; a simple journey to the mall is a three-hour endeavor without a car.

I stared at my mom. "You do realize that the only job within walking distance is the country club, right?"

Maya nearly choked on her bacon. "Oh my god, Audrey. You in a polo shirt!"

Mom smiled. "The country club would be nice, sweetie!"

"I'm personally fully on board with this plan," Maya said, laughing. "You could learn some manners, some country club sensibilities. This will be good for you."

I cut the remains of my omelet up into eggy crumbs. "No one is going to hire an inexperienced fifteen-year-old, so don't get too excited."

Dad went for an encouraging smile. "It's a matter of trying and learning."

"I *know*," I said. "I'll try. I'll apply to the country club."

"Wait," Maya said, a sudden flush to her cheeks. "I need an after-hours teacher, a happiness mentor." She grinned at me, always my sunbeam. "For when Clarisse is too much, has fumbled my mind with critiques and formulas and—"

"Don't talk with your mouth full," Mom said.

"*Audrey*," Maya said. "You can tutor me so that I don't forget to dance like no one is watching." She looked at Dad. "That counts as work, right?"

Dad chuckled. "Sounds more like you two making a mess and ending the night with a door-slamming fight."

"That's the point!" Maya cried. "Keeping the messy fun in ballet." Which made my throat tight, that she would think I'd be good at that, but she went on, "I need this, Mom. Otherwise it's going to be a summer of Clarisse madness and sadness. Audrey will help me further refine my dancing techniques *and* relax."

I found my voice. "I'm especially skilled at the art of being lazy, which is key for relaxing." I looked at Mom. "And, if you do recall, a summer of madness and sadness prior to a ballet audition is *not* good."

Mom sighed.

Maya leaned back. "Such a summer could even lead me to dancing straight off that stage and then *bam*, you have two glum ex-ballerinas in your home."

"But there's nothing wrong with that, if that happens." I pointed a finger at her.

She nodded. "That's certainly true—"

"*Okay*, okay," Mom said, laughing. "*Enough*. Audrey can tutor Maya, whatever that means, in the evenings and on your off days, as Clarisse allows."

"And Audrey's pay?" Maya asked.

"We continue to feed her," Dad said.

"It was a good try." I shrugged at Maya.

"You girls." Mom shook her head.

"So, to summarize"—Dad pushed back his plate—"Audrey will help Maya prepare for her audition, as well as proceed with her local job hunt."

I lifted my water glass to Maya's and we clinked. "Cheers to forever happy dancing, sister."

"Cheers to *you*, sister."

Mom sighed. "Now, which one of you is making brownies?"

Maya took the dibs for brownie making, and I pushed at my food, chewing at my smile. I knew I wouldn't be applying at the country club anytime soon, and not just because the idea of catering to the likes of the OC Housewives shot a rifle of panic into my chest. I already had plans for the next day (Brooks). And I had plans for the day after that (Brooks), and now frequent evening dancing (doing nothing, doing everything) with Maya—helping her get closer to achieving her dream, pursuing her thing, even if it meant simply rolling around on the floor and goofing off and unwinding.

Maybe, at some point, I'd find my dream too.

Under the table, my phone buzzed. It was Brooks.

Think you can come out tonight? Want to tell you all about my day. Want to hear all about yours.

The already warm thump in my chest turned hot and bright, and it dawned on me that Brooks could be my thing, my ballet, my fire. I had never felt so necessary. No one had ever felt so necessary in my life.

22

10:20 A.M.

Back in the truck, I U-turn away from the barricade, the soon-to-be mandatorily evacuated neighborhood.

"He wasn't being an ass, you know," I say. "You shouldn't have been so rude."

Grace blows her bangs from her face. "The dude was withholding information. Pisses me off, and I thought you wanted to check it out."

"We are."

"You going to call Brooks?"

"No." I glance over at her flip-flops. "You should have worn different shoes."

23

Chatter

Brooks and his dad live in the west side of Coto. The four-bedroom three-point-five-bath house was built with the intention of a larger family, but it's just the two of them. The furniture and drapery and rugs are elaborate and dark—rich burgundy and soft browns. It's icy cold and drafty, with the ceilings droning the constant rumble of the AC. I wonder how high their electric bill peaks.

The first time he had me over, that second day of July, not even a week after the Balboa trip, Brooks explained that his dad gave his secretary his credit card and instructed her to make the house a home. One January afternoon, Brooks came home from school to painted walls and cluttered rooms. He hates it, prefers simple and clean, light—industrial even.

"When Mom came down for my graduation," he said, "man, she laughed—said we were living in a funeral showroom."

Brooks's mom is still in Seattle, teaching art history at the University of Washington. I asked Brooks why he didn't stay with her if he loved Washington so much, and he shrugged and opened the stainless-steel fridge, dug out two bottles of beer with a pond on the label.

"There was drama at my old school, and my mom and I don't get along well, so I figured I'd mix it up senior year." He cracked off the bottle tops on the side of the counter. "Challenge myself, you know?"

"Was it worth it?" My knees were shaking. I was in his house. I was alone in his house, and he was scruffy and beautiful. "Mixing it up?"

He handed me a beer and smiled. "I met you, didn't I?"

A skinny gray cat rounded the island counter, purring madly. Brooks scooped her up, nuzzling his face into her fur, into the darker cloud-like splotches on her neck. She wasn't wearing a collar, and her purring rumbled as he struggled to contain her. She clawed at his arms until he finally dropped her to the wood floor.

"Shit." He rubbed his scratches. The cat had disappeared, but I could hear the whisper of her meow. "Don't let her chatter fool you," he said, but with a grin. "My dad's cat is a beast."

I smiled. "I'm more into dogs anyway."

A photo hung on the kitchen nook wall: Brooks, maybe six or seven or eight, gawky with a buzz cut and gap-toothed grin, sunburned skin. The other boy is taller, slightly older, also blond. They're on a trail canopied with evergreens, both in khaki, wearing bandanas on their arms.

I held my finger just above the glass. "You and Cameron?" I asked, looking over my shoulder. "You guys were adorable." Brooks swigged from his beer, eyes set on the frame. "Where does he go to school?" I remembered the drive through the canyon, Cameron moving east, ending the backpacking tradition.

Brooks squinted, the place where the dog struck him creasing. "He doesn't anymore."

"He dropped out?"

"In a sense," Brooks said. "He's dead."

24

10:37 A.M.

What most people don't know about mandatory evacuations is that, in some states, legally, a resident cannot be forced to leave his or her home. You'd be something of a fool to hang out in a fire's path, but, in some states, there's nothing the law can do about it but knock and ask in a stern voice and holler threats and repeat the word *mandatory* again and again on an intercom until you're convinced. *Yes. I must leave. Yes.*

And you *should* go. They're evacuating you for a reason. You're not safe.

In California though, it's a criminal offense to not obey evacuation orders.

Yet last summer, during the Falls Fire down in Lake Elsinore—a community also bordering the Cleveland National, forty minutes south on Ortega Highway—two brothers ignored orders and stuck around. Photos show the red-faced men on their driveways wielding garden hoses, flames visible in the hills above. Yeah, they look somewhat freaked, but no one died in the Falls

Fire, so they must have survived. And as far as I can find on Google, they weren't punished for their supposed criminal offence.

So it can't be that big of a deal, right?

Like I said, in some states, if you really want to stay home, you can.

Maybe it's because of this that I don't feel anything. No guilt, no remorse, no fear. I ditch my truck on the side of the road, cross the park up to the manicured slope—where I smoked my first and only bowl, where I played hide-and-seek when I was ten—and climb through the sage weed and crunchy grass. I take the more rugged route home, and I don't feel a thing.

Grace and I clamber up the bank. It hurts to breathe. I take off my hoodie and hold it to my face. Can you get sunburned if the sun is covered with black and brown and gray sheets of smoke? The air hisses with the venom of a rattle-snake. My shirt clings to my back like a wet leaf on glass.

I'm being dramatic. We've only been walking for ten minutes.

Grace's tank top is tied around her mouth. "Have I mentioned I hate you?" she asks.

She hikes in her bikini top and shorts, my car keys clipped to her belt loop because my pants won't stay on my waist with the extra weight. Flies hover by her tan legs, the sweaty curve of her waist. I could never strip off my shirt outside, and I envy the fact that she does it without a second thought.

"This was your idea," I say. "Checking out my house."

"I wasn't imagining a hike through the freaking desert," she says. "Was more thinking of a meet and greet with some fireboys, maybe a tour on a truck. You know, led by *your boyfriend* or whatever."

I roll my eyes. "Because a wildfire is like a brewery."

"God." Grace sighs. "A cold beer. How good does that sound?"

Hot air blows. I can taste it, taste the smoke, charcoal, and dirt. My lips are papery, glued shut. I step and pray that the rattlesnakes have retreated into their caves as I listen for a whisper below the crackling crunch of dried bottle-brush and hawthorn shrubs.

The land is the same sad color of the sky—brown and beige, the reek of death and wilt and decay. The home association used to send landscaping crews back here—these hills between parks, between neighborhoods—to prune and trim, but it's been months since a gardener last walked these slopes. Two years ago, it was green and lush, the land studded with bright wildflower buds after a few seasons of decent rain, smoke-free autumns.

But here's the problem: Fire *is* necessary. Like Brooks said. A good year of rain—of rich land and fast growth—practically guarantees that the next dry year will blow up in smoke. We haven't had a big blaze since I was thirteen, and this region has been in some level of a drought since I was conceived—a drought that jumped to critical conditions last winter, when the average January temperature was seventy-six degrees.

We were long due for a fire, Brooks told me. *Inevitable.* That's what he said.

The slope we climbed is behind us now. My breath hitches. The wild stretch of fire laps out southeast—a raging pool of flames with black fields in its wake. The man at the barricade was right: We are surrounded. The fire is bursting everywhere. We stand on the hill that rolls down to my yard, facing the larger bank that looms over my house. I can't breathe. Higher up, the black smoke entirely engulfs the hill, the land behind it, the trail I've walked my entire life—the fire zigzagging just below the smoke line like a river of lava snaking down to my home.

"What did I tell you?" Grace says. "Your house is good as gold."

I'm going to be sick.

25

Stars

On that second day of July, my first time at Brooks's house, after he told me his brother was dead, all I could manage to say was, "What?"

Brooks touched my arm, urging me away from the wall, the photo. "Last September, the day before he was supposed to go back to school."

He yanked open the patio glass door, pulling it so hard that it slid off its track. He wouldn't look at me, only shoved the door back into place. We stepped out into the dimming afternoon, and I tried to pull up words, think of the right thing to say.

His brother. Cameron. Dead.

I'd been imagining him alive, strong and tan and blond like Brooks, with a sharp jaw and wide eyes. Tall too, maybe hovering over Brooks by an inch, sprinting up sandstone Ivy League steps, clutching an armful of books to his chest, living somewhere that requires sweaters made of wool, a state not under constant threat of wildfires. My chest swelled, and I thought of Maya. She's nearly another limb. To lose her, my heart cracked at the thought of it, and at the memory of when I thought I would lose her. Those were the worst days I know.

"Brooks," I said. "I'm so sorry."

He rubbed his bad eye. "You know the band Stars?" I shook my head, and he slid the door into place, closed. He leaned against the glass, looking out past the trees lining his neighbors' property. "They were Cameron's favorite. Canadian, older. Poppy indie or whatever. I never understood the appeal, but Cameron—you know."

I didn't know. Not about Cameron or the band, but I said, "Yeah."

"There's this one song, from the early 2000s—" He glanced at me. "This guy talks before the music even starts, saying, *When there's nothing left to burn you have to set yourself on fire.*" His arms were crossed lazily over his chest, his expression calm, as if he were reciting some anecdote at a party, not explaining his brother's death. "Cameron posted that online the night before he died. *When there's nothing left to burn you have to set yourself on fire.* The next morning, he went down to Alki Beach and dumped gasoline on himself."

I tried to breathe, but it was like sand had filled my lungs.

"Fire," I said, wanting to ask, desperate to ask, if this was really why he was so obsessed.

"His final words to the world." Brooks's voice was even, so crisp, but his hand clenched and unclenched around the Zippo. "A bullshit line. And then, he lit himself on fire." His voice finally cracked. "He was my best friend."

My skin seared. I stepped closer to him, his grief panging through my body. It suddenly all made sense, his aloofness at school, the scowl that's set into his face, the way his hands often shake—still in mourning, soaked in grief, learning how to *be* without his brother.

"I'm so sorry," I said again.

"Me too." And he almost smiled. "But it happened. You know, now it's just something that happened." The same line he gave me about his parents' rocky divorce.

I wanted to ask if Cameron's death was why Brooks and his dad had moved, the cause of the divorce; I wanted to ask if Cameron had shared Brooks's deep voice and shyness; I wanted to understand, but rocks sat on my tongue. Instead of saying anything, I reached for his hand.

There's a fire pit in Brooks's backyard. The gas fire pit—one of those Home Depot portable deals—sits in the middle of a pebble circle with two wood chairs on either side. Brooks and his dad, or maybe the plastic-wielding secretary, apparently forgot to purchase cushions for the chairs.

"Took me a whole day," Brooks said. "This setup."

"You did this?"

It was twilight—the sky a stretched-out topaz sheet above, bleached and tie-dyed orange and pink and red. A hot summer, newly July, and already blistered afternoons and coffee-brown hills. But coastal California guarantees a nearly year-round evening cool down, so I didn't think twice when Brooks struck the long match, turned on the gas, and filled the metal bowl with light.

"We had a permanent pit back in Seattle," he said. "I needed one here—a backyard bonfire is a necessity. But, well, fire hazard on the dead grass and what not, so solution! Pebble garden and non-wood burning."

He was hyper, earnest, as if he hadn't just explained his brother's death by fire a few moments before, jumpy in the way that felt as if he were acutely skirting pain.

"Pebble garden." I swallowed a mouthful of beer. "I like it."

We sat on the ground—the rocks still warm, the day's heat soft through my jeans—our knees touching. The flames licked at the metal cage. I wondered if Brooks and Cameron had sat in the Seattle rain around a fire pit.

"I wish I'd met you sooner." Brooks's eyes wandered my face, memorizing me, mesmerizing me. "All winter, every night, I was here. It would have been so nice to have been alone with you."

I ducked my head, smiling. *Alone with you.* "You were out here even when it rained?"

"What, those four drizzly nights?" He tossed a stone into the fire. "Yes, even then."

I whistled. "Dedication."

A minute or two passed in silence. I wanted to ask Brooks if he had a favorite Californian tree, and I wanted to ask if Cameron had ever visited the Golden State, but the risk of stumbling over my words was at an all-time high. I was there alone with him, and he was still looking at me, eyes so green against his sage tee.

"But we have now." He kissed my knuckles. "I'm lucky to be alone with you now."

I didn't know how to say that I felt the same—so stupidly lucky. "Why did you sit next to me?" I asked. "At senior prank night? I don't even understand why you went. You didn't sit next to anyone all semester. And you barely knew Grace. Why me?"

"It was my last chance to approach you." Brooks touched my chin, nudging me to look at him. "And I wanted to. You looked as lonely as me."

I looked at my hands. "Lonely."

"Audrey," Brooks said, his left eye watering. "You should know I really like you."

I was dizzy and my feet were asleep and we'd only hung out a few times and ten minutes earlier I'd been drenched in his grief, Cameron's death. But right then, there was a surge in my chest, hot and bursting, like sparklers on the Fourth of July. Can you fall for someone in such a fragment of time? I never thought I'd be the kind of girl to fall for a boy over a few summer nights. I didn't hide my smile, didn't bite down.

"I really like you too," I said.

Brooks kissed me then, his hand on my neck, fingers in my hair, slow and sweet like the saltwater taffy we shared on the way home from Balboa. It was my first kiss, if I don't count my kiss with Ross Bower in the fourth grade. I never count the Ross Bower kiss.

Brooks pulled me closer so that no pebbles were between us. Every inch of my skin buzzed. We'd only been hanging out for a few days, but he was eighteen, so this was inevitable. I didn't like to be touched, I've never liked to be touched, but this felt oddly okay. This felt safe. But I couldn't calm down, couldn't steady my pulse. He was so close.

"I *really*, really like you," he said again.

The July sky darkened into night, and the stone in the fire popped and, with my eyes halfway closed, the sparks looked like a fury of fireflies. I forgot about Cameron and his suicide, instead thinking how nice it was going to be to turn sixteen and have been kissed by a boy who *really*, really liked me.

26

11:02 A.M.

Five minutes pass. Grace and I don't move. The flames crawl just over the ridge of the bank above my home—brush I've walked through hundreds of times to get to the trails above. It is loud, a crushing, unfathomably bright roar. My house is drenched. A crew points hoses at the roof of terra-cotta tiles, spouting out water thick with chemicals that will keep my home soggy for hours. I squint through the haze to the glaring mound in my backyard. Our outdoor furniture has been shoved into the middle of the lawn, a blanket of foil draped over the sides. The pool shimmers with a film of ash. My skin is sticky, my body overheated, and for the first time in years I ache at the thought—with the desire—to undress and dive into the murky water.

I'm on my feet again. Huffing into my hoodie and trying to slow my breath. I squint until my vision blurs, trying to make out the figures below. Is Brooks down there?

No. He wouldn't be. He's just a volunteer reserve.

"Why the hell are they not spraying the fire?" Grace takes photos as she talks.

"Protocol," I say.

My house isn't receiving special attention. My neighbors are also being watered and wrapped. When a fire threatens subdivisions—especially high-priced subdivisions—the attack approach changes. Burning houses is what brings fires fame and exclusive coverage on the TV. In a remote area, a blaze can burn hundreds of thousands of acres, and yet, if no structures are threatened, it'll never receive a place on the 5 o'clock news. It's all about the houses. Save the homes. Save the memories. Defeat the monster nipping at the million-dollar boxes.

Brooks isn't wrapping homes in aluminum foil like they're sweet potatoes ready to plop into the oven. At least not willingly. He says it's all for show, for the media, for politics, for money—the mind-set that fire is a villain to defeat. "Fires are meant to burn," he says. He doesn't believe in focusing on the homes. He hates that they turn a blaze into a million-dollar-a-day event.

"What do we do now?" Grace asks.

"We watch," I say, but I'm not watching. I'm planning. I'm thinking about Maya dancing, Maya still thinking her kitten is safe. I check my phone. 11:10 A.M. The audition started at 10:00 A.M. Is Maya still on her toes, blowing the committee away?

I need to be able to tell her I saved Shadow. My ultimate congratulations.

Midway up the pluming slope, a line of firefighters hunch over in an effort to dig out a line of earth that will be brush-free, a ribbon to halt (or at least pause) the flames above—flames that appear frozen in place, as if licking at an invisible force field.

"It's so slow," Grace says.

"Fire climbs faster than it falls."

"That doesn't make sense."

I'm too thirsty to explain the science of it.

A helicopter sweeps above us. Can they see us? Have the firefighters below noticed us? *Breaking news: Two dimwits evaporate from dehydration and heat exhaustion, next up on Channel 4.* Embers drift up, floating to where we stand. We need to leave. We need to move. But the fire is above my home, beautiful and mesmerizing, pluming out mushrooms of gray smoke.

"Can we go?" Grace asks. "I need to pee."

It's undeniable. Fire is fascinating. Brooks told me so. How the word itself is derived from Latin, how it only shows enough of itself to lure you closer. He explained this on the beach at Balboa, but I didn't really believe it until now. I can't look away. You can't look away.

Last night, I asked him, "*Aren't you worried?*"

And, last night, he said, "*Not really.*"

And last night, Brooks's hands everywhere, the light dimmed. He kissed me, and the chandelier swayed in the wind rustling through the open balcony door. I was ablaze, no longer under him. He yanked my jeans off. I yanked off his. He was breathing so hard, asking, *You really want me now, you really still want me?* I was dry and it kind of hurt and now Grace says again, "*Audrey*, shit."

Because I'm back on my knees, dry heaving.

"I'm so sorry," Grace says. "You have total permission to cry. I don't know how you've been so calm."

I'm not crying for my house.

No. That's not right. I'm only crying for my house.

I wipe my mouth with the back of my hand. My skin streaks black with grime, with the dirt spinning from the sky. Last night and Thursday night and today—it's not a series of Lifetime Special–worthy coincidences. A wildfire storming after I lose my virginity. No. It's not nature overlapping with reality. It's something more.

"Can you stand?" Grace asks. "We need to get you water." She glances at her phone. "And I need to get home, get ready before Quinn comes over."

She helps me to my feet. And I hear it again, that phantom meow, that low purring sound. The fire is still at the top of the bank, as if it hasn't moved an inch—but it's like a Las Vegas mirage, not real, a trick. My house drips with liquid chemicals, sticky yellow and gray, as if attacked by seagulls with a vendetta. The firefighters have moved on to the next house.

Grace helps me up. "Let's go," she says.

"Stay here," I say. "Can you stay here?"

"What are you talking about?"

"I have to save Maya's cat."

"What cat?" She stares. "No, you *don't*. That's insane. You—"

"Just stay here." I hand her my hoodie.

I turn. My feet take hold and I run. My legs pump, lungs fill with smoke. I'm in the air. I'm flying downhill. I'm going home. Grace is screaming my name like I've never heard her scream before. I don't stop. I'm hauling down the bank. I run through the high brush toward the flames. I run home.

27

Hunting Ground

Orange County is more than the pristine beaches and towering palm trees and glassy cliffside mansions depicted on TV. We are more than the home of Disneyland. Drive twenty minutes east (or forty, depending on the hour), gear a tad south, look past the countless subdivisions and glammed-up shopping centers, and the land ripples out in waves of chaparral—sagebrush and cacti, oaks and lilac. The banks give way to hills, and the hills give way to mountains that roll out to Mexico some hundred miles south.

This is my home.

In the sixth grade, I did a report on the area's history. I'm a freak for remembering this, but I do. The thing is, I've always clung to facts. There is safety in what can't be changed.

Back in 1908, President Roosevelt created the Cleveland National Forest—protecting 1,904,826 acres of land that sprawls out and encompasses the counties of Orange, Riverside, and San Diego. And good thing he did, because ultimately, what wasn't protected was inevitably bought and sold and crafted to our needs. Million-dollar homes plotted on hillsides, tucked into valleys, flagged on crests. Shopping malls and strip malls and artificial lakes.

The Cleveland National Forest borders my home. It is my home.

Coto de Caza—originally envisioned in 1968 as a hunting lodge—was complete by 2003. A lavish, gated and privately guarded master-planned community of eventually some four thousand homes (and growing), two eighteen-hole golf courses (each accompanied by its own clubhouse), an equestrian center, a general store, and, later, the setting of a Bravo reality television show. Coto de Caza: painfully whitewashed and lacking in diversity. Last I checked online, the racial makeup behind the gates is apparently around 90 percent white, and, despite our proximity to Mexico, only 8 percent Hispanic or Latino.

Coto de Caza. It's Spanish. Obviously.

Translation?

According to Google: hunting.

According to SpanishDict (because translation is never simple): a legally regulated area for hunting, or (if used colloquially) a hunting ground.

This is my home.

Though I love it here, I can acknowledge the stereotypes exist for a reason.

We hunt for the best lots with the best views. For drugs to make us numb or wild or smaller or larger. For perky boobs and line-free faces, for muscle-strung arms and tight asses and enough space between our legs for the Santa Ana winds to swing through. The sparkly Mercedes and Escalades, the greenest lawns and most elaborate pools, straight white teeth and glossy hair and perfect tans and sparkle-bling-sparkle jewelry, the most extravagant parties and king-size candy to offer on Halloween.

We hunt one another.

But don't let the media fool you. We're no worse than anywhere else. Like everywhere, like everyone, we simply want to be happy. This is our truth. We hunt for hope. Don't you?

Enjoy the sprawling natural landscape, they invite online, *the winding trails that take you to the reaches of the Cleveland National Forest and Caspers Wilderness Park. One of a kind. A distinctive way of life. The most sought-after community to live and play.*

And that's great and all, but the problem with the natural landscape we've claimed and molded to our preferences is that, like all land, eventually it has to burn.

28

Wire Hanger

Another summer night, late July, sitting on the warm pebbles. We each held an unwound wire clothes hanger to the fire—a marshmallow on the end burning gold. Brooks had bought a bag of Jet-Puffed just for me. I hadn't had a marshmallow in years. I thought I hated marshmallows. My hands and his both sticky sweet, the burnt sugar melting against my teeth, I decided I loved marshmallows.

Brooks brushed my hair from my face, so tender I felt weightless.

"What are you thinking about?" he asked.

Before him, I couldn't comprehend the compulsion to want to spend every moment with a person. I didn't know the ache that comes when separated, like a bruise on a rib, and then the swell of relief when together again. I understood then.

I wanted to tell him that I was thinking I was scared, that I was thinking that it made me nervous whenever his cell wailed with his station's ringtone, calling him closer to an emergency and farther from me.

But instead I said, "I'm thinking that you should really invest in outdoor cushions."

We never sat on the chairs, always on the ground. It was an unspoken rule. The chairs kept us separated. On the ground, our knees touched.

Brooks wrenched the wire hanger from my grasp—tossed it and his own off to the side, our roasted marshmallows melting into the pebbles—and pulled me onto his lap. His body was hammered from the pack training, from the hikes and mop-up runs, from the hours lost at 24 Hour Fitness, strapped into a machine, so he'd be prepared to conquer rugged land when the time came.

"This better?" he asked.

I kissed him in response. "It scares me," I said. "The idea of you in a fire." I rested my hand on the curve of his cheek, nervous; he always did the touching. "I don't want you to go away," I said.

He leaned into me. "I'm not going anywhere."

"You could die."

Die. His brother, not even dead a year.

But Brooks didn't notice, didn't react. "Risk of the job," he said.

"What are *you* thinking?" I asked.

"That I've never felt so happy in all of my life."

A kiss. One, two, three, four. Marshmallow-sticky lips, a sweet tongue. The word *kiss* from the Middle English word *cyssan*: to kiss. It was Brooks who told me this, and Cameron who had told him—Cameron who studied Chaucer his first year in college and relayed the juicy translations.

Brooks's tongue was tracing my teeth when his dad's cat jumped from the bushes onto us with a snarling meow.

"Shit." He shoved the cat and me away. I landed on my elbows, the cat curling around my back. "That thing—" He looked at me. "Did I hurt you? I'm so sorry. It scared me."

I ran my hand over her matted fur, feeling her spine curve at my touch, her body vibrating with her purr. My body ached from his push.

"What is the *thing's* name?" I asked.

"Cat."

"You named a cat *Cat?*"

He fiddled with his Zippo. "It seemed fitting."

"I thought she's your dad's."

Brooks waved his hand. "So?"

I bit my lip. "You can't have cats outside around here. She'll be dead in days."

"You and death tonight. You're obsessed."

"You live in a canyon!" I said. "You of all people should know that we're surrounded by mountain lions and coyotes and deer and all sorts of crazy cat-eating animals."

An eyebrow rose, a pointedness in his gaze. "Deer eat cats now?"

"That's not the point." I nuzzled the kitten. "Poor Miss Cat. So neglected."

"How do you know it's a *she?*"

"Does it matter? Males can claim *Miss* too."

He scrunched his nose. "I've never seen you so worked up before, Audie. It's a nice change." An attempt at a smile. "I thought you were a dog person."

"That doesn't mean I don't care about a cat's life!"

We stared at each other, his shoulders wide and tense. I didn't understand the roll in my stomach—my irrational desire to get the cat safe inside.

"Don't worry so much," Brooks relented, pulling me into him again. "I'll talk to my dad about keeping her inside. Making Cat an indoor cat, okay?"

His lips were on mine, mine on his, because I was desperate for the good to come back, the moment before Miss Cat jumped at us. But before I could find the earlier sweetness, his cell went off with a wail. The station's ringtone. He pressed his head against mine with a sigh, and I moved from his lap, voluntarily this time, back onto the pebbles, my arms around my knees, elbows still stinging.

"This is Vanacore," he answered.

I checked my own phone. I had three missed texts from Maya.

We still on for baking cookies while sashaying tonight?
Where are yoooooooouuuuuuuuu, sister?
I'm going to fire you!

I texted back my apologies, my having lost track of time. I told her I'd be home soon and I'd make it up to her, that I'd try. Because, his phone pressed to his ear, Brooks fumbled with the fire pit, killing the flames, and I knew he was hoping to hear he was being paged to fight a larger blaze elsewhere. I knew, regardless of what he was hearing, he was going to end our night to join a fight. I gripped my phone and kept my eyes on the bushes, looking for the cat who'd already slinked away.

When Brooks dropped me off twenty minutes later, Maya was waiting in the hall between our bedrooms. Her legs were propped up against the wall—toes pointed, her torso relaxed. Her headphones were in, her eyes closed, head bobbing, as she sang, "*Look how far I've come, look how far I've come, look how far I've come.*"

I tapped her with my foot, and she jumped.

"Oh, look who it is, my prompt older sister slash ballet relaxation tutor," she said, throwing her headphones aside. "Only two hours late for our cookie-baking-and-plié session."

I sat beside her. "I fail, I know."

She let her legs fall to one side and rolled onto her stomach. "You're suffering from boyfriend syndrome," she said. "I've seen it happen before."

"You're thirteen."

"Sam had a boyfriend at ten!"

"That's ridiculous," I said. "Boys are gross."

She rolled her eyes. "I suppose."

"Is nine too late to start our cookie-baking-plié tutoring?"

Maya sat up. "*Hmmmmmmm.* Hell, hell, *hell* no," she said. "I'm about ready to throw away my pointe shoes out of sadness, so the situation is desperate," she said, already more sarcastic than me at thirteen. "I must learn to dance like no one is watching ASAP."

"Did someone say cookies?" Dad called from the bonus room, where an action movie played loudly.

"Did someone say *hell* three times in a row?" Mom yelled after him.

"Yes!" I shouted.

"Guilty!" Maya laughed.

"Language, sweetie," she yelled. "Bad language is not proper for a ballerina."

Maya rolled her eyes. "I can't tell if she's being serious or if she's joking," she whispered.

"Probably both," I said.

"Don't forget the baking soda this time," Dad yelled again. "And the salt. And to tell us when they're finished!"

I motioned to the stairs and stood with a twirl. "Prepare to be schooled, sis. Schooled in the art of risky baking and dramatic spinning."

We tumbled down to the kitchen and stayed up past midnight, eating cookie dough and dancing around the kitchen with *Practical Magic* on the TV in the background.

29

11:13 A.M.

My rescue mission to save Maya's cat isn't playing out like it did in my head.

I am wheezing. My arms are bleeding from a fall into the bramble. I am sweating through my tee, and snot drips down my nose as I scale the gate that borders my yard. Fire trucks line the street. Shouts of firemen ricochet from my neighbors' house. I run up my driveway, through thick, suffocating smoke. Pray I'm not seen. I slip on the foam they sprayed. Fall on my ass, get up. Run to the front door. It's locked. I locked it for Dad this morning, and Grace has the keys on her belt.

I'm trapped. But this is my house, my home. I look up at the bank where the deer stood this morning, and now, where the deer stood, there is fire. Where the hell did the deer go?

The fire is raging down to where Maya and I grew up. It's so hot I think my skin might burn from the heat alone.

"*Hey!*"

Brooks's colleagues. They see me. Two of them are approaching. A woman. A man. They wear helmets, bandanas around their mouths, thick goggles.

"Honey, you need help?"

"Miss, this entire area has been evacuated."

"Miss, you are breaking the law."

And I say, "DON'T TOUCH ME!"

I push past them, run to the garage, pound in the key code. The metal door lifts.

"You can't stay here," they call, "it's not safe."

I roll under before they have a chance to catch me. I sprint to the button on the other side, punch it so the door rolls back down before anyone can move in after me.

"Please, listen—"

The door shuts, seals, and I'm immersed in darkness. I am home.

30

Twisting

It was supposed to have been Grace's and my summer. That's what we'd planned. Sleepovers stretching for weeks, late night meet-ups with Quinn and Rich and the rest of the gang, maybe we'd both get jobs at the Irvine Spectrum, maybe we'd find a piercing parlor that wouldn't ID us, and we could get our belly buttons pierced like Quinn.

But none of that happened.

Grace and Quinn became more serious, and I found Brooks. I cancelled plans and slipped away. I tried to explain. I tried to articulate to Grace what was happening, what I felt, but how could I? All I knew was that I wanted to spend every waking moment with Brooks, that he was my *thing*—that I'd finally found what was most important to me.

"I miss you," Grace said, twisting around on a park swing, mid-July, a diet Coke in hand. "Why does it always have to be all or nothing with you?"

I sat on the swing beside her. "It doesn't."

"Either all ballet or no ballet. Aiming for a four-point-oh or you don't give a shit. You hang out all the time or you're antisocial." She untwisted her swing, knocking me in the shoulder. "I'm just saying, I sense a pattern."

"I don't like doing things halfway, you know that."

"AKA you have an obsessive personality."

"AKA I'm a human being."

"Setting you up with another loner was a bad idea," she said. "You two have just retreated into each other. Why can't you guys hang out with other people together? I know Brooks has anxiety issues but—"

"One, you didn't set us up," I said. "And two, the retreating, so not true." I pumped my legs and flew. "We came to your Fourth of July barbeque, remember?"

She snorted. "Oh, yes, that glorious hour, how could I forget? You've totally retreated, Audrey," she said. "I hate it."

"Like you've never cancelled plans with me to be alone with Quinn."

She glared at me. "Not at the rate that you have in a mere few weeks."

Grace wasn't being fair. Was there ever a point in our friendship that she wasn't obsessing over some girl or boy, proclaiming me the third wheel, talking her throat dry with tangents over the most petty of fights? No. There wasn't.

"I only mean that your relationship shouldn't define you."

"Brooks helps his dad out at his office," I said. "And he has the volunteering at the station. I swear he cares about it more than he cares about me, and he has his crew, his workout partners—"

"And what about you?" Grace said, feet on the ground now, swing stable. "Take out Brooks and what do you have?"

I swung and I laughed because it stung and I said, "Well, duh, *you*." But I kicked my legs hard, because now that he was in it, the very idea of subtracting Brooks from my life was paralyzing.

"Do you ever wonder if some of the rumors were true, about the fights, juvie—" Her bleached hair was tousled around her ears from the swinging. "I thought he was a sexy hookup, Audrey, but a *boyfriend*—" She kicked at the woodchips. "Dude, I'd rather you be with Hayden."

"Oh gosh. You're joking."

"Hayden hates Brooks, by the way."

My stomach tightened. "*Hate* is a strong word," I said. "Especially for Hayden, who *you* claimed liked Brooks."

Grace ignored me and asked, "Do you feel safe?"

"I feel *safest* with Brooks," I said.

Grace jumped from her swing. "Come on," she said, holding up her phone. "Quinn will be here soon."

We headed to the sidewalk as Quinn rolled up in her Mini Cooper. She parked, only to leap from her car in a black peacoat for the seventy-degree night—her long dark-brown hair up in a high bun and her taupe skin highlighted with golden blush. Her lips broke into a wide smile when she saw me.

"*Audrey Harper?* Am I really seeing Audrey Harper, flesh and blood, before me?"

"Dearest Quinn." I laughed. "I've missed you."

I've always adored Quinn, even if I'm sometimes jealous that she's replaced me as Grace's number one. But she makes Grace happy, loves Grace, and smiles at everyone. She's the person at the party who makes it her mission to ensure that everyone feels welcome, and she seemingly succeeds—a beacon in bright lipstick.

And Quinn has always been relentlessly kind to me, taking me on as a friend immediately—never, as far as I know, having an issue with my frequent solo time with Grace, unlike Brooks.

She pulled me into a hug and then pulled back to look at me. "Uh-oh. Did you and Brooks break up?"

"Nope," Grace said, and she nudged Quinn's shoulder. "I told you, Q, you're a terrible face reader."

"Well, is he meeting us at Rich's kickback?"

Grace coughed, totally not on my side, and, a coward, I looked down at the grass.

"Wait, *you're* coming to the party, right?" Quinn asked. "*Audrey*. You have to come. A girl squad, remember? We need a girl squad to defeat the beer pong zealots that await us."

I cocked my head. "I've never won beer pong in my life."

"Because you haven't given yourself enough chances!" Grace whined.

"It's not the same without you," Quinn said. "It'll be low-key, I promise."

I couldn't stop myself from smiling—warmed by their want, by the kinetic energy of being with two good friends who were eager to be around me. I wanted to go, I did. I missed last semester: the low stakes and ease of being with Grace and Quinn and our friends, sitting back and watching their party chaos unfold. But my mind was already made up, so I pulled out my phone, looked at it like it was my ball and chain.

"I need to hold back," I said. "I'm waiting for Maya to let me know if we're having one of our ballet relaxation nights. I'll stay here, try to get an answer, and either head back home or get Brooks to drive me to Rich's."

"You're a better sister than me," Quinn said.

Grace eyed me. "We'll see you soon then, maybe?"

I said maybe, and I hugged them both, and they headed away.

I am a liar. A terrible friend. I didn't text Maya because I knew she had plans with Sam. I never went to Rich's party. I stayed at the park, swinging higher— until Brooks got off work an hour later and showed up with two spiced hot chocolates and a kiss that tasted like cinnamon. Safe.

31

11:27 A.M.

My chest might burst. I've never run like that before. I wonder if they'll break open a window and drag me out of the house. I wonder if they'll arrest me.

The smoke trapped inside chokes me. It's dark from the gunk the firefighters sprayed over the windows. And it's somehow hotter than it was outside.

I run upstairs into Maya's room. Her door isn't closed. Did I close it? Her closet door—it's open too. Did I shut it? When I was running around this morning, evacuating, did I close any of the doors? I shove off the pile of clothes, the boxes and junk. And there it is. A litter box. That bottle of vanilla body spray. A crate. Stuffed toys.

No kitten. No cat.

I search under her bed. Cat poop and a torn up sock, but that's it.

"Shadow!"

"Shadow!"

"Shadow!"

And I scream, because I have to scream: "*Cat, Miss Cat!*"

There is no Shadow. There is no cat. There is only the pounding on the door downstairs and the yells from outside.

I move through the house. My phone is vibrating in the back pocket of my jeans, but that's the least of my worries. I go from room to room, calling "Shadow" and "Cat." Thinking of how I'll tell Maya. How I'll have to tell her I didn't save her cat.

I stand in my room and stare at the ampersand pillow on my bed. The hat from Balboa. The dried rose from an apology bouquet a few weeks back. I don't take any of it, but I grab the silver Zippo on my desk. I let the Space Needle imprint into my palm.

I pause on the stair landing and call her name again.

I can't leave. I have spent every day of my life with this house as my home. I may bitch about Orange County, the heat, the drought, our obsession with designer clothes and slick cars—but there is nowhere I'd rather be. This house is my family. I could stay and wait it out. But no, I can't. I've been inside for fifteen minutes, and through the window I see fire where this morning I only saw smoke. I see flames so bright and alive against the brittle, brown land.

"Shadow!" I call one last time.

Nothing.

I can't go yet. I sit on the couch in the family room. Olive green and warm, this couch was here before me. I cuddle up into the corner of the cushions and count to thirty and pretend I'm not crying. My heart is beating too fast. It's hard to breathe. This is my home. I lose count and start again. One, two, three. I can't see the fire from here. Is it still there? I can stay. Twenty-four, twenty-five. I never meant for it to get this bad. What if I stayed? The firefighters would probably take an ax to the door.

I hit thirty and force myself up. I stop crying. I walk out the back door. The noise almost sends me to my knees—a helicopter swinging just above my street. The man and woman from earlier are waiting for me, as if they'd been watching me through the windows. But the man holds an ax. They were going to come in and save me. I don't need saving.

"Miss, you need to come with us now."

Guilt soaks me. They've wasted precious time. They're asking more questions. They're talking medical talk. I see Grace through the haze, still on the ridge from where I came.

"The cat wasn't there," I say. "The cat wasn't inside."

"Honey."

"Have you seen a cat? A kitten?"

"Let us check you out."

"I need this cat."

"An open window, maybe."

"She was sick, I think. My sister—she found her."

"Miss, you need to lie down."

"I'm fine," I say, still gripping the Zippo. "No."

"Miss, please."

They don't believe me. They think I need to be checked, and maybe I do. But I am supposed to be keeping it quiet, staying low. That's what Brooks said.

"Miss, what's that in your hand?"

One, two, three.

I duck between them and run, sprinting to the back corner of the yard, where the pool's fake waterfall rocks offer a step to hop over the gate. I hurdle it like a pro.

I think they're going to chase me up the hill, but they don't, so I stop running because I can't run anymore. I climb to Grace with all the energy that is left in my limbs, and they don't follow me.

"What the hell, Audrey?" Grace says, face red, hands clenched. "What the actual hell was that? I didn't know what do. I didn't know if you were coming back or—"

"I had to save Maya's cat."

"A cat?" she cries. "You risked your life for some *cat*?"

"I can't believe they didn't catch me," I say. "I can't believe they didn't take me in."

She's shaking her head. "Who took you where?"

"The two firefighters." I motion down at my yard, but they're no longer there.

"You need water," Grace says. "We need to get you water now."

We start the trek back to the car. My heart is breaking, and my phone is buzzing in the back pocket of my jeans again. Like it'd been buzzing when I was in my home, back in those dim, smoke-drenched rooms. I pull out my phone, and it's my mom. She's turned on the news. Will she be able to hear the fire's roar, the helicopters, the shouting and sirens and the *danger* when I pick up? Can she see me on the TV now?

"Mom," I say.

The whoosh of her shaky breath and then, "Hon, don't freak out, everything is okay. Okay?" At the sound of her voice, the creak of comfort, familiarity, my eyes fill again. And then she says, "Maya and I are at CHOC."

"Wait." I press the phone to my ear. "What?"

"The hospital."

CHOC. As in, Children's Hospital of Orange County.

I fall back on my ass. "What?" I say again, because it's all I can say.

Grace nods in the direction of my car.

"She fainted during her audition," Mom says. "She's okay, they're doing tests, they don't know if it's the—they don't—I want my girls together—" Her words cut off, and I know she's crying, her wrist held to her mouth. "I want you away from that fire, okay?"

This I didn't do. This is one blow too many. Lifetime worthy. My sister fainting. My sister back in the hospital we thought she was done with, on today of all days, the day that was supposed to be her day.

All I can say is, "Yeah, okay, I'm coming," and I push myself to my feet, leaving my home, the cat, and the fire behind.

32

Meet the Parents

I managed to keep Brooks a secret from my family until August. It helped that they were busy. Mom and Maya with ballet. Dad with work, his LA commutes and out-of-state conferences. I let them assume I was spending my summer afternoons with Grace.

But then Brooks dropped me off when Mom was gardening in the front yard. A goodbye, a maybe-too-long kiss, an *I'll see you later*. I stepped out of the Audi and slammed the door, and Mom emerged from behind the tall rosemary bushes. I froze. Did she see him? Did she see me kiss him? Mom watched Brooks zoom off on his way to save the day, to answer a station page.

"Honey." She wiped her gloved hands on her jeans. "Who was that?"

"A friend," I said.

She shaded her face with her hands. "Was it someone you didn't want me to see?"

"No," I said. "It was just a friend from school."

"A guy?"

I nodded and said, "Yeah, Brooks," and she asked me to tell her about him, and so I did, not mentioning that he'd graduated that spring, or how he liked to speed through the canyons at the foggiest times of night, and sometimes even let me drive despite the fact that I only had my permit.

I told her that Brooks was into existential philosophy and that he interned at his dad's firm through the school year. I explained how he's good with words and brilliant too. "Quiet though, like me," I said, "not so into the party scene." I explained that he and his dad had moved down from Seattle, and that Brooks spoke of the Pacific Northwest with such love, I'd decided a trip north ought to be our next family vacation.

"That's how great he is," I said, bending over to a pick a sprig of rosemary. "He makes me excited for a family vacation."

"Are you two together?"

I looked at the cracked pavement. "I'm kind of with Brooks, yeah," I said. "But, I mean, I don't see the big deal with labels."

She smiled at this. "Fifteen and yet so wise," she said, not suspecting that my lips were chapped from kissing in the Audi the night before. "Invite him to dinner on Sunday. Dad can barbeque." She fanned her face with her hat. "I want to meet the boy you've deemed worthy of your time."

"If I say okay will you let me go inside?"

"Deal."

Brooks came to dinner three days later.

He was horrified at the request but, after some pleading on my part, agreed. Mom and Dad went overboard. Rib-eye steak and grilled prawns. Rosemary roasted potatoes. Citrus arugula salad. The weathered patio table in the backyard was set. A candle in the middle. Wine for the adults. Cucumber water for the rest of us.

"*Mom*," I said. "You're going to freak him out. This is too much."

She waved her wooden spoon. "Oh shush. No one ever minds being treated nice."

Brooks was freaked out.

I sat upright, trying to trigger my appetite. "This looks delicious," I said. "You guys haven't barbequed all summer."

"False," Maya said. "You simply have missed all barbeque nights."

"Your sister makes a good point," Mom chided.

I clicked my tongue. "Still. Good work, Mom and Dad."

Brooks sat beside me and stared at his plate, as if he didn't know how to proceed, how to enter the conversation. His hair had grown out all summer, and for the first time, the blond tangles that fell near his ears didn't look rugged or sweet but rather vulnerable and sloppy.

"Glad you finally could join us for a summer meal," Dad said to me, and he looked at Brooks. "Especially you, Brooks. It's a pleasure to meet you."

"Thank you, sir," Brooks said, making eye contact. "Likewise."

So formal and foreign, and my heart swelled at his eagerness to gain my parents' approval.

"Kevin," Dad said with a smile. "You can call me Kevin."

Brooks nodded and I said, "He's been busy at the station or we would've done this sooner."

"Oh yes!" Mom clapped. "Firefighting! I want to hear about the firefighting!"

Dad cut his steak. "Such an honorable job. What initiated your interest?"

"Was it the uniform?" Maya asked, yanking a tail from a prawn. "I bet it was the uniform."

"Excuse Maya," I said. "She's entering her boy-crazy phase."

"Am not!" She plopped the shrimp into her mouth.

Brooks set down his fork and knife, like he'd read online that this was the way to be polite at a dinner—to not hold your utensils while talking. "My brother," he said. "My brother initiated the interest. Cameron." A broken name. He shifted in his chair, and under the table, he pressed his hand against his pocket where his Zippo waited. "He was into it, so—"

"Is Cameron also a firefighter?" Mom asked.

I nearly choked. "Tell them about the family road trip!"

He glanced at me nervously. "It's okay," he said. "My brother died last fall."

My parents took in a collective breath. Maya stared at him, brown eyes instantly glossy.

"Oh," Mom said. "I'm so, so sorry."

Brooks picked up his fork and knife, cut into a potato. His left eye was acting up, and I wondered if my parents thought it was the start of tears.

"Thank you," he said. "It's okay."

I wished I could hold him and tell him that he didn't have to explain a thing. He took in a breath, and I was relieved my parents didn't ask how Cameron had died.

"But firefighting, my interest—" Brook started again. "I went to this summer camp as a kid, up in northeastern Washington," he said. "People typically assume Washington is always raining, no droughts, you know? Not true. The summers dry out quick, especially once you diverge from the coast."

"Such a beautiful area," Dad said.

I turned to him. "You've been?"

"Of course, my parents used to—"

"Kevin," Mom said. "I want to hear Brooks's story."

Brooks's cheeks flushed. "It's not much of a story." Which was so strange to hear coming from him, after all the stories he'd told me with such earnest passion. "When I was twelve, there was a fire near the camp. Usual deal—wiped out the entire area. The camp was evacuated. The town too. The community destroyed from this seemingly uncontrollable thing. This fire."

"That's terrible," Mom said.

I stared at him. He'd never told me about a summer camp. He'd only mentioned the family road trip to Oregon.

Brooks swallowed a prawn and winced. "I remember seeing the firefighters—throwing themselves into that heat to save lives, trying to tame what can't be tamed." Brooks gulped his water. *To tame what can't be tamed.* I'd never heard him respect—let alone acknowledge—the danger of a fire. But I'd never seen him tell a story with such tepidness either. "I guess I knew then," he said.

"Is this your long-term career goal then?" Dad asked.

"I think so," he said. "Don't think I could handle an office job—have to keep moving." And he ran his fingers through his hair, as if proving his struggle to remain still.

"I like to be on my feet too," Maya said, her voice a boom box compared to his.

I smiled. "On your toes to be precise."

"Ah, yes, you're a ballerina," Brooks said, his relief at the change of topic tangible.

She wrinkled her nose. "I wish. No. I *practice* ballet. Not yet a ballerina."

He paused. "A ballerina in training then?"

"I guess," she said, shy now too.

I was exhausted by all of the nervousness at the table, by the anxiety of the meal. I pulled my remaining prawns out of their shell one by one.

"She was invited to audition at the Institute up in Newport this October," Mom said. "An incredible academy. Ninety percent of their alums join companies worldwide."

"Mom, I'm not in yet."

"But you're auditioning," Brooks said. "That's big, right?"

Dad clapped. "Thank you! I've been trying to tell her that all summer."

"Well," Mom said. "Audrey was en route to ballerina status herself not long ago."

I almost choked on my water. "Mom. No."

"Really?" Brooks perked up.

"No," I said. "Not really."

"She was awesome," Maya said. "She danced the main solo in *Red Shoes*."

"He doesn't know what that is," I said. "Because it's irrelevant."

"I really think, honey," Mom spoke, holding her glass, waving one hand, "that you were on your way, that—"

I cut my steak into six bites. "I wasn't happy."

Brooks stared at me. "Audrey dances. I had no idea."

I stared back. "Danced."

"She taught me everything I know," Maya said.

"Wow. Audrey and ballet." Brooks leaned back. "I never would have guessed."

"I don't know why you'd keep it a secret from him," Mom said.

"What secret? That it was the pits of my life? I wasn't happy," I said again. "But Maya, dude, she *breathes* for the shit."

"Audrey," Dad says. "Language."

Maya smirked. "Beautifully said."

"Thank you."

But then Maya added, "But still, I doubt I would've gone back to it if it weren't for you"—she smiled at me—"you dancing for me when I was sick."

Brooks shot me a glance. "Sick?"

And there was this pang of silence, because I guess that's also something I should have already shared with Brooks. Maya having had cancer. But he'd never asked about her, and it'd never come up—because she was better, she *is* better, and it was only something that happened, something she endured and conquered.

And Maya said, "When I was younger," as if she hadn't had that scare just three years ago. "Burkitt lymphoma. It's gone now." A smile. "All better."

"Yeah," I said. "Because you whooped it in the ass."

"Honey," Mom said.

"Thank God for that," Brooks murmured, relaxing even more, somehow.

"Ass whooping." Maya beamed. "What can I say? I'm a pro."

"Well then," Mom said. "Audrey, will you pass the salad?"

Maya peered at Brooks's plate. "Hey," she said. "Where are all of your prawn legs?"

He stared at her. "My what?"

"Oh god," I said.

"You've been eating the shells?" Mom asked. "Oh dear! You must be miserable." She laughed. "No, honey, you peel them—have you ever had prawns before?"

Brooks face was red and my chest tightened, and Maya and Mom and Dad laughed and made idiotic jokes, and Brooks tried to laugh too, but he looked ready to flee out the door—his face redder than I'd ever seen. I wanted to take him away, shield him from my family's noise, lead him to his fire pit, where it could be just him and me alone.

"It wasn't too bad," he finally said, an attempt at a smile. "Gave the shrimps a good crunch."

"I do it all the time," I added. "Forget."

"Man," Dad said to him. "You are a trooper."

Before he left, Brooks kissed my cheek. He shook Dad's hand and waved awkwardly at my mom and Maya. And then he was out the front door, and that was that.

He sent me a text from the car: *I'm sorry I'm so miserable. They hate me, don't they?*

I wrote back: *No. You're charming. They adore you.* Though I wasn't sure if that was true.

"Well," Dad said. "I think Brooks is a nice guy."

Maya clanged a plate into the dishwasher. "I can't believe you managed to snag someone even more socially inept than you."

I flung water at her. "Shut up."

"It's not a bad thing. You two were clearly destined in the stars with your awkwardness, that's all," she said. "Though I will never forget that your first boyfriend basically ate a bucket of prawn shells."

"Neither of us is awkward." I insisted. "And *yes* you will forget it."

"Oh yeah?" She smirked, and she said, "Prawn shell, prawn shell, prawns," sashaying into the family room and turning on the TV.

"Really, honey," Mom said. "He's a sweetheart. I could tell he really wanted our approval."

"He did," I said.

She shook her head. "But, my, he's gone through a rough time. His brother dying only a year ago," Mom said. "He must still be grieving."

I stared at the wood floor. "Of course he is—it was terrible."

"How did he die?" Dad asked.

"An accident."

"Just remember, it's not your responsibility to take care of him," Mom said. "I know what it's like to feel like you need to save someone, but that's not on you."

"I'm proof," Dad said with a laugh. "Mom tried to save me, and it was a disaster."

"Brooks doesn't need me. Are you serious?" I tried to hide my agitation. "He's fine."

"Okay, okay," Mom said. "Regardless, you shouldn't have been so nervous about us meeting him."

I turned back to the sink. "The age. I wasn't sure if you'd be cool with his age."

"As long as he respects you. Knows you want to wait." She couldn't even say the word. *Sex.* As if the three letters combined into something more foul than a curse.

I lowered my face into the hot water's steam, grateful for the task of washing the dishes, for a reason to face a corner. "He does," I said, but my voice shook.

"Communication, Audrey," Mom said. "Just remember that."

"He's a good kid, respectful, great work ethic clearly," Dad said. "He was nervous, understandably—which is a good sign. A good kid would be nervous."

I glanced back as Dad raised his wine up to the light, and he squinted, maybe looking for a fly in the red. But there was nothing. His wine was clean, so he raised it to his lips and took in another mouthful, and he said, "I'm not concerned."

33

Let's Talk About It

Y ou want to know what I think about sex?
  Here's what I think:

I don't know.

I thought it would be like jumping into a pool: You don't know you like the water, want to swim in the water, until you're plunging into the deep end.

Sex wasn't like swimming. I actually really like swimming.

I don't know.

What do I know?

- Before this week, I was a virgin.
- Before this week, no hands but my own went below fabric.
- Before July, I didn't know what a kissing daze felt like. Rolling on the ground, out of breath, fully dressed kissing, nuzzling, for hours beneath a white star sky.
- Because before July, I'd never been *kissed*-kissed.

But how do I feel about sex?

I'm not a prude. I'm not. But even if I am, so what?

I don't think this should be such a big deal, but I don't know how to make it *not* a big deal when all of my friends rave relentlessly about sex, when everyone expects me to be famished for it. But when you're stuck with your body all day and all night and become aware of its growth, of its bends and dents and scars, and hate those bends and dents and scars, it's not quite so simple. The idea of going beyond kissing feels confusing. I flinch when my mom pats my back while I'm doing the dishes, when Grace catches me off guard with a leap attack, when Dad tries to hug me good morning.

This is just me. This is just my head. I'm not comfortable with the vessel I inhabit.

So I breathe through my nose, and I know I'm fine, that there's no reason, no explanation. Because then again, maybe it *is* rational, because how can I be okay with someone touching me, being so close, when I so desperately want to peel off my skin and scoop out my layers and burrow myself beneath blanket forts?

And that was fine. I was mostly content with that, with not wanting to be touched. But then I met Brooks, who was so tentative, so tender, so also alone, and his being close was exhilarating, reviving. I lost sense of myself when I was in his arms, just us and the fire pit or the beach or the Audi. And so, slowly, I let Brooks come closer and closer, and the warm summer days dripped into one long gasp, until he wanted to feel my skin on his, and I kind of wanted to feel his skin on mine. And last night, Saturday night, I thought I needed all of him, that he deserved all of me.

But I didn't, and neither did he.

It's so dumb. I know it's so dumb, but some days I wish I were still ten. Because, most days, okay, all days, sex doesn't even interest me—it feels entirely abstracted from kissing, rarely a plausible action in my life. Maybe my head and heart are broken. Maybe I simply haven't fully matured, or whatever. Maybe I need a new body that doesn't feel so foreign and strange. Maybe this is entirely normal, and I simply haven't found others who feel the same. Maybe the others are all remaining silent like me.

Maybe I'm simply not there yet. Is that not enough of an answer?

So, I don't know what I think about sex. I wasn't raised religious, and all my parents told me was not to be stupid and to communicate and to be in love and to use my brain, but I felt safe—though not Thursday night—and I loved Brooks and he loved me, and he wanted to be close, and maybe I wanted to be close too, so why was I so hesitant, still wanting to wait?

I don't think I've answered the question yet.

34

12:40 P.M.

Back at Grace's house, we drink several glasses of water. We smell like smoke, and our skin is sticky with sweat and ash. Her parents are at Costco preparing for the worst. Hayden is quiet in his room. I shower again. The stench of smoke bleeds from my skin, filling the bathroom in waves. Hayden showers here too. I squirt on green body wash. It smells like Hayden, like peppermint.

Maya. I said I'd be a better sister. When Maya was dancing again and I was no longer dancing, I told myself I'd keep her close. But I didn't. I stayed in my room, door closed. I stayed out, phone on silent. In mid-August, we let the notion of my tutoring her in happiness-dancing fall away. She's the love of my life, and I failed as a sister. I didn't save her cat. She's in the hospital. She fainted. The cancer might be back. I stand under the shower's spray and hold myself.

I grab the strawberry shampoo, squirt it into my hands, rub it into my hair.

It smells like Grace. I am crying again. I thought I'd never be one of those girls who gets a boyfriend and disappears. But I was and I did. All summer long, I pushed Grace away. I can be better. I will be better. I'm crying because I'm underwater, and it's finally safe to break. So I cry for my house and my family and what Brooks and I became and for the land that's burning. I cry until I can't anymore, until my body is pink and I know I've used more than my fair share of water.

I leave the bathroom. I'm fine. I'm clean. Everything is okay. It will all be okay.

Except it's not.

A text from Brooks, sent three minutes ago:

I love you. I'll win this, for you, us.

I write back:

Call me?

My smoky morning clothes lie in a heap in the corner of Grace's room. Why the hell did I only grab one pair of jeans?

And I text him again:

I love you too.

And he ignores my question, my want for a call, and simply sends back:

Be safe.

I take a breath. Another breath. Two full minutes of breathing and 911 is typed into my phone. I count to ten. I clear it out. I pull on my sweatpants from freshman-year gym and head downstairs.

Grace scrunches her face at me. "You can borrow some of my clothes," she says, standing at the stove.

"You're practically ten feet taller than me."

She raises her eyebrows. "Really though, *gym* pants?"

"I'm going to the hospital, Grace. Not the mall."

While I was in the shower, she was busy in the kitchen. Scrambled eggs with spinach and cherry tomatoes. Fried jumbo-size tortillas on the skillet and thick-sliced bacon. Salsa and sour cream and shredded cheese and avocado. A pot of coffee still brewing hot. Orange juice—the good kind, fresh, with extra pulp.

A lifelong Disneyland nerd with flair in the kitchen and a want to escape Southern California, Grace's dream is to attend the Disney Culinary Program in Florida.

I stare at the food. "Um."

"When did you last eat?" she asks.

"At Starbucks."

"When did you last *eat*-eat?" she says, because she knows I sometimes forget, knows I sometimes don't forget and would just rather stay empty. "You freaked me out back there. I thought you were going to die on me."

"This is awesome," I say, "but I *need* to go. My mom—"

"Food!" Grace claps and piles eggs and bacon and avocado onto a tortilla, slides it in front of me. "You're not allowed to drive until you lose your dizzy-eyes."

But right then Hayden walks into the kitchen, and there's no way I can eat now because my throat clenches. His hair is a mess of curls, and he's wearing basketball shorts and an old shirt I've seen him in a million times. Because I've seen Hayden a million times. But everything is different because of last night and Friday afternoon.

He makes a slight show of pausing at my presence on the stool, as if he didn't know I was here, like I haven't sat here hundreds of times.

And for whatever idiotic reason, he asks, "You make it to bed okay last night?"

Grace scrunches her nose. "What does that mean?"

"With the smoke," he says, not so smoothly. "It can be difficult to sleep."

I cut into my tortilla. "I slept okay. Thank you." I meet his eyes. "Seriously."

"Good." He's nodding. "I'm happy to hear it." He snags a slice of bacon from the pan, smiles at Grace. "I love it when you make second breakfast. What's the occasion?"

She waves a spatula in my direction. "Audrey decided it was a good morning for a fire hike."

"A what?"

"I had to get back into my house," I say.

"You were evacuated."

I nod. "Hence the *get back*."

"Evidently Audrey doesn't need me to train her to get up to speed in track," Grace says. "You know the giant hill behind her house? She was running up and down it, and the fire was like *right* there across the street, and she was running all around, and I was like, *dude*, where did you get such fine cardio—"

"That's definitely not what you said," I say.

Hayden's stopped eating. He's staring at me. "You could have been massively hurt."

"I wasn't," I say.

"May I ask *why* you went on this venture?"

"Maya was hiding a cat in her closet," I say. "I had to go back. She's going to be devastated."

"In other words, we didn't find a cat," Grace snaps.

I glare at her. "Not like you helped me look. You stayed up on the ridge."

"You were acting crazy! I didn't know what you were doing!" she says. "I mean, seriously, forgive me for my sanity. Do I look like someone who is just going to run into a fire? Not to mention the fact that *you* demanded I wait." Grace turns to the sink.

I check my phone. 1:11 P.M. "I have to go."

Hayden pushes at his glasses. "Where?"

"The hospital. Maya passed out." I speak calmly, so whatever, because I have to believe this is a fluke and has nothing to do with cancer. I have to hold on to the possibility. "She's probably fine."

"Oh. I'm so sorry," he says, and he's going to say more but Grace shushes him, shakes her head, nudges him out of the kitchen, and then he's gone with a call of, "Nice seeing you, Round Table."

"Why did my brother just call you *Round Table*?" Grace asks.

I fake a shrug. "He's your weird-ass brother."

"Oh no." She drops the spatula in the sink. "My brother is developing a crush on you. *Oh hell no.* What a goon."

My cheeks burn. "Chill out. It's an inside joke from psych. And how is *Round Table* in any way an endearing name?" Thank goodness he left off the *Lady.*

154

"I don't trust him." She gestures at my plate in a huff. "Your food is getting cold. Eat."

I don't want to eat because my appetite evaporated back at my house, but I know I need to eat to make it through this day, so I chew and swallow and gulp until half the burrito and a quarter of my orange juice have been consumed. Mom texts me again. Mom says Maya is probably fine, just dehydrated, probably just needs support, but she's fine. But why am I not there yet?

"Grace," I say, when her back is turned, when she's at the sink, scrubbing a pan. "Will you come with me to the hospital?"

She stops washing and I remember. Big Sur with Quinn, who will be here in only a few hours. I'm finally asking for help at the worst time.

"I can reschedule the trip," she says, turning to me. "Quinn will understand. It's not like I have all the details ironed out, and she'll get it—"

I stand to rinse off my plate. "Don't you dare," I say. "I forgot, that's all. Not a big deal." I'm scared to go alone. I'm scared to absorb the news. But I say, "My mom would probably rather it be just the family anyway."

"Text me, whenever, constantly," she says. "I want updates."

I can't stall any longer. My mom texts again. It is time to go. I've sat in this kitchen for over twenty-six minutes. I'm running out of time.

Grace shoves my dirty clothes into her washing machine, and I repack my backpack. I appease her by taking off my sweats and tugging on a pair of her old denim shorts. I haven't worn shorts in years. It feels almost okay. I zip up one of her old hoodies, a black one with neon skulls and devil horns.

"It's over a hundred degrees," she says. "You really need a hoodie?"

"Comfort," I say.

"I can call Quinn *right* now," she says.

"No," I say. "You two are having your night, okay?"

I hug her again and start to leave. But I'm halfway down the drive when Hayden runs out of the house, calling for me to wait. An echo of last night.

So I wait.

35

Sitting Water

In early August, I invited Grace and Quinn along on a morning hike with Brooks. We drove through Trabuco Canyon, the canyon walls high and scarred with starved brush and withered sycamores. The riverbed that runs beside the dirt road was an endless stretch of hot white boulders.

Brooks had accepted my last-minute decision to invite my friends with a silent shrug and an *okay, cool, good idea.* But now he was silent, gulping from a thermos of coffee—his knuckles tight as the Audi hit potholes and rocks, at times the back wheels spinning out.

"We should have borrowed my sister's Jeep," Quinn said. "You sure we'll make it?"

Brooks laughed, but it was warped, almost cruel. "Don't underestimate my Audi."

Grace reached forward and tousled my hair. "That's right," she said. "We must never estimate our *Audie.* She's a gem."

I grinned back at her before Brooks could react. "I am something of a glorious rock," I said.

"Audrey," Brooks said my name pointedly, looking at me, like he'd never made up the nickname, like Grace had never heard him say it in passing. "My rock indeed."

Quinn whispered to Grace, warmth in her tone, a coo. Brooks's cheeks were red. The wheels hit another dent in the road, and I jumped and he sighed. He didn't talk the rest of the drive.

We hiked the shaded trail in silence. Grace and Quinn held hands and raced through a tunnel made of dried branches and leaves. Brooks and I kept close, sometimes close enough that our arms pressed into each other. I wanted to apologize for sabotaging his plan: a quiet hike, alone together. I also wanted him to apologize for his often brash treatment toward my friends.

"I should have brought Hayden," Grace said. "He's spending his entire summer holed up in his den of a room, and it's making him even crankier than normal."

"Can you really judge him for that?" I asked. Hayden's summer was entrenched with advanced classes at Saddleback College, preparing for the ACT, and spending his mornings coaching a middle school summer camp basketball team. "His schedule sounds exhausting."

"If he can be judgy of my *fun-centric* lifestyle," Grace said, "I can be judgy of his repulsive dedication to his precious four-point-whatever GPA."

"I didn't find Hayden's dedication repulsive," Brooks said dryly. "He seemed well-balanced to me."

Grace smirked. "He was putting on a facade for you, trust me."

"You just miss antagonizing the poor boy twenty-four seven," Quinn said. "*You've* been the cranky one ever since he stopped studying in the kitchen."

"Whatever," Grace grumbled.

I was surprised by Brooks's comment, surprised he even *remembered* Hayden, let alone defended him. I wanted to hug him for this, but he walked at a distance, his face absent.

"Mind if we do a sprint?" Quinn asked.

"A what?"

Grace lunged her right leg. "Get some training in so we don't have to go to the field later," she said. "We'll meet you up the trail?"

I nodded and they took off—their feet bounding over branches, their arms rhythmic. Quinn's long braid swung behind her, Grace's hair pulled back into the tiniest of pigtails—their legs strong, bodies bounding forward. They seemed invincible, and I ached for it.

Brooks took a swig from his water bottle. "I didn't know they were girlfriends," he said, which made sense. He'd only met Grace at her house, working on his statistics project with Hayden, and then he'd run into her and Quinn in passing at the senior prank night. "That's cool," he said.

I eyed him. "Cool?"

"Your best friend is a lesbian." He shrugged. "Why didn't you tell me?"

"She's bisexual," I said, kicking a rock into the dried creek. His silence tightened my throat. "And you would've known if you'd hung out with my friends more often." I faltered over my words. The morning was already too hot, his sadness thick. I was making it worse. "It's not like it's a big deal. She's Grace. My best friend."

He squinted. "Do you ever wonder if she has a crush on you?"

"You're joking, right?"

"She clearly likes you a lot."

"She's my *best friend*," I said. "Not to mention the fact that she's head over heels for Quinn."

"Why are you so upset?" He slowed his pace.

I circled to face him. "You're making ridiculous assumptions." And I couldn't help it, I had to say it, because Fourth of July had been a disaster, and the party we had visited last week ended with him walking out of the house silently, rudely, so I had to say, "And I don't understand why you can't be nicer, why you act this way whenever we're with my friends. You're not *nice*—you act so different. You're, I don't know, rude—superior—silent."

Brooks's left eye leaked, his lips slightly parted, and he stared at me like I'd wounded him, because I had, and I'd never insulted him before. We'd never argued.

"I'm trying, Audie. I am," he finally said. "And I said Hayden was nice, yeah? I know I'm no good, that I embarrass you, or whatever, but I'm trying. I thought you understood."

I dug the heel of my sneaker into the dirt. I didn't know what I was supposed to understand.

"You are good," I said. "Of course you're good."

"It's hard for me. It's hard for me to be around people." He rubbed his neck. "I freak out, okay? I used to freak out real bad. So it's easier if I'm quiet. If I'm alone. It still hurts." He stepped forward. "Every minute reminds me of him."

Him. Cameron. The wind danced parched leaves onto the trail.

"I only know how to be with you," he said. "That's my truth."

I nodded and wrapped my arms around him. He held me tight and I said, *It's okay*, I said, *I understand*, because I did. I've always felt out of step, out of place. He kissed my forehead and there was a shake in his legs and I apologized, I said he didn't have to say more than he wanted to say around my friends, *It's okay*, I said.

"You don't know how much you mean to me," Brooks said, lifting my chin.

The oaks spun above. He was comfortable with me, with only me, and that alone made me dizzy. I was selfish: ecstatic over the fact that I was the only one to know him—*really* know him. I kissed his lips.

"*Hellooooo, lovey love birds!*" Grace called from up ahead. Brooks stiffened. "We've run to the end and back, and dear goodness, wait until you guys see the glory of the waterless waterfall. It's intense!"

Quinn popped over Grace's shoulder. "We can be mermaids, it's so lush!" And she waved her arms, as if a bird were related to a mermaid, laughing. "Hurry your butts up!"

Brooks and I continued our hike, hands held.

"I'll try to do better," he said. "For you."

The four of us rested at the end of the trail—where, it turns out, there was no longer a waterfall but only a sun-bleached rockslide and a warm green pond. Quinn and Grace rested on the slope that led to the Saddleback Mountain trail, and Brooks and I sat farther below by the water. As he promised, Brooks was being social, likeable—utilizing his one topic: firefighting. He was erratic, overcompensating, his words clipped, loud then soft. I didn't mind because this was *him*. My Brooks—self-conscious in the most surprising of ways, eager for approval.

Brooks had spent the winter months researching the politics of fire-fighting, the infrastructures, the escalating fire seasons, the beetle issue in Colorado, and the impact of deer hunting laws in Yellowstone. He spoke with authority on this that afternoon, with shaking hands too, like a smoker antsy for his next fix.

"How can something as small as a beetle have such impact?" Grace asked.

"It's bigger than the bug," Quinn said, clout lined in her words, as if she thought Brooks should have mentioned this, but then she glanced to him. "Climate change—right?"

Brooks nodded. "Exactly."

Even after two months, his passion still enthralled me. That he cared about something so intensely. I wanted that. I wanted his urgency to sink into me like osmosis. I forgot about the stiff drive to the trailhead, about his earlier grief. I sat back and listened as he entertained Grace and Quinn with his fervent anger toward the poor foundation of the very notion of firefighting, waxing on his belief that fires should be allowed to burn.

"Why do it then?" Grace asked. "Why join if you think the system is so flawed?"

"You can only instigate change from within." Brooks peeled an orange, the fruit spraying out mist. "How can I attempt to change a system if I have no experience with it?"

He handed me a wedge and I chewed, the citrus acid sharp on my teeth. I'd taken off my sneakers and socks and was soaking my feet in the warm green pool.

"Always so deep," I said.

"It just needs to happen," he was saying now. "It *can't* not happen."

"Rain?" Quinn smiled.

"*Fire.*" He looked at her as if she'd asked him the color of the sky. "It's going to happen soon. I can feel it."

"Whoa there," she said, tossing a pebble into the water. "No thank you."

Grace narrowed her eyes. "What do you mean *feel* it?"

"We're surrounded by matches just waiting to be struck," Brooks said, waving his hands at the trail, at the dry hillside where Grace and Quinn were sprawled. "It'll happen."

And it wasn't that there weren't any fires. Smoke consistently mucked the horizon—from the hills of Malibu, Temecula, Los Angeles, as far as Big Sur, even Yosemite. California was always burning, but nothing was large enough or close enough to our Orange County community to merit a first-year volunteer facing the heat.

"You're used to Seattle." Grace laughed, waving a hand. "This dryness isn't that abnormal."

"That's so not true," I said. "We had real winters as kids. Remember the rainstorms?"

She shrugged. "Not really."

"I do," Quinn said, her eyes wistful, her hand now on Grace's. "The storms were bliss. God, Grace, how damn good would it feel to run in the rain?"

She whistled. "It'd definitely beat running in one-hundred-degree heat."

Brooks prodded at the pocket of his shorts, and I knew he was looking for his Zippo, something to clutch, but he'd left it in the Audi. "It's only a matter of time," he insisted.

"Brooks," I murmured.

"It's healthy!" His voice cracked. "Part of the ecosystem—"

"I so do not need another Brooks science lesson." I waved my face with my hand, overheated from the hike.

"It's more dangerous to soak your feet in sitting water," he said, an edge in his throat.

"Okay," I said, trying to diffuse.

Brooks lowered his voice, spoke only for me. "Come on." He gestured to the dry rocks of the waterfall, the shallow pool, the mosquitoes and bees and other black flying things hovering. "I can't save you from West Nile virus."

"I don't need to be saved," I said, yanking up my feet.

"I know you don't." He kissed my ear. "But maybe I need to do some saving."

36

1:22 P.M.

Hayden is running down his driveway, asking me to wait.

"Hey," he calls. "Audrey, hold up!"

He's still in his basketball shorts and that faded green shirt, his eyes still water blue, his hair a mess. He holds a hand to his chest, and I understand. I feel it too. It's growing more difficult to breathe. The smoke is thickening. With each minute, the fire grows.

"You okay?" I ask.

He's baffled. That's his question. *You okay?* I see it in his eyes that that was what he was going to ask me. "Yeah, yeah." He shakes his head. "I wanted to make sure you're all right."

Every hair on my body is on end. "Why wouldn't I be?"

"Well, for starters, you were evacuated and ran into a fire—"

"Do not fall prey to your sister's dramatics."

"And you don't look okay."

"Gee, thanks." I feign a grin. "Need I remind you that looks can be deceiving?"

"I heard you," he says. "In the shower, I heard you crying." My mouth goes dry. "And you're about to drive to the hospital to see Maya. I know how—"

"She passed out," I say, too loudly. "It happens when you're dancing sometimes."

Hayden looks at me. "Last night. You weren't all right last night, Audrey. You can't ask me to lie to Grace about that."

"I didn't ask you to," I say. "You can tell her the truth."

"And what's that exactly?"

"I drank too much and needed a ride home." I hitch my backpack up my shoulder and turn to trudge down the driveway. If only it snowed in Orange County, it'd make a nice sledding slope. "That's the truth."

Hayden walks with me. "Did Brooks try something?"

"Nothing I didn't agree to do."

"What about Friday?" His voice is high. "At lunch, what you said—did."

And I remember the pulse of Hayden's lips on mine, his hands finding the curve of my waist. But he can't say it. He can't admit that we kissed. He still doesn't know how to communicate, how to be angry. I am a terrible person because I'm grateful for this.

He pushes his glasses up his nose. "Audrey, I'm—"

"I'm sorry. I have to go." I look at my phone. 1:31 P.M. I can't do this right now. We've been standing in the smoke, and I can't talk, right now I can't talk about it. "Maya. The fire."

"What did Brooks do?"

"You and Grace," I say. "You guys are so convinced Brooks is this monster." My heart hammers. "What if it's me that's the problem?"

"I know you. I know it's not you."

I start walking again. "Isn't Friday enough proof?"

A pause. "But that wasn't only you," he finally says. "Friday. It wasn't just—" And it's the first time he's admitted it, that he was an active participant until he shoved me away. And now he says, "Let me come with you. I heard you ask Grace. I can drive you."

"I don't need a babysitter, Hayden."

The hurt hits him quick. I see it. The way he stops. Steps back. The way his already-dying smile fades, and he can't look at me. "I'm not asking to be your babysitter. Let me help you," he says. "You're not just my little sister's friend." He sighs. "After Friday—how can even you say that?"

I can't focus. Call me crazy, tell me I'm exaggerating more by the hour, but I swear—right then—the sky darkens to a charred red. I wonder what Brooks is doing right now. Grinning at the flames. Hacking fire lines. Sprinting away. Maybe he's in Mexico drinking a piña colada. No, he hates the idea of Mexico and beach drinks. His face is probably streaked black with soot, his hair wet and sticking to his forehead. He's working. He's proving himself. *Yay, Brooks.*

"Audrey," Hayden says.

"I need to get to Maya. And I can go alone. That's all I know." I unlock my truck and toss my backpack inside and ask, "Are we still on for tonight?"

"You sure?"

"Maybe we can do some dancing," I say. "For the memory experiment."

He's nodding, playing along. "If that'd be helpful."

I smile. "I think it's maybe even necessary."

And he looks like he's about to eliminate the space between us, but I step up into the truck. I close the door on him, start the engine, and roll down the window.

"So, Sir Cumference, I'll see you tonight?"

"Tonight, my lady."

37

Overdone

It wasn't long after Brooks met my parents that I met his dad.

We'd just walked back inside after two hours out in the pebble garden. Two hours with a random kiss (or five), some conversation, but mostly silence, mostly being alone together. It was after nine. He poured me a glass of apple juice, poured himself a glass too. I liked these quiet moments best. He hugged me, his arms around my waist, and I looked past him to the living room fireplace, where four framed photos stood on the stone mantel. Every shot was from Brooks's and Cameron's childhood.

A blond toddler and a chubby baby in his lap. A large-eyed woman holding both of their hands, surrounded by evergreens. Cameron displaying a hooked fish, mouth wide in a scream—he can't be older than eight. Both boys on bikes on a trail; was this the day the dog swiped at Brooks's eye and Cameron tried to scare it off with a stick?

That night, Brooks kissing me, tasting like apples, I thought of him and his brother on bikes, chased by a dog, and I thought of their camping trips to the fiery quaking aspens. Cameron and Brooks trekking into the autumnal mountains to watch trees shake in the chilled wind. Cat slinked around my feet. The stories he'd told me. The images I'd created in my mind.

And that August night in his kitchen, I pulled away from Brooks and asked, "Can I see the backpacking photos?"

He squinted. "The what?"

"The pictures from your camping trips with Cameron, the quaking aspens."

"I said I would show you those?"

"So I could see your favorite tree," I said, thinking of my Google search, how it wasn't really the aspen I wanted to study. "Remember?"

He laughed, but it was stuck in his breath. "We're kissing, and you're thinking about trees?"

"You like trees."

He kissed my nose. "I like you more."

And then I asked, "Did he look like you?"

Brooks stilled. "We're kissing, and you're thinking about my *dead brother*?"

"It's just—" I said. "Those pictures from when you both were young—" I nodded to the mantel. "They're hard not to notice. I was only wondering if he looked like you when he was older."

He glanced back, as if he'd never seen those photos before. Then he turned to me, his face twisted into an expression I couldn't read. "That's not cool," he said. "Did I *look* like him? It hurts—it's not okay for you to ask questions like that."

My throat tightened. I kneeled on the kitchen floor and let Miss Cat lick my hand and hide between my knees. I could feel Brooks watching me.

A minute passed, and I said, "I didn't think—"

"No," he said. "You didn't."

The wood floor needed sweeping. Had Brooks ever swept a floor before? I tried to focus on this then, housecleaning, because it didn't seem fair that something Brooks talked about daily—Cameron—was off-limits for me to mention. The hurt in his voice didn't make sense, my one question hitting him so hard, when all summer he'd been spewing monologues about Cameron.

I stood tentatively. "I'm sorry."

Brooks sighed and pressed his hands against his eyes. "Hey," he said. "It's fine. It's just hard. A sensitive subject, you get that, right?"

"Yeah," I said. "Of course."

"I miss him so bad."

Before I could respond, kiss him, make it okay, the front door banged open down the hall. Brooks looked pained. "My dad," he said.

I'd expected his father to be intense, ready to rope in a multi-thousand-dollar settlement for dog attacks on the minute. But he was soft and tired, tall and heavy, with a mop of thick blond hair and a sloppy smile. His skin sagged along the jaw. He looked exhausted, overdone. In comparison to Brooks's hyperactivity, his dad was lethargic. He walked into the kitchen with a shuffle, tugging at a navy blue necktie. He paused when he noticed me.

"Dad, this is Audrey," Brooks said. "Audrey"—he motioned with his glass—"my dad."

"Hi," I said.

"Luis," he said, a smile. "About time I met one of Brooks's new friends."

I swallowed at the word. *Friends.*

"Dad." Brooks croaked. "Seriously?"

"You're a lone wolf. Nothing to be embarrassed about." Luis turned to the fridge. "Any calls today?" He tossed packets of sliced cheese and meats onto the counter, opening a jar of Dijon mustard and untwisting a loaf of bread. "Or was the extent of your employment further patronage to the gym?"

"Actually," Brooks said. "I spent the morning at the station for a mandatory drill." He gripped the counter's edge. "Learned everything there is to know about ladders—climbing up them, climbing down them, putting them away. Also helped with some truck maintenance. Didn't have time for the gym."

I shoved my hands in the front pockets of my jeans. "Partly my fault," I said, feeling an urgency to contribute to the conversation. "I was needy today."

"Right, well." His dad bit into his sandwich. "Your mother called."

"Okay."

"She asked why you haven't returned her messages."

"Because she's only calling out of obligation," Brooks mumbled, and it struck me that he'd barely mentioned her, only once or twice, and always quickly and shoved aside. "And I'd rather not have my day ruined by her perpetual disappointment."

"That's not fair," Luis said. "Just call her back."

I pointed feebly at the fireplace. "You have some great photos."

Luis glanced at Brooks, because I'd totally again said the wrong thing, because the previous ten minutes had nagged at me like a scab. I had to keep picking at it. I wanted to scream: *Those framed photos are agitating and fascinating and I'm curious, so be it.*

"Thank you," Luis said. "Those were good days."

"I'm so sorry for your loss," I said.

Luis studied me, glancing at Brooks fast. The kitchen was hot, as if the oven had been left on broil all day. My words had been simple, sincere. My pulse sputtered.

Brooks gripped my shoulder. "You needed to be home by nine, right?"

"Yeah," I said, though this wasn't true. My summer curfew was eleven, and my parents were never strict about it. "I do."

I tried to think of something more to say, to prove my worth, but I could still only think of Cameron, of siblings, of the empty space. Luis losing his eldest son to suicide by fire, and Brooks's inability to fill the gap, his mom up north, isolated in their old home.

Brooks headed out of the kitchen and into the foyer. "Let's go." A grunt.

I backed away from his dad. "Nice meeting you," I said.

Luis waved his sandwich. "Have a good night now."

Outside, the darkness was still. "Very smooth, Audrey." Brooks opened the passenger door for me. "You're a charmer, aren't you?"

Inside, I fumbled with my seat belt. "Your dad seemed nice," I called.

Brooks slid into the car. "He is."

"Is everything okay with your mom?"

He stared at me. "Excuse me?"

"What you said inside."

Brooks laughed, shaking his head. "My mother and I don't communicate well." He turned the key in the ignition, muttering under his breath. I couldn't hear him. I didn't think he wanted me to hear him—only wanted me to acknowledge that he was upset. "You wouldn't understand," he finally said. "My family has never been like yours."

I bit my tongue. "What is that supposed to mean?"

"All happy. Your parents ready to throw confetti at every achievement."

I wanted to tell him that that was far from the truth. I wanted to ask him if he'd remembered about Maya, about the years of Maya being sick, and tell him that it was unfair for him to boil my family down to such simplistic notions. I wanted to tell him about my mom's struggle with depression, and how hard she'd cried when I quit ballet, how my dad lost his temper about the money I'd wasted, about how I felt chronically empty and far away. But in many ways he was also right; my parents have never been anything but supportive, and their slips were human.

"Why are you so angry?" I asked.

"You didn't even drop it with my dad." He pulled out onto the street. His hands gripped so tight around the wheel, like he was worried that if he let go he might lose control. "You had to mention those worthless photos to him."

I didn't have an excuse for not dropping it, because I didn't even understand why I hadn't, other than an itching desire, a curiosity anxious in my chest. "Why does this matter so much if they're worthless?" I wanted to point out that he talks about Cameron all the time, that I didn't understand why it was suddenly off the table for discussion.

Brooks took a curve too fast, tires screeching. I watched him as he closed his eyes on the road for a moment. "We are talking about *my* dead brother," he said. "How can you not see that every time you mention him it feels like he's dying all over again?"

"They aren't worthless," I said. "Those photos are not worthless."

"Yeah, well." He steered the car with his knees, sighing the way Maya sighs when she's about to cry, when she's pretending to be angry but really she's hurting—a performed breath to cover a sincere wound. "You probably ruined my dad's night by mentioning the photos. He'd rather it'd been me. Cameron alive, me gone. Him and my mom both."

The pain twisted in my stomach. "Hey." I sounded like him in the kitchen. *Hey.* "How can you say that?"

"Audie, just stop," he said.

I wanted to cry. "Are you really okay?"

A pause and then, "You know. I ask myself that every day."

A deeper ache spread through my chest. I reached for him slowly, worried he'd reject my touch, but he didn't. My hand on the curve of his warm neck, he slanted his head closer, as if relieved by my skin. I thought he'd explain, maybe talk about Cameron more, maybe this would be a turning point. He'd let me in, let me absolve his grief, let me save him. We could get through this together.

He reached for the stereo knob, turning the music too loud. I stared at him. The way his jaw clicked. The Zippo in his right fist, the flicker of silver as he passed it between hands, fingers long around the steering wheel. The way his eyes stayed on the road with such effort—blinking, blinking, blinking. His chin wasn't high. He was hunched into himself. He hadn't had his hair trimmed in months, and it curled around his ears.

"Will you please find something else to stare at?" he asked, a crack in his throat.

I looked at my chapped fingers, my green nail polish, freshly painted that morning. I understood Brooks wasn't angry. That night in the car, I saw myself in the way he held his head—sad, strung so tight, and anxious with guilt too thick to find the surface. And I understood that he needed me, and that—as terrible and confusing as it was—I was in love with not only his passion but maybe his sadness too.

38

1:48 P.M.

This drive to the hospital is kind of (totally) sucking.

I check my phone. No more texts from Brooks.

I wish he'd call. I miss his voice. I miss what we used to be.

Stay quiet, stay low.

I'm too awake now, too caffeinated, too well-fed, too aware. Too okay to be alone. Why did I tell Hayden no? Alone, I'm only me, my thoughts sparking like fireflies on a July night. Like on Thursday—the land igniting. But if I think about the past few days, I'll cry. So, fireflies. I'd rather consider the fireflies.

We talked about fireflies recently, Brooks and me. A nighttime conversation as we drove through the canyons.

No fireflies in Washington, but sometimes—if we're lucky—we can see the northern lights, he claimed, though I'm sure now it was a lie.

The west coast would be perfect if we had fireflies, I said.

And he asked, *Wouldn't you prefer the aurora?*

And I said, *Yes, no, I don't know.*

But last night, I said yes. And while I don't want to think about it, I *do* think about it, because it's weird to no longer be one: a virgin, I mean. I hate that I care. I didn't lose anything but a label, a social construction. That's what girls say online. But that's also bullshit, because if it meant something to me, then it's that simple: It meant something, *means* something.

One day I hope to go farther north than San Francisco, I told Brooks.

Then let's go, Audrey, let's go north, all the way to Alaska.

The Zippo is still in my hand. I drive with it pressed against the steering wheel, speeding past fresh crops of suburban neighborhoods in the valleys. Eighty years ago this was a sea of orange groves. These new houses—all of Orange County's houses—are better off than those in mountain communities, up in Big Bear or Tahoe, where fire can leapfrog from tree to tree, lightning fast. A crown fire, that's what that's called.

Even in Washington, I've seen fire jump above my head, Brooks once said. *The crown fires are the royalty of all fires.*

But even still, even if my high desert home isn't worthy of fire royalty, watch out: See that lovely russet field of sun-fried grass? That land not yet developed into little box communities, perfect for teenagers to make out in beneath a new moon if they're not afraid of dirt and rocks and mosquitoes and twigs in their hair? You see that rolling valley, right there? There might be a baby fire waiting for the perfect moment to attack, so small, even its smoke is too minimal to detect.

Dun dun dun, as Brooks would say.

Shit shit shit, he said on Thursday.

And what did I say? I said nothing, before and after.

I take the curve onto the 133 Toll Road that can carry me to Laguna Beach or the Irvine Spectrum or Disneyland or the Children's Hospital of Orange County, which is not far from OCIB, not in the least. I hold the wheel and the Zippo with one hand and pinch my waist with the other. No more crying is allowed, but the fire is too big and I didn't call 911—and Shadow, my little sister's cat, he's gone.

Another cat probably burned alive.

Robot Lady speaks: *In one mile, take the I-5 North exit 10B toward Santa Ana and merge—*

I follow the thinning smoke north, and my phone starts buzzing. A number that's familiar but not in my phone.

Brooks's dad is calling.

39

Sixteen

The day before I turned sixteen, in late August, Brooks and I returned to Balboa to a beach house on the peninsula. A house planked blue on the outside, all creamy white and hardwood inside. It sat on the boardwalk, a single hop from the sand. He said one of his fellow reserves owned the house. It didn't matter. My mom and dad thought I was at Grace's for the night, an innocent birthday sleepover.

"I wanted to do something special for your birthday," he explained.

My stomach flipped. The bed upstairs. *Something special.*

We spent the afternoon on the back patio, observing the bustle of the boardwalk and the pier. Families on bikes passed, tanned girls in bikinis, young guys in shades and high socks.

We were approaching summer's end and Brooks's hands were hot on my waist. I was soaring and flailing in the same breath. *I'm too young to be here, I'm so lucky to be here, I don't want to be here, I don't ever want to leave here.* My toothbrush and face wash and nighttime moisturizer were inside. I shouldn't have said yes, but then he never really asked. *Scored us a premiere escape for your birthday night. You liked Balboa, right?*

My palms were sweaty. I checked my phone. I texted Grace. Brooks and I had never stayed together for a whole night.

We waited until sunset to walk onto the still-hot sand. Brooks wore blue swim shorts, his OCFA shirt. I wore black jeans, a tank top under a loose tee. No swimsuit for me. I hadn't brought one. I told him it was an accident, but it wasn't. I tried to kiss Brooks, but he shook his head, nodded at the setting sun, the swaying lights of the boats sailing home from Catalina. I hadn't seen him this calm since early July, the first night on the pebble garden, our first kiss. His calm, his hush, not sad or hyper or shy—I wanted to swim in it. We watched the day's colors fade from bright to dim night.

When it was over and there were only indistinct stars in the sky, Brooks said, "You know, I think I might love you."

I fell back onto the sand. He followed my lead, curled up next to me. He kissed my neck.

"Thank you," I said.

"Thank you?"

"For thinking you love me."

Looking up, searching for a bright star to wish on, I cursed the fog, the clouds, the light pollution. I wished on the bright red light of a helicopter—a silent plea that this feeling wouldn't fade.

"Thank you," I said again. "Because I think I might really, really love you too."

We were still cuddling when a yell rang down the beach.

"Where's my fabulous birthday girl queen? Audrey, Audrey, come out to play!"

I squinted up to the lights of the boardwalk, where Grace, Quinn, Rich, and Hayden stood, a giant gold balloon floating above their heads.

"You invited your friends?" Brooks asked. "I wanted this to be our night—*just us*—you know."

I'd only told Grace about my plans and where we were. I said she could stop by, that I wanted her to stop by, because it was my day and I was missing her so bad. I didn't know she'd bring Quinn, and I definitely wasn't expecting Hayden or Rich. But I also didn't think Brooks would be bothered by it. Or maybe I did and I didn't care. Maybe I knew exactly what his plans were and wanted something to interfere with them.

I stood up, brushing the sand from my pants. "It's my birthday."

I ushered Grace and Hayden and Quinn into the beach house.

"We're not going to stay long, I swear," Grace said to Brooks, and then to me, "but how could I not see you on your final day of being fifteen!"

She drew me into a hug, lifting me off my feet. Hayden had tied the balloon's string to my wrist, so it floated with me, bopping along on the ceiling.

"You're the best," I said. "Thank you for coming."

"Are you kidding?" Grace asked. "I squealed when I read your text. Quinn, did I not squeal?"

"You definitely squealed." Quinn sat on the couch.

"My ears are still ringing," Rich said, pulling me into a hug. "You need to return to the world of the living, Audrey. I miss you."

I smirked. "I miss watching your drunk-ass attempts at break dancing. That's special stuff."

"Why, *thank you*," he said. "You're one of the few who appreciates my dancing."

"Sorry. I've been keeping Audrey busy." Brooks leaned against the fridge, arms folded across his chest. A fresh beer bottle in hand. "My apologies," he said.

My face was hot. I stared at him and Rich stared at him and Quinn stared at Grace and Grace stared at me. Hayden shuffled in from the corner where he'd been lurking and gave Brooks a weird side dude-hug pat, because Brooks had been an ass during the initial hellos—had only strutted past them, sliding open the beach house door with too much force and beelining toward the fridge.

But then Hayden said *hey*, and Brooks side-hugged him back.

"It's good to see you," Hayden was saying to Brooks. "I hear you made it through the fire academy, that you're actually doing it. Congratulations."

Brooks tipped back his beer. His hands shook. "Thanks. Doing it and loving it." And then, not even asking how Hayden was, what he'd been up to, Brooks nodded at me. "I didn't know you and Audrey were close."

Grace chuckled. "Did you forget Hayden is my older brother? Of course they're close."

Which is funny because Grace is typically touchy about my being *too* close to Hayden.

But then Hayden said, "I'm really only here as a designated driver."

My balloon may as well have popped. I opened the fridge, stared at the eggs for tomorrow's breakfast.

"Thanks for that," Brooks said. He tried to smile. "Maybe you're saving me from receiving a crash call tonight."

I wanted to crawl into the fridge, but I slammed the door instead. I looked in the freezer. A meat lover's double-pepper pizza. Brooks's favorite.

"That's a chipper thought," Grace said.

"It's what I do," Hayden said. "Help friends out."

Brooks nodded. "A good civilian." It was like when he called my dad sir, so formal and quiet, with the best intentions.

I clutched his hand, but he didn't even react. Grace had introduced him to me. He wouldn't even know me if it weren't for her and Quinn, and I guess initially Hayden, and yet he acted as if they were gnats. I stepped away from Brooks and Hayden, and Brooks asked Hayden about basketball. He could do this. He could be social. I sat between Quinn and Rich on the couch, the balloon floating above us.

"Move, *move.*" Grace shoved Rich's shoulder, trying to take his place. "Go ensure my brother doesn't say something idiotic to Brooks and let me sit next to my best friend," she hissed.

Rich jumped up. "Whoa, dramarama."

"Just like Audrey," Hayden interjected from the kitchen, an awkward laugh, turning away from his small talk with Brooks. "You two dancing around the house together in fits of dramatics since elementary school."

"Oh shush," Grace said.

Rich pointed his finger at her. "I'm so going to beer pong your ass tonight," he said. "It's on, Dramarama. It's so on."

"Please don't." Quinn swatted him. "I rather not spend the night cleaning up puke."

And then Brooks interrupted, too loud, too sudden, "I've never thought of Audrey as dramatic."

I blushed and the others laughed, and Grace wrapped her arms around me—letting the chaos of the room drip away.

"Happy birthday," she said, presenting a purple hemp bracelet threaded with silver gems, sliding it over my wrist. "I know, crazy simple, not to mention a copycat." She waved her cluttered wrist, showcasing the bracelets I'd made her over the years. "But you're always making me these things and I always adore them. I wanted you to have something from me for once."

My throat tensed, because that had been one of our summer plans—me teaching her how to braid hemp bracelets and her teaching me how to jog without getting shin splints, like summer camp but with hot showers and wine coolers. I'd missed all of it—letting the weeks pass without following through on a single plan.

"Who taught you?" I asked.

"YouTube," she said. "Is it terrible?"

I hugged her. "It's perfect. Thank you."

"*My* gift to you is my presence," Rich said. "You're welcome."

"I'm honored." I laughed.

Hayden's eyes fell on me, and I couldn't look away. He rocked on his heels and clapped his hands. "I should have baked you a cake," he said. "Carrot cake, that's your favorite, right?" He rubbed his glasses on his shirt. "I'll bake you a cake and bring it to class one morning. A post-birthday surprise."

"Class?" Brooks asked, walking in from the kitchen.

"We're taking AP Psych together," I said.

"You were in Stats last spring." Brooks stared at Hayden. "Didn't you graduate?"

"My brother," Grace said, "likes to keep things advanced in preparation for premed."

I smiled at Hayden. "A surprise Hayden carrot cake in class sounds awesome."

"You do love your sugar." Brooks tossed his beer bottle in the trash—the glass smacking loudly—mumbling something about calling the station to check in, heading for the stairs. He took the steps too loudly, every beat a needle to my head.

Grace whistled under her breath. "Uh-oh."

"Is he okay?" Quinn asked.

"He's fine," I said. "I'll be right back."

I walked up the stairs slowly, the balloon dancing behind me. Brooks was in the bedroom, sitting on the edge of the bed.

"This isn't even my house," he said. "I said it'd only be us. No parties. I promised."

"They're only saying hi."

"Right."

"We're here for *my* birthday," I said. "Grace is my best friend—you're being rude to her, to everyone. They're important to me."

Brooks looked at his hands. "Tonight was for you and me," he said. "*Us.*"

How could I tell him that I was nervous? That even after two months I still wasn't ready? That we spent so much time alone, and I missed spending time with other people?

I kissed his head. "I'm going to say goodbye to them, okay?"

"Okay."

Downstairs, Hayden stood—his arms stiff—and the rest sat on the couch.

"I'm sorry," I said. "Brooks had stuff planned. And, you know, he doesn't like crowds—"

"Because four is a crowd," Rich said.

"Four is *kind of* a crowd," Quinn said. "Especially when you're involved."

Grace stood. "Don't you dare apologize for him," she said.

"I'm not," I insisted, because I was apologizing for myself, that I was choosing him over them.

"Anyhow," Grace said. "It's okay, we were a surprise. And we're late anyway. Hayden is chauffeuring us to a party so he can get back into the spirit of Safe Ride." She smiled. "Sure you don't want to ditch Brooks and come too?"

I looked up at the balloon. "I like quiet birthdays," I said.

Grace hugged me. She whispered in my ear, "Tonight? Are you going to do it tonight?"

I didn't want to let her go. "No." I let her go. I backed away. "No way."

She nodded and pulled back, "All right, okay. Well, call me, whatever the time, if you need to escape."

I smiled too. "I won't need to."

Grace and Quinn ran out of the house for a pre-party sprint across the sand to the waves. Rich followed them behind, pleading to be let in on their track-speed fun. And then it was only Hayden and me, following them outside to the boardwalk. We stood in silence for a couple minutes. My feet were bare, and I distracted myself by rubbing my heel against the sandy asphalt.

Hayden took in an audible breath and said, "I offered to DD because I wanted to see you."

"Oh."

Quinn and Grace attempted cartwheels on the sand. Rich fell on his face.

"It should be noted that, in my opinion," he said, "I think we're close."

I warmed. "Me too."

He shuffled his feet. "I don't like this. Leaving you here."

I tugged on the balloon string, made it dance. "I'm stronger than you think."

Hayden laughed. "I think you're plenty strong."

And I laughed too, clumsily, because I didn't know what I meant—what being strong had to do with my sleeping in the same bed as Brooks. A wind blew, and Hayden raised his hand to my face, as if to brush the hair from my eyes, only to stuff it back in his pocket.

"I hope your birthday is sweet," he said.

"Like the carrot cake you're going to bake me?" I teased.

"Yes." He grinned. "*That* sweet." He looked back to the house. "Brooks rubs me the wrong way. I don't like him. Can I say that? I don't like this."

I faltered. "My relationship?"

"Him. I don't know. He's intense."

"His intensity—I love it," I said. "I've never known anyone more passionate."

"Passion doesn't always equate to something good, Audrey."

My throat throbbed. He didn't know Brooks, didn't know how he treated me, how he made me feel. And Hayden, he'd never cared about me, not like this.

"Brooks is gentler than he lets on, different when he's not with a group of people." I twisted the purple bracelet around my wrist. "I'm *safest* with him," I said, the same thing I'd said to Grace, because it still felt true, even if Hayden's gaze fell. "I want to be here."

He bit his thumb, a shared habit with Grace. "Good, that's good." His dark curls fell over his glasses, and I thought he was going to hug me, and I thought maybe I should hug him, but neither of us made the move. "I'll see you," he said. "Okay?"

I nodded, confused by the tightness in my chest, the static of flutters. Hayden crossed the boardwalk to the border of the sand. He shouted that they had to go, that he didn't have all night—he needed to get to his reading. And I went inside, locking the door behind me, pausing at the sight of Brooks in the kitchen. Waiting and watching, a nervous smile to greet me.

40

2:18 P.M.

I'm driving to the hospital and Brooks's dad is calling me and can this day just please cut me a break?

"Audrey, it's Luis," he says.

I press on the brakes. "Oh," I say. "Hi."

I want to ask if something happened to Brooks, but it's like my mouth is stuffed with dirty cotton. I focus on driving, and I try not to think, because I'm not going to think about what I heard Luis say last week.

"I need you to be honest with me," Luis says, two notches too frantic— like father, like son. "I'm sure he's told you—Brooks—I'm sure he's told you all about Cameron."

My stomach flips and the road spins. I pull off onto the shoulder. The GPS Robot Lady demands I take the on ramp for the I-5 N in a quarter of a mile, but I'm thinking of the burning grass and a beach I've never seen. I can smell the gasoline, and I can hear a boy's scream. I've parked the truck. I'm resting my head on the wheel.

"Audrey?" Luis asks.

I can't think about what I heard Luis say last week.

"Yeah," I say. I choose my words carefully. "Brooks told me all about Cameron."

"With all that's happened," he says, "I had to call."

The tangle of speech, the chopped sentences. Luis talks like Brooks talks when Brooks isn't okay. He sounds like how Brooks sounded all September. Cars whip past, each one a muffled roar, a brief gust that resounds through my truck. I clock the cars with my eyes. Seventy-seven mph. Eighty-four mph. Sixty-seven mph. Eighty-eight mph. Ninety-one mph. Seventy-three mph. Ninety-nine mph. The speed limit is sixty-five. I've been on the side of the road for approximately 174 seconds.

"Have you heard anything from him?" I ask. "Is he okay?"

"Audrey," Luis says, so smooth now, so slow, a recording voice. "Do you have any reason to think Brooks started the fire?"

I hurdle over the bench and push at the passenger door. I'm not thinking right now. I'm clammy and hot and shivering. I get out of the car and fall into the yellow weeds with my head between my knees, pressing the Zippo into my thigh.

"Audrey?"

"I don't understand," I say.

"Did Brooks start this fire?"

"Why would you even ask me that?" I say.

Brooks asked me the same question Thursday night. *Why would you even ask me that?*

Luis is laughing. No, Luis is crying, though it almost sounds like laughing. "Maybe I made a mistake. Supporting him with this whole firefighting deal. Guilt—hanging around for so long, blamed for your brother's death. I don't know if he'll ever get past it."

It's like he's dropped me into the Pacific in December and I'm trying to swim, the ocean filling my lungs.

"He was only a boy," Luis is saying. "Just a kid. Just an idiot kid."

"A boy," I echo, because it's confirmation. Just boys. Just idiot kids. It doesn't fit. Maybe it could. Because I still see a boy on a beach, drenching himself in gasoline. I mean, Dad calls me a kid all the time and I'm sixteen. *How's my girl,* he says, *good morning, kid,* he says.

"Audrey," Luis says.

I almost scream *shut up.* I almost scream, because I wish he'd stop saying my name that way, as if we're on the same team. He knows the facts. I know the lies. Brooks lied and he lied and he fucking lied.

"I just want to know that my son is okay," Luis says. "I need him to be okay. My boy."

I hold my hand against the speaker of my phone. Inhale. Exhale. I wish I were swimming. I wish Luis had tossed me into the ocean. I'm wishing I were anywhere but here—illegally parked on the side of the Toll Road, my ass in the dirt for the billionth time today, on the phone with my boyfriend's dad who is crying and implying that my boyfriend was blamed for his brother's death.

"Did Brooks start this?" Luis asks again.

Guilt like that.

It takes you places.

And in Balboa, the night I turned sixteen, what did Brooks tell me?

That I don't know guilt. That I don't know what guilt can do. I didn't really know what he was talking about then. I didn't have a clue.

"No." My words taste like the ash suspended even here, some fifteen miles away from the flames. My words taste like lies, like the way Brooks's voice sounded in mid-July. "Brooks would never. *Fighting* fire," I say. "That's his passion."

Luis is breathing into the speaker and I'm staring up at the slouched eucalyptus trees that border the Toll Road, the 133. The whole row is yellowing. Trees usually a rich olive green, native to Australia, considered resilient to California's severity because they suck up all the water, hog it for themselves, Brooks told me—no—Brooks *notified* me of the eucalyptus's selfishness. I don't care. The eucalyptus is mine.

Selfish like me.

"I'm so grateful, Audrey," Luis now says. "I'm so grateful that he has you."

"I have to go." And I don't wait for his response, his goodbye. I end the call and drop my phone and hang my head between my knees and breathe through my nose.

I read once that it helps if you stick out your tongue, so I stick out my tongue. It doesn't help. I thought I was okay. I thought I was done, but I'm not done. I heave up water and breakfast and I want to cry but I can't cry, because I can no longer pretend and I just lied to a crying dad, a dad who only asked for honesty.

Guilt like that.

It takes you places.

I just lied for the last time today.

41

Why

The morning before I turned sixteen, Brooks bought two cupcakes, and that night in the Balboa beach house, my friends gone—Brooks acting as if my friends had never even been there at all—he lit a candle and sang. He was surprisingly on key. I blew out the flame.

Sitting on the white kitchen stool at the high counter, I tried to eat the chocolate cupcake. It was too rich, too heavy. My legs shook. The house was so empty without Grace and the others. The balloon now tied to a chair, blowing limply in the breeze. I thought he'd make a comment about Hayden, ask about him and me, but he didn't. The stool was cold through my jeans, and Brooks was too quiet and I was too quiet. I wished I were home, and I nudged the plate aside, said, *I'm not hungry*. I was already so full from the night.

Brooks threw the chocolate cupcake into the sink.

"You're angry," I said.

He ran his hands through his hair, as if trying to shake out the sand from the beach. "I'm sorry it's not carrot cake."

"That's not fair," I said.

Brooks leaned against the counter. "I know," he said, soft but slow. He lifted his head and met my eyes, "I love you," he said. "God, do I love that I can say that out loud now." He held my hand like I was made of glass. "I love you."

I kissed him in reply.

Upstairs in Brooks's coworker's parents' master bed, I was a child in gym shorts and Dad's old In-N-Out shirt. Brooks's cell phone rested on the bedside table. He clutched me against his bare chest. I was lying on pins, so acutely aware of every inch of my skin.

My shirt drooped off my shoulder, and he kissed my spare freckles. His finger ran around my neck, trailing down my collarbones, my shoulder blades.

"Happy birthday," he said.

I rolled over to face him. "I can only kiss you."

He laughed as if we weren't alone, as if he were worried my parents might hear. "Still? You're serious?"

"Yeah," I said. "I am."

"I thought tonight—your birthday—" There was a strain in his voice, an annoyance he couldn't tamp down.

I didn't know what to say. "I'm still me," I said, though I wasn't entirely sure what that meant. "I'm not ready."

"You're safe with me," he said. "You know that, right?"

Waves rolled outside. The new school year was less than two weeks away, and we were in the fold of unflinchingly hot days, no breeze, still time left before the dry Santa Ana winds. Yet even with his skin warm against mine, I felt as cold as ice. He tugged on my shirt, where the flesh on my hips is swollen, bones replaced with wet sand.

"I know I'm safe," I said, because that's why I was still there, why I hadn't left with Hayden and Grace, because I believed I was safe. But to peel off the fabric, to be so close, I didn't know how. "I'm just not ready," I said, because it was the truth, the simplest way to articulate my muddle of a mind. "Is that not enough?"

His left eye lost a tear, and he nodded but asked, "What are you waiting for?"

And I said, "To feel as comfortable with myself as I do with you."

He kissed my forehead, cocooned me into his arms, and we slept.

But that August night in Balboa, I woke to the smell of sulfur and burnt wood. The clock read 2:49 A.M. Brooks sat on the hardwood floor with a box of matches, striking one after another.

I lifted myself up on my elbows. "What are you doing?"

His hair veiled his face, but I could see his arms, his knees, his hands—see how he let the matches taste his skin. "How do you think it feels to know I'm not enough to make you happy?"

Rage bit my chest, so foreign and sudden. Half-asleep, I said, "You can't guilt me into sleeping with you." A line I'd heard in a movie, I must have, because my voice didn't sound like me, the accusation was a surprise.

Brooks just laughed. "Shit. You don't know guilt."

"That's not fair," I said. "I do."

When he spoke again, his voice was quiet. "I know you haven't lost Maya to fire," he said. "And I know you can't understand the guilt that would come from that."

It hit me. "This is about Cameron."

He laughed again. "You won't ever get it," he said. "What guilt can do, *real* guilt."

The room was hot. My skin seared. I haven't lost a sibling, but I almost did. I haven't lost a sibling to fire, but guilt—I know guilt. I know what guilt can do.

But the night I turned sixteen, I didn't tell Brooks this. He didn't need to hear it. He didn't need to hear what a terrible sister I am when he no longer had the chance to be a terrible brother. He needed me to fill the holes his brother's death had left.

He moved from the floor to the edge of the bed. "Audie," he said. "I'm sorry. I'm so sorry. I just miss him. I miss him so bad." He pressed his cheek to mine, and the night stood still. "I love you," he said, the words still new.

He wasn't a boy with plans to save the world, prepared to fight fires and protect me from earthquakes. He wasn't the boy who taught me the beauty of a quiet night outside, the necessity for passion. He was a boy with grief tacked on to his shoulders and scars on his wrists and hands. A boy playing with matches on the floor, crying for what he couldn't have, worn down.

I reached for him, circling my arms around his back, resting my head on his shoulder. We fell back on the bed, curled into each other. I tried to remember how we'd been in June and July, because it hadn't been this. This was a new Brooks. It hurt to breathe, and I wondered if this was what it was like to have a panic attack: a balloon in my chest, filling too fast, cards shuffling in my head.

"I'm sorry too," I said, because I wanted to hear him say it was okay, but he didn't.

And I *am* sorry. I'm sorry I don't know how to make myself better, and I'm sorry I couldn't save Brooks. Instead of soothing the embers, I offered more kindling. I'm sorry, because if I'd listened closer, if I'd acted better, if I hadn't interrogated, if I'd used my phone—

I know guilt. I now know what guilt can do.

42

2:24 P.M.

The ground is warm. I've wasted six minutes. I need to drive away, before a cop or a Good Samaritan shows up to help and sees me pasty and shaking and asks me what happened. Because I'll tell them, I swear, right now, I'd tell anyone who asked. Say it all. I'd tell them the truth. The words would slip out from my mouth, and that would be it. That would be the end.

I flick the Zippo and burn a dry blade of grass. It smolders and curls in on itself so fast.

Call me back, Luis. Let me tell you a story in exchange for a story, the tale of Brooks and Audrey for the tale of Brooks and Cameron. Give me another chance. Let's have a chat.

I'm tapping on my phone, but I'm not calling Luis. Let him have some peace for a few more hours. Let him breathe, take a nap, drink a beer. Whatever. My phone is in my hands, and I'm tapping the screen, but I'm not calling Luis because I'm calling his son.

I wonder if the phone is sitting in some pocket of his shell jacket or if it's in the fire truck. And I wonder where he is, if he's running or if he's digging or if he's taking a water break, but it doesn't matter, because it rings and it rings and he doesn't answer.

This is Brooks. Leave a message after the Robot Lady.

And it's funny. I didn't know that's where I got the term *Robot Lady*. The GPS on my phone, Robot Lady. She came from Brooks.

"It's me," I say, not knowing what I'm going to say, but knowing I'm done, knowing my voice sounds strong because I am strong, I am. "You need to call me. Now. I talked to your dad. He told me about Cameron, what I told you I already knew. Brooks, you need to call me—"

I'm rubbing my eyes and I'm pushing off from the ground and brushing the dirt from Grace's shorts and my voice sounds good, sounds steady because I am steady.

"Your dad," I say, wondering if Brooks will hear the rage of the road, of the rushing cars and the wind. "Your dad asked me if you started the fire. He said you were blamed for Cameron—" I inhale. "Brooks, you better as hell be alive, you better be okay, because you need to call me because I can't lie anymore and I want to hear you say it, the truth, and if you don't call, I'll turn myself in. I'm going to tell. People are homeless—all the homes. We need—"

The voicemail beeps, cutting me off. I'm not done, but I don't mind. It's enough. He'll listen to it. He listens to and saves every message I leave. He'll call me eventually. He'll hear me.

So I climb into the truck and turn on the engine and push it into drive. Click on the blinker and accelerate into the flow of traffic and heed Robot Lady's advice and take the on-ramp for the I-5 N to my little sister.

43

THURSDAY

Late Thursday night, Brooks texted me.

Come outside? Wear sneakers.

I was writing back, asking why, when he sent:

It's a surprise.

I hadn't seen Brooks since Luis's work party Saturday night, so I snuck out the back door.

We climbed the bank across the street from my house, the dry brush snapping beneath our feet. Brooks walked ahead, moving up the slope diagonally.

I hadn't climbed the hill in years—it only leads to more scrubby hills of dead spiky weeds and stubby cacti and dried-up flowers, to trails that twist behind Coto de Caza through the 460,000 acres of rolling land. Nowhere.

Brooks carried a large pack and wore his black work boots, black baggy pants. No beanie on his head. He looked ready for a bank heist. Or a fire. His arms were bare. The hot wind was sharp. We ascended the ridge, and I looked back down at my home: so small and insignificant at the curve of my dead-end street, only our back porch illuminated—a beam to lead me back.

I headed with Brooks deeper into the inky night. Round a bend, a few steps farther, and we were on the trail. Brooks pulled out a corked bottle of red wine, and we passed it back and forth. I took too many sweet gulps.

"The trail closes at sunset," I said. "You know that, right?"

"Of course." He reached for my hand. "Do you trust me?"

The silence was loud. Our feet hitting the hard ground, frogs croaking, the chattering of crickets, a howl far off. I gripped his hand. There is no real fence protecting the protected land—the occasional rusted gate, the random warning sign, a sagging string of barbed wire that gives way to cacti and bottle-neck brush. Brooks trekked as if he'd studied the trail, as if he knew the land like he knew fire. We left the path and pushed into the knee-high crackling grass, down another slope, wind whooshing across the valley.

Brooks stopped, pulled me into him, and kissed me deep. I was dizzy.

"Happy anniversary," he said.

44

3:00 P.M.

I walk into the Children's Hospital of Orange County and am greeted by fluorescent lights and sunshine-and-ocean murals. It took me twenty-six minutes to finish the drive. My cell is in the back pocket of Grace's shorts. It has yet to ring.

Right now, the priority is Maya. I hold her stuffed elephant against my chest. If Maya were ever to admit that she still clings to Donny, it would be while hooked up to an IV.

And, okay, fine: I needed the stuffed animal's comfort too.

I see Mom before she sees me. I call to her, which is a mistake, because it startles her and Mom is a crier and crying is more contagious than yawning when the crier is my mother. She rushes to me and holds me tight. I'm so grateful I showered twice, that I've consumed bacon and eggs and more coffee than one should ever consume, because my morning rum-breath stench has been replaced with positive I Am Healthy I Ate Breakfast evidence.

Ignore the fact that I puked it all up on the side of the road.

Thinking about bad breath is a good way to not think about crying.

Thinking about bad breath is preferable to thinking about why I'm close to crying.

"Oh, honey," Mom is saying. "This is a day for the books, isn't it? Look at you." She shakes her head. "You should have come with us."

"No one would've been home to save our stuff if I had," I say.

Mom touches my cheek, soft, so soft. She's in her Mother audition clothes. Pressed linen pants, peach silk blouse, a brown scarf draped around her neck. "I don't care about *stuff.*" Her dark hair is swept back in a bun, turquoise drop earrings bright against her white skin. "You shouldn't have had to experience that. *I* wouldn't even know how to react—"

"Mom, *Maya*," I say. "Can we focus on Maya?"

Mom shakes her head, not a no, but a denial, an *it's fine it's fine it's fine* headshake. "She's okay, going to be fine. I don't think it's the lymphoma, I don't think—" She brushes back my hair. "I'm just so relieved you both are okay."

Yeah, we're okay. We're so okay.

Maya is still under the lights of her MRI and CT and a PET, tests with results that will eventually reveal what's under her skin, so we have time. Mom leads me to the bathroom, where I blink at my reflection, and she wields her magic wand of cover up—mascara, blush stain, lipstick. She insists that I'll feel better with a fresh face (she and Grace must be conspiring) and wipes my skin with a cleansing cloth (always so prepared with her oversize leather purse). I think it makes her feel better.

Mom holds my chin and explains the morning's events. A standard beginning: Maya stretching, Maya drinking coffee, Maya complaining about not having access to her cell phone, Maya eating the aforementioned light breakfast, Maya begging Mom to have five minutes with her cell phone, Mom not relenting, Maya quiet during the short drive from the hotel to the school, her legs shaking, nerves, the standard nerves.

Mom asked Maya how she felt, and Maya smiled and said fine.

"Mom," I say. "*Fine* never means fine."

She uses her thumb to blend in blush on my cheek. "You and your clichés."

"Obviously I'm right. She passed out."

"Well, *fine* didn't mean fine *this* time."

They signed in for the audition and Mom kissed Maya's cheek and Maya vanished into the leotard sea for warm-ups and barre and floor and, later, when she was one of the fifteen selected from the fifty, her stage solo—the final round.

And then Mom had to wait. She read a book in the lobby with a twitching foot (because one daughter was auditioning and her other daughter was alone in fireland). But then she heard the sirens, and Maya was wheeled out on the stretcher after collapsing onstage—not a failed leap or a twisted ankle, but a hard fall; she passed out and hit her head on the rise, cutting her scalp.

"Audrey, please don't cry." Mom sighs. "She's okay. It's okay. I'm sure it was only exhaustion. The last time she relapsed—she was sick for months—it was gradual, remember? She's healthy." Mom nudges me to face the mirror and combs my tangled hair with her fingers, starting a braid.

My jaw throbs from clenching. I want to sink to the tile floor and cry into my knees and let Mom hold me. I'm far gone—this summer and last weekend and Thursday night and last night and the fire flickering secrets to the sky. I am so afraid. I am afraid Brooks will die in the fire. I am afraid Maya is sick-sick again.

I want to show Mom my bruises, the ones under my shirt and the ones she wouldn't see. I want her to feel the blister on my palm, its heat, and I want her to tell me I don't have to be strong, that I can call it quits on today, call it quits like I did with ballet.

Mom's braiding tighter now, tugging at my head, inspecting my reflection in the mirror. So I inspect her: her skin dull in the bathroom light, her exhaustion intensified—the inward drop of her usually pulled-back shoulders, the weight beneath her dark eyes, the deeper lines in the angular slope of her face. She yanks my braid and twists it up into a tight coil.

"I'm scared," I say.

"Oh," she says, and the shiver in her speech scalds so deep. "I know, baby," she says, and I'm still hearing that waver in Luis's voice—a father so broken and scared—and I'm wondering how my mom isn't on the floor herself, how she isn't crying into her knees.

"I'm so sorry," I say. "I should have been there. Last night, today."

Mom massages her fingers against the back of my neck. "You're here now. Are you okay?"

I only shrug, smile, because I am not okay. Not yet. Because I don't know what to do and maybe I'm not ready to tell all the truth and nothing but the truth.

"You were so happy this summer," Mom says. "But the past few weeks . . ." and I hold my breath because I hate that she's noticed, I hate that I've made her worry. "And now today." I hold my breath. "Audrey, what's going on?"

I can't give her another reason to cry. "There's a fire," I say. "We were evacuated—and now Maya—what's happening is I'm worried about Maya."

I turn back to the mirror, and I smile because my makeup is complete and my hair is braided back into a twist. My face is *fresh*. I don't look like a daughter who drank too much the night before, whose face got chafed from her boyfriend's scruff. I don't look like a daughter who was woken at 5 A.M. to a huff-puff-puff on the front door and who puked at the sight of her house surrounded by fire only to run straight into it.

Mom rubs my shoulder. "Honey?"

"I need to see Maya."

In the mirror, I look like me. Perfect posture beneath the slouch-friendly oversize hoodie, muddy eyes and angular rouge-smacked cheeks. I look like my mother's daughter. My sister's sister.

45

First Day

On the first day of the semester, after Psychology, I admitted to Hayden that I was hesitating on taking AP Literature.

He narrowed his eyes. "Why?"

"I'm not sure if it's worth it," I said. "The time, the effort—"

"You can absolutely handle the extra effort," he interrupted. "And it could make a difference. I've heard you talk about your dream to go to that small school in Colorado. You want to get in? Work for it."

My breath caught on the word *dream*, had I used that word? Yes, I was intrigued by the Rocky Mountains, a small college campus, an education that pushed me, a chance to explore, but was it a dream?

Hayden opened the classroom door, and we walked out into the hall.

"It's easy for you." I shrugged. "School stuff—it all comes naturally."

He shook his head. "That's quite the assumption."

We exited the hallway into the dry heat of the courtyard, and I turned to face him. "Well, aren't you making an assumption? Claiming I'm not working for what I want?" But then I added, "And maybe I don't care about school like you do. What if I don't want to work as hard?"

Hayden raised his hands up in defeat. "Fair enough," he said. "But think about AP Lit, will you? Archer is a fantastic teacher. I think you'd love the class."

"Sure, whatever," I said, like a child, like his little sister's friend.

But he smiled. "Do as you please, Miss Round Table."

I spent two days in Junior English, bored and sketching outlines of maps and mountains in my notebook, and I thought about what Brooks had asked the first night we met. *What do you love?* And I'd said school, learning something new that I never thought I could understand.

Like in ballet. The feeling of nailing down the most complicated piece of choreography after working on it for weeks—nailing it three times in a row, that hum in my body, the adrenaline in my heart, the euphoria.

In class, drawing in my notebook, I realized I was missing *that*. Challenging myself with something new—the promise of effort and reward, no matter how slight.

And so I transferred into Archer's AP Lit, and not because I needed to believe I had a thing but because I realized that the trial and error of learning and eventually understanding was the most satisfying experience I'd yet to find.

46

3:36 P.M.

The ER isn't a sea of pastels and rainbow murals. It's pale and gray and smells like bleach; a long room broken by limp curtains with a soundtrack of wailing babies and sobbing kids and beeping machines. I hold my breath and follow the nurse to the end, Mom behind me, until we reach my sister, who looks more bored than sick, more amused than devastated.

"Hey, you made it for my final act!" Maya calls, sitting on the edge of her raised bed, swinging her legs, an IV taped to her hand. "I call this the *Dance of the Pathetic*: a seated allegro of death." She raises a pointed foot for a rond de jambe. She's not yellow and collapsed and pinned to her bed. She's restless and glowing. Apart from the IV, she doesn't fit the scenery.

I rush to her, hug her, laugh into her hair. "You're alive!"

"Did you expect a corpse?" she asks.

"Cold and stiff," I say.

Mom swats my shoulder. "Not funny!"

Maya sticks out her tongue at Mom, and we're both laughing when an emergency physician sweeps past the curtains with his tirade: low blood sugar + low blood pressure + high stress = Maya probably experienced an everyday vasovagal attack. No reason to raise an alarm. A perfectly normal event in a perfectly healthy human, even if said healthy human was once whittled down with lymphoma. *Fainting accounts for 3 percent of ER visits.* And though Maya hit her head hard enough to merit six stitches in her scalp, she's concussion-free. *Eating nuts throughout the day will help prevent future incidents,* the physician explains.

The oncologist is next to arrive with the real-deal verdict. Good old Dr. Shoe and her high blond ponytail and bundle of folders under her arm. She's all hugs and smiles and *look at you girls!* She claims I've grown, but I know I haven't, and I'm going to stomp her feet if she doesn't get to the point, because my heart is riling up and I need an official answer stat.

She repeats what the EP shared: this is no reason for a freak-out. Not all of Maya's results are back, but what has returned points to near-perfection—tumor-free scans and in-range numbers. Her body is still behaving like a body in remission, a body that simply had a minor glitch this morning.

"We won't have the final results for a few days," Dr. Shoe says, "but I'm confident we're in the clear."

She goes on and on and on and laughs and jokes about Maya needing to eat before four-hour dance auditions, but I'm not listening, and I don't think Mom is listening either, because I'm kind of crying and Mom is totally crying and Maya is rolling her eyes.

She's okay she's okay she's okay.

But I have to tell her about Shadow.

Mom follows Dr. Shoe out to circulation to sign her name on a dozen forms, and a nurse arrives to check Maya's vitals prior to release. Her heart and her lungs and the pumping of her blood. I can't stop staring at her.

I hug her again. I'd wrap her in bubble wrap if I could, if she'd let me. I clutch Donny against my chest.

"Were you afraid?" I ask. "When you fainted. When you woke up."

Maya shrugs. "I was more confused."

Years ago, when I was scared for her and she walked in on me crying in bed, she rubbed my back and told me not to worry, that she knew she was going to *beat stupid cancer* because she was *stronger than it*. She was my little sister and I was her older sister and she comforted me. Bald, thin, and with sores in her mouth from the chemo, she'd dance around the house, telling me she was going to be the first bald prima ballerina. She'd taunt me with her glissades and promenades, laughing, *Do one! Do one! Mine are way better than yours. I'm so more prima than you!*

And I wish I could tell her this—how it's because of her that I'm not total dust—but I don't because she'd pretend to gag, call me cheesy, oh so dramatic, which yes, fine, I am.

The nurse asks Maya if she needs help getting dressed, and Maya waves her away, nodding at me, telling the nurse she has me. *She has me.* The nurse leaves for another curtain room and another damn rock sits in my throat, ready to crack from the heat. I have to tell her about Shadow.

"What's up with you?" she asks, eyeing me, my made-up face and braided bun, Grace's shorts and hoodie. "And *what* are you wearing?"

The gray tile floor is speckled with gray. Gray on gray on gray. An ER in a hospital for kids. *Just a little kid*, Luis said. *Just an idiot kid.* How can I tell her about the fire, the evacuation, her poor cat?

"It's been a long morning," I say. "Like you wouldn't even believe."

47

Burned

A blistering September. Summer was over and school had started for both of us. Back at Tesoro High for me, Saddleback Community College for Brooks. We were busy—reduced to random canyon night drives, texting, and sporadic meetings.

The second Friday of the semester, I stopped by his place with a gift. Anxious to see him, anxious for proof that things were still good—that we were still good even though it all felt so heavy, so strained by time constraints and grief. I craved the pebble-garden nights of summer and hadn't been at his house since I met his dad weeks before. I missed his house, missed Miss Cat, missed *him*.

But when Brooks opened the front door, his hair was disheveled and there were pillow creases on his cheek. It was 4 P.M. He was wearing gray running sweats and a white OCFA shirt a size too big. He hadn't shaved since I'd seen him earlier that week, his stubble grown in messy. I wanted to fold into him, or fold him into me. He never napped. He was always go, go, go. Full alert for *the* call. Hyper-giddy, hyper-passionate, no time for sleep, no reason to sleep, but he looked like he'd been sleeping so I asked—

"Were you sleeping?"

"Trying."

I was dizzy from my early morning and the beginning-of-the-school-year rush, so I curtsied and sang, "*Surprise!*"

"Surprise indeed." He nudged me to him. "Hi."

It was too cold inside—colder than a December morning, the AC set too low—and it smelled like sautéed onions and garlic. It also smelled like something burnt, meat gone sour. I listened for the familiar purring, the sullen meow.

"You cook?" I asked.

"Last night," Brooks said, "Dad and I attempted a family meal. Unfortunately we have no carrot cake leftovers, sorry." Before I could react, he nodded at the small box I held. "What's that?"

"A gift," I said, and he peeled back the gold paper, his face scrunching at the reveal of a peppermint tea box. "It's inside," I added.

But when he pulled back the cardboard flap, he closed his eyes. "Audrey."

"It's adorable, right?" I pulled out the purple collar from the tea box. With the tiny bell jingling, I showed him the metal heart-shaped tag engraved with MISS CAT and Brooks's cell phone number. "She's snooty, don't you think? So I figured *Miss* was necessary, even if you refuse to admit it." When he pulled out his Zippo from the pocket of his sweats, tossing the silver between his hands, I added, "If you don't like the color, we can go pick one out together. I just figured, you know, you wouldn't care. And purple, purple is neutral—good—"

"Oh, Audrey," he said.

He was so sad it made it hard to think.

I kneeled down on the floor and shook the collar so the little bell clanged as loudly as it could as I sang, "Cat, Cat, dear Miss Cat, where are you, Cat, Cat, I miss you, come here, Cat," until Brooks yanked me up and pulled the collar from my grasp. He tossed it onto the counter.

"Cats aren't dogs," he said. "They don't come when you call for them like a child."

"But she likes me," I said, hearing how pathetic I sounded.

Brooks glared up at the ceiling lights. "She's not here. I haven't seen the cat for weeks."

Vertigo swayed. *"What did you do?"*

His cheeks hollowed. "You think I did something?" He released me in a breath, a choke in his throat. "I love you, and you think I'm a beast."

My body went slack. My eyes stung. I gazed past him at the wall. The photo of him and Cameron on the trail was gone, and the frames on the fireplace mantel were all set face down. The sight swept me with nausea.

"Brooks," I said, "that's not what I meant." But I wasn't sure if that was fully true, I wasn't sure what I'd meant. "Cats die around here all the time, remember, I said that?" I sighed. "It's just—you said you would keep her inside."

His breath was shallow, and he pulled me back to him. "I forgot, Audie. I'm sorry. It was an accident." He wasn't making sense. He was holding my arm so tight again. Did he know he was holding my arm so tight? "It's been killing me—that I lost her—I know how much you loved her."

I was biting on ice. I wanted to rewind. Go back. Take the cat home with me and name her something pretty and sweet. We'd keep her safe, keep her home. I wanted to go home. I wanted him to come back. My Brooks, the one who had swept me off my feet in June and July.

"Please don't cry." His hands fumbled around my chin. "Audrey, please—"

And I know what you're thinking. Why didn't I leave him then? Why not run out the door and never speak to him again? Why not tell Grace or my parents? Someone, anyone, what was happening?

Because here's the deal: The signs were there all along. I should have seen. I *did* see. I knew something wasn't right. Brooks wasn't okay. And yet I wanted so much for it to be okay, for him to be okay. That first month, those weeks, were magic, and I wanted that back. He was my thing. I needed to pretend it still felt good, or that it at least could be good again.

So that hot September afternoon, in the frigid ice block of his house, after I gave Brooks the collar, I told myself I was only crying for the cat. Brooks's hold was a gentle embrace. He hugged me, a hand on my neck. Holding me in the safest way I knew, in a way I recognized. It was only the hot winds—September in Southern California—the Santa Ana winds change everyone; I told myself this. And Brooks still didn't have a fire to fight, and he'd wanted a fire so bad, and his brother had died last year at this time. Once the winds stopped, it'd be okay. We'd be like we were.

"Audie," he said. "I'm sorry." He wiped my cheeks. "I'm terrible. I hate that I'm terrible. It's just. Cat leaving—and my dad, it gives my dad another reason to hate me, and I really did like Cat," he said. "And with what Cameron used to do to cats—" I felt him swallow. "It's been a year. We're almost to the one-year anniversary of Cameron's death, and you know, it's getting to me. It hurts too much." He ran a hand gently up my bruising arm. "Did I hurt you?"

"What did Cameron do to cats?" I asked.

A pause. I breathed in the whiskey. It'd had to be whiskey. Another pause. As if he were deciding if this was worthy of spreading more pain.

"You have to understand," he said. "He was sick."

"What did he do?"

"He burned them alive."

48

3:55 P.M.

I've been reunited with Maya for some twenty minutes, and the ache behind my heart is only growing.

"It's been a long morning *how*?" Maya asks again, tugging on her hospital gown.

My phone buzzes. A full body shock. But it's not Brooks, it's only Grace asking if Maya's okay. I don't answer. Maya's looking at me as if I have blood pooling from my mouth. And I'm a coward, I'm not ready to talk about Shadow, so I ask a question I didn't think I'd ever ask.

"You *really* love ballet," I say. "Right?"

And it's the most idiotic question because duh, yes, she loves ballet. Right away I know I did wrong.

"It's not cool how you do that," she says. "Just because ballet made you miserable doesn't mean it has to be a bad thing for me."

"That's not—"

"I'm not you," she says. "Why would you even—after this summer, you *know* I love it."

"I was only checking," I say, which sounds so lame. "I want you to be happy."

"Uh, ditto. I want you to be happy," Maya says. "I'm happy. What about you?" An accusation. And she says, "You're always sad, even this summer."

"I'm fine."

She lets out a breath. "Really?"

I think of this morning, watching the flames swim down to my house, and the slam of it—my heart both too fast and too slow—it's what I feel now. All these years, I thought I'd done such a good job of keeping Maya in the dark, unaware of my sludge. But she saw and she sees. I sit on the bed beside her. Maya's words hang high, sustained by the whir of machine beeps.

Is there a diagnosis for severe insecurity? With Brooks, in the beginning, I started to feel okay, because he was something to focus on, and he numbed the hurt of being stuck with myself, but now he *is* the hurt, and I don't know where that leaves me.

"Come on," Maya says.

I promised I'd be honest—that I wouldn't lie for the rest of the day. But I don't want to talk about this—not now, not today, not ever.

"I'm good," I say. "I have you, Mom and Dad, Grace, and Brooks and Hayden." But these names are making me stumble because of how complicated it all is, because since when did I think of Hayden in the same breath as Brooks?

Maya is narrowing her eyes, not convinced, so I go on.

"My life is so good. I'm so lucky. Where we live, our home—" I stop. "How could I be sad when I have so much?"

"Then why are you crying?" she presses.

I wipe my cheeks with the back of my hand. "It's been a bad day."

She ignores this and softly adds, "And you never seem to eat anymore, not as much as you used to, at least."

Maya is staring at me. She's not going to drop it, and my heart feels too swollen to hold on to all of my secrets, all of this weight. So I speak before I can stop myself, "Sometimes I hate eating because it doesn't feel good to be full when I don't like myself. Most days I feel like shit and I don't know why. Okay?"

"No," she says. "No, that's not okay."

I wrap my arm around her, and she leans her head against my shoulder. "You're too mature for your own good," I say. "I mean, you're in the ER after passing out at your audition, and you're worrying about your older sister? That's silly."

She laughs. "It's not silly! Can you please—I mean, will you talk to someone?" she asks. "Like, at least Mom? Or someone at school?"

I cling to Donny. "Maya."

"What?"

"I'm going to get better," I say.

"Pinky promise?"

I twist my pinky with hers, and when we release our fingers, we sit in the loud silence of the ER until I ask, carefully, "But how are you doing?"

"Aside from the whole fainting during my audition and stitched-up-head crap, I'm fantastic," she says.

"Yeah?"

"Yeah," she says, and then, "but, uh, is there a reason you're carrying Donny around?"

I look down at the faded gray elephant in my hand. I take a deep breath. "Maya—the fire. We were evacuated."

Finally, Maya looks sick enough to be in a hospital.

49

My Trees

It was mid-September, and we were already in the mud of the semester. My backpack was heavy and my locker full: AP Psychology, AP Literature, Geometry, World History, Spanish II. Homework with Grace. Occasional study sessions with Hayden. Even without my late-night drives with Brooks, my 6:23 A.M. alarm chimed too early.

But those drives were often our only chance to see each other. He was busy too, with the firefighting drills, station calls, and sixteen units of courses at the local community college.

One night, on the side of an oak-canopied road, he asked, "Have you decided yet?"

"Decided what?"

"Your favorite tree."

"Oh," I said. "No."

He smiled. "Audrey."

I smiled too. "Brooks."

"I gave you a whole summer to choose."

I thought of my house. "Cedar, oak, and olive."

"Right," he said. "All trees that can easily be found in your backyard."

"What? My favorite trees can't be accessible?"

He tossed his Zippo between his hands. "I worry you didn't think this through."

"Oh, I did," I said, because I had. In June, after our first date, I tried to decide on a favorite tree, but never found one that felt right, so these trees had become the top contenders. "Cedar is connected with healing, protection, cleansing. Oak is all about courage. And olive trees—well, you know, to extend an olive branch—"

"Hey, our relationship does not need repair."

I pulled at the drawstring of my hoodie. "I'll tell you my favorite tree if you show me your photos of the quaking aspens."

He messed with the Zippo. "Like you haven't already googled it."

"I mean the photos from your camping trips with Cameron." I needed to see them because I needed to believe him, believe *in* him. "You told me you'd show me them, and I want to see."

Brooks snapped the Zippo closed. "You're kidding, right?"

"No." My throat hurt, but I couldn't drop it. It bothered me that he hadn't shown me the photos, had bugged me ever since the night at his house when I met his dad and he'd thrown that fit. Bugged me more since Miss Cat went missing, since he told me what Cameron did to cats.

Brooks pushed the Audi back into drive and pulled out onto the road, too quickly, without looking. Maybe there never had been any photos. Two boys—a teenager and his young brother—trekking through the woods. Would they really be all that concerned with taking photographs?

Maybe Brooks had wished they *had* taken photos, and in the speed of all of our talking—the lust, the frenzy—Brooks had made up the fictional photographs without thinking. And now he didn't want to admit his tiny lie. If that were the case, then I needed him to own up to it, so I could understand why none of this felt right.

"It's not like I have the photos on my phone. Our last trip was years ago. I was still young," he said. "And Cameron hated online shit, social media, whatever. Him and me both."

"Oh."

"Most of them are probably on my mom's hard drive, up in Washington."

"Okay."

"Why, *of course!*" He slapped the steering wheel. "Cameron's phone. The camping photos must have all been taken on *his* phone. Would you like me to track down my dead brother's cell phone so you can examine a photo of a tree you've already seen? I'm sure there's at least another bar of battery in it. The phone has to be hanging around *somewhere.*"

The easy plunge of his words grasped around my ribs—how quickly his mood had crashed, how careless I was for pushing on the topic. I wanted to apologize, because that's what I'd usually do. But I felt sick to my stomach and more angry than sad.

"If there aren't any photos you can admit it," I said. "It's not the end of the world."

"Do you really think the photos are what's important here?"

I asked him to take me home.

"I'm sorry," he said.

I was a bitch. His brother committed suicide, and I was interrogating him about childhood photograph. I was sinking. "Me too," I said.

He still gripped the steering wheel and stared out at the street. "Quaking aspen trees," he said. "They often grow in colonies. Did you know that?" I shook my head. "An individual aspen lives up to some one hundred fifty years but—the root system—the colony—it, I don't know, prevails for ages." He flicked his Zippo, up and down, up and down. "For thousands of years, a colony of roots shooting up new trunks as the older ones die. Saplings flourishing from the old, the roots staying alive."

I covered my palm against his hand, the Zippo, its Space Needle. "That's incredible."

"A colony of aspens is considered one living entity. Intrinsically, inextricably rooted together, always." His left eye was watery, the scar somehow darker in the dimmed light, and he nodded. "You and me, we're like those quaking trees."

My heart banged softly. "Oh."

He pressed his thumb to my lower lip. "You and me, Audie," he said. "You and me, always."

"Always," I said.

But that night, when I returned to my room, I opened my laptop.

I stared at the screen.

And I typed in *Brooks Vanacore, Cameron Vanacore* and clicked Search.

50

***

4:02 P.M.

S till in the ER, going on an hour in the hospital now, Maya sits back on the bed and grips the sheets. I sit beside her, because I know that while today has been a horror day of all days, what I'm about to say is going to kick deep. She asks me about the evacuation, about what happened, what I saved, who knocked, who rang the bell, if I ran, if I cried, if I could see the fire in the morning light.

She's chewing the inside of her cheek again, and I know she's dying to ask me, imagining the worst when the worst is probably the truth. Her bare feet shake.

There's no easy way to ask, so I spit it out, sudden, rushed, "Did you have a cat in your closet? Is that what you were going to tell me yesterday?"

She looks up, a gasp of a smile. "You found Shadow!" But then she sees my face. "*Oh.*"

"I ran into Sam at Starbucks. She told me."

Maya pushes off from the bed. "We have to go get her."

I nudge her back down. "I already tried. I went back. She wasn't in your closet or your room. I searched the house. The firefighters—I had to go. The fire was too close." My throat threatens to seal. I don't want to tell her how close the fire was. I can't let Maya lose all hope.

"She's dead?" Her eyes fill.

I pull her into me. I did this, and it's hard to not hate myself for it. "We don't know that. Maybe she got out." I rub her shoulder. "And the house might be okay. The firefighters were all over it. Anyhow, cats are resilient. You found her outside, right?"

Maya nods. "She was so skinny."

And I can't not ask. "Was she a kitten or just a skinny cat?"

"I don't know."

"What did she look like?" I'm talking low, as if there's a risk of Brooks overhearing, like he might pop out behind the curtain and insist *she's gone.* "Grayish with some darker cloud-like spots?"

"I guess, yeah." Maya shakes her head. "Why does it matter if she's *dead*?"

"She's not dead," I say, willing it to be true, and a shiver shoots through my toes.

"You actually went back to look for her?" Maya asks.

"I think I almost got arrested."

She rubs her nose. "That's crazy. What if you got hurt?"

"Sam said you loved her."

"But still."

"I wanted to save her for you, Maya."

"You saved Donny." She steals the elephant from me, hugs him close to her chest. "You're not as selfish as you think."

"Why didn't you tell me you found a cat in the first place?" I ask. "We could have gone to the pet store together, found her a collar." My chest is tight. I still have the purple collar for Miss Cat on my desk, if my desk isn't ash by now. "You can always come to me, you know that, right?"

Maya nods. "You're more of a dog person. And you've been, well, kind of grumpy all week."

I rub my eyes. "I'm so sorry. This week has been—bad."

"What happened?"

The Zippo is heavy in my pocket. My phone is quiet. I want to tell her. Tell my sister something, even if only a fragment of the truth. But Mom stops me, pulls back the curtain right then. She takes in our puffy faces and our tangled huddle on the bed.

"You broke the news?" she asks me, and I nod and Mom says, "Okay. It's okay. The house will be fine. Let's get going and see if we can find something to cheer us up."

"Wait," Maya says. "Is Brooks out there?"

"Yeah."

"When did you last hear from him?" This comes from Mom.

"A few hours ago."

"Are you worried?" Maya asks.

I only came to say goodbye.

"Audrey?" Mom says.

My mind froths. "Maybe he's already dead."

51

Muddy

A week after our tree talk, Brooks and I sat on the overwatered grass at the park near my house. The intention had been to relax, to kiss, to simply be together. But he was too frantic, too angry, pulling up fistfuls of grass.

"Nine hours of crawling on my hands and knees," Brooks said. "Nine hours of crawling through nothing."

He'd called me down from my bedroom where I'd been studying. I was a sponge, intended to soak up his misery.

"They chauffeured me all the way out to *Riverside* so I could press the back of my hands to the ground." He nearly shouted. "I was *praying* I'd feel something hot just so I could do something other than inch around like a dumbass."

"Did you?" I asked.

"Did I what?" he asked.

"Feel something."

"No. The fire was done. Eighteen thousand acres." He held a sliver of grass to the flame of his Zippo and let it shrivel in his grasp. "All of it done."

"Well," I said. "That's good, right? You guys got it out."

"Right. You're right."

"Brooks." It was past midnight. The triple-digit days were now stacked into weeks—the heat exhausting. The high winds building too quickly—my skin chronically dry and wind-burned. I had to wake up in a few hours. I had a Geometry quiz and Psychology unit exam waiting. I wanted to go home, go to sleep. "Are you okay?"

"I'm tired of missing him," he said, under his breath, squeezing his Zippo. "I'm tired of feeling inadequate, you know?"

"You do so much," I said. "You're so far from inadequate."

He closed his eyes. "Please don't."

I reached for his shoulder, and he jumped at my touch, his hand still holding the Zippo. His fist flew out, white knuckles, silver flashing. I lurched back onto the ground, my arm protecting my face. A response I didn't know I had in me. A fear I didn't know existed.

"Audrey," he whispered. His hand was now open, twitching but relaxed, the Zippo dropped in the grass. "Audrey, what the hell was that? You didn't think—"

"You're not inadequate," I repeated, slowly, sitting up. "Stop saying that."

We headed back to my house, to where the Audi was parked. The wind pushed against us, and we walked tensely, Brooks's low mood still palpable.

"How is it still so hot?" he muttered.

I managed a laugh. "Welcome to fall in Orange County."

It felt like a midafternoon on the hottest day of summer. But I didn't mind it: The night sky was so bright, as if the ninety-degree temperature gave it a finer shine. The trees that lined the street swayed erratically, somehow so loud, their leaves wind chimes. And, across the road, the hillside that rolled up to the national forest rustled, from the wind or from animals or both.

While others complained about the Santa Ana winds and the heat, I secretly loved the season. Nostalgia made the winds take on a tint of magic— my pulse high when branches smacked and scratched my bedroom windows while I slept, the feeling that the morning gusts could push me into flight as I walked to the bus stop.

I was feeling it then—the hum in my chest from the wind—as Brooks and I walked that night. And it was obvious that he was spellbound too. His dry lips were parted, looking ahead to where a large branch had splintered from an olive tree and fallen across the sidewalk. We walked around it in silence, and I wanted to say, *See, I told you so, the worst has yet to come, these winds bring the fires, you'll get what you want soon,* but I was afraid it'd only set him off again. And I didn't want his dream of a wildfire to come true.

We approached my house, where my mom's beloved oak swung its branches against my bedroom window and—before heading up the drive-way—I turned to him.

"Eucalyptus," I said.

"What?" he asked.

"I decided," I said. "The eucalyptus is my favorite tree."

I was thinking of the Toll Road, how the line of eucalyptuses always feels steady, like home. I was thinking of Grace's room, her incense, and the oil she burns by her window to set a mood. I was thinking of Vick's VapoRub, my mom slathering my chest when I'm sick, the scent calming the aches in my head. I was thinking of pressing the eucalyptus oil onto Maya's wrist when nausea from chemo slammed.

I was thinking of a solid tree, tall but lean, always there, somehow reviving.

"You would pick a selfish, explosive tree," Brooks murmured.

The wind gusted and my hair tangled behind my back. "What are you talking about?"

"Do some more research," he said, a small smile, not bothering to push his own overgrown hair from his face.

So I did.

Eucalyptus trees are not only total water guzzlers and invasive to California, but they're supposedly horrifically flammable. Ignited, the tree can explode. But otherwise, combustive tendencies aside, with its thick and regenerative bark, the tree is exceptionally fire-resistant.

So the eucalyptus might be a tad temperamental, a wee bit selfish, but at least it's a survivor.

I decided it was still my favorite tree.

When I was done studying the eucalyptus—had decided that it was indeed the tree for me—I paused on my homepage. The cursor blinked.

I tried again. The same keywords I'd used the night before, and the night before that. I squinted at my laptop screen, trying to find some hint of a puzzle piece that would give light to the story.

Cameron Vanacore

Seattle, WA

Stars, "Your Ex-lover Is Dead"

Suicide by fire

Fire suicide

Alki Beach

Self-immolation

Cats

Burning cats

Brooks Vanacore

No internet search has ever been so unsuccessful.

Brooks said Cameron was twenty years old when he committed suicide. Not a minor. Something about his violent public death would've been reported online, right? But there was nothing. Not one report of any self-immolations in the state of Washington. I weeded through gruesome images of Thích Quảng Đức—a monk who self-immolated himself during a political protest—yet there was no evidence that a Cameron Vanacore had done the same. No evidence that a Cameron Vanacore ever even *lived*. No school records. No awards. No recognition. No old Facebook page, dead and floating. No obituary.

Brooks hadn't given me an exact date of Cameron's death. Only ever said it was a year ago this month. *September*. It was mid-month, so the anniversary had maybe already passed—that would explain Brooks's mood, the change. And suicide. Brooks had never talked about the Cameron before death aside from when they were kids—had there been a trigger, years of mental illness beforehand? And was Brooks okay, was Brooks seeing anyone to help with the loss? I was too afraid to ask, wouldn't dare suggest it.

I searched every day of September of last year, paired with *Seattle* and *suicide*.

No link led to Brooks or Cameron Vanacore.

When I finally slept that night, I dreamt of a bathtub full of cats, burning alive.

52

***

4:29 *P.M.*

Apparently Sunday is the day for shopping, and apparently the vast majority of Orange County is not the least bit deterred by the fire swarming the southeastern portion of the county, because I've rolled through Row A and Row B and Row C and I still haven't found a parking spot.

Released from the hospital, Mom and Maya returned to OCIB on a mission to request a makeup audition—to explain the fluke of the fainting incident. I was sent to the Hilton to pick up their bags from their stay last night, because if I didn't want to accompany them to the academy, I might as well make myself useful.

Our plan was to meet at our new hotel in Foothill, but a text from Maya directed me elsewhere: *YAYGOODNEWS! Meet @ Fashion Island for happy early dinner in 30ish minutes! Picking up Dad from airport and then Fig & Olive for yummy time.*

Fashion Island. Of course. Thank goodness Grace convinced me to wear her shorts. Forget cooking, she should get into the business of fortune-telling.

Fashion Island, though not an actual island, is just a short drive from Balboa Island—where Brooks and I evolved into a *we*. It's also practically down the street from OCIB and some twenty minutes west of CHOC. I've only been here once for a dance-friend's birthday party when I was ten. Each guest was treated to a salon makeover and handed ten bucks for individual shopping sprees. I bought blue eyeliner and pocketed the rest. I'd probably do the same today, only trade out the blue for black.

I'm kind of cracking. Maya is okay. She's great. And I told her I'd talk to somebody about my depression, getting help, and that's good. I think I really will. But right now I'm losing it, because now that I know Maya is fine, now that I've confessed about the muck in my brain, my focus is lost and my mind is all live wire. Shadow is probably howling in our home as she burns alive, and the fire, Brooks—

Another text comes in, breaking me out of my spiral.

It's not from Brooks but from Hayden.

How's it going? Still on for the memory dance tonight?

A minute passes, and I'm rolling through the lot. Another text from Hayden arrives.

I mean work on our psych project, sorry, that was dumb.

I could hug him. I should have. I will.

An empty parking spot in Row F. I park but don't get out, because I drove too fast so I'm here early, and I'd rather wait alone in my car than alone in a restaurant.

I swipe at my phone and reread Hayden's texts and write back.

Memory dance is so on. Logistics to be confirmed at a later hour.

I read Grace's texts next. Questions about Maya, proclamations of love, and photos of her and Quinn on the start of their road trip: Quinn with crown braids posing in front of her car trunk filled with camping gear, her smile a laugh; a selfie of them on the road, Grace grinning so big; a blurry photo of the central coast.

I reply: *These texts give me life. You and Quinn deserve the happiest of times. And, more good news, Maya is healthy!*

But then I turn to the not-so-stellar news. CNN. The *Orange County Register*. NBC. Big surprise: The fire is growing strong.

What was originally considered a small, contained brush fire was aggravated late Saturday night when erratic offshore Santa Ana winds collided with onshore coastal winds—

Air currents from the fire, creating a microclimate that made fighting the fire more dangerous and unpredictable—

Within an hour, the fire's containment dropped from 50 percent to 10 percent; it is now 4 percent contained with over 20,000 acres burned—

Crews hope to find reprieve with the lower nighttime temperatures, but what they really need is rain—no moisture on the ten-day forecast—tomorrow a high of 103 degrees—winds with gusts up to sixty mph—

Ten minutes of reading and my mouth is chalky and my hands are sweaty and any calm in my bones has been sapped dry. It's only getting worse. Thousands of families floating, lost, breaking. Do they feel this crack in their hearts?

Eleven minutes lost to crying.

But that doesn't stop me from searching: *Audrey Harper, Brooks Vanacore, Caspers Fire, Orange County, California* . . .

Nothing.

I have to stop. I jump out of the truck and inhale deeply, leaning against the warm cab.

Here, minutes from the coast, the inland smoke is subdued. Compared to back home in the canyons, the frantic Santa Ana winds are almost cool and tamed—the oven no longer on broil. Don't mind the rusty clouds smudging the mountain line. Really, it's just another beautiful Sunday in Southern California. A warm, glowing October.

I'm officially falling apart. I close my eyes for a beat and then push off from my truck. I make my way through the parking lot. I pretend my legs aren't shaking, that my palms aren't sweating. Grace was wrong about my need to dress to impress: Today is a day to get away with sweatpants. Fashion—attempts at exterior perfection—loses meaning when you've lost what keeps you rooted, when your roots are being turned to air and ash. Many evacuees wander toward the mall in gym clothes, oversize shirts, and leggings with patterns you wouldn't normally see in public. I know which ones are part of my community by the finger-brushed hair and stricken expression. Sadness blooms even here. Hands are clenched around shopping bags, around children's hands, around Starbucks cups. Eyes are puffy, too red for concealer to hide. Arms are locked around loved ones, clutching what remains.

My heart bangs in my throat.

I want to text Brooks and ask him why he hasn't called me back and what the fire looks like up close. I want to tell Brooks I'm scared and I miss my home and I'm ready to call it quits. I want to tell him to go home to his dad. I want to inform Brooks I'm done, we're through. *Goodbye, thank you for last night.* I want to text him and remind him I love him, tell him I forgive him. That I'm sorry he's hurting so bad. That I'm sorry I kissed Hayden, that I'm confused. That whatever happens, it's okay. Everything will be okay.

I want to text him a simple question: *how are you?*

Instead, I hop from the asphalt to the sidewalk and yank lavender from a jumbo-size planter outside of Nordstrom's. Stealing lavender is a necessity because my sister had a day as shitty as my own, and she received good news from her oncologist and probably good news from her dream dance academy.

I should have walked slower. Here I am: Fig & Olive, a rustic breezy place.

Did Brooks get a lunch break? Was the Starbucks muffin the last thing he ate?

A hostess leads me to the patio. My family always eats outside when it's time for celebration. The patio's exposed honey wood beams and pillars remind me of a house—the outlines of where that wall, that room, that life will go. It reminds me of a house after a fire has torn through it: only blackened foundation and spare beams remaining. What does our house look like now?

I don't think I have a house anymore.

Dad and Mom and Maya sit by the massive cement fireplace in the center. Even today, the fire burns. Dad looks beat with travel-fatigue, but when he sees me, he stands.

"Our warrior," he says. Dad hugs me and I hug him, almost crying, so I pull away fast, too fast, because there's no way am I going to make a scene in a restaurant. He grasps my shoulders and looks at me. "I'm so proud of you," he says, and I have to blink.

It's just past 5 P.M. and I'm going strong, because I'm fine, but I wish I could just go hide in my bed. I don't know if I still have a bed. And it's so absurd—eating out and celebrating after today, when we don't know if our home is okay.

"Audrey hugging," Maya says from the table. "Where's the camera?"

"So what happened?" I lower myself into the empty chair. My water glass is filled, a lemon slice floating above the ice. "What did the committee say?"

"It turns out Maya fainted in the two last *minutes* of her solo," Mom says.

Maya sips her water. "And *supposedly* my first eight minutes were simply spectacular." She's topped her navy blue leotard with an eyelet lace blouse— the cover up left behind at OCIB when she was carted away on the ambulance.

"Don't say it like that," Dad says. "You clearly were spectacular."

"Not to mention the first two rounds—the barre and floor work," Mom adds.

I hate when they do this, hop around the point, keep me out of the loop a beat longer than necessary. "So are they letting you make up the audition or not?" I ask.

"Not," Mom says.

"Because I'm in, in, in, in, in, in, in!" Maya sings.

They cheer and I cheer, tossing the lavender at Maya, which she puts behinds her ear. Mom explains that, providing Maya's test results from today prove she's really okay and her fainting was just tiredness and not a sign of doom to come, Maya will be set to start at the academy the first week of the new year—on schedule. And now I *am* crying because this is everything we wanted and what we thought we lost. Finally something good. Maya a step closer to a career in ballet.

Today is a good day.

It is, it is good. But my exhaustion hisses and my heart beats so fast it hurts and I hiccup over my tears. Because, not far from where we sit, hills are engulfed. The couple that sits at the table across from us holds hands and cries silently and I can't stand it. I can't stand what this grief and guilt is doing to me. Is this how Brooks has always felt?

It's a good day but for too many hours, I thought Maya's cancer was back, and the hospital was so bright and numb, and she knows I have a problem with sadness, that her cat is most likely dead. And somewhere out there my boyfriend who was blamed for his brother's death is inhaling smoke, and I lied to his poor dad, and I'm as guilty as him, as Brooks, I am, and so it's really difficult to convince the parts of myself shuddering from the past fifteen hours that *right now* is a moment to be happy.

"I knew you'd be fine," I say to Maya. "They'd be fools to turn you away."

She grins. "You think everyone is a fool."

A waiter with a goatee arrives. Mom and Dad order the goat cheese ravioli and the Chilean sea bass to share. Maya goes all out with the forty-buck sirloin.

Now they're all staring at me, and it's my turn to order. I think of what Maya said in the ER. Will I talk to somebody? I will, once I get through today.

"I'll have the truffle risotto," I say.

Dad calls for a bottle of wine. We've survived a fire and we've survived a medical emergency and he survived a supposedly shaky flight, so wine! I want to clarify that I survived the fire. Not him. Not Mom. Not Maya. Me.

I survived the fire. But our waiter retreats to the kitchen, and my family has launched back into conversation—discussing the pros and cons of Maya living on the OCIB campus or living at home. I'm considering the pros and cons of calling the Orange County Fire Department and inquiring into whether or not a Brooks Vanacore is still alive.

"This is a day for the books, isn't it?" Mom sighs. "Can you guys believe this day?"

"I can believe it," I say. "Because, uh, it happened. It's happening."

"In, like, thirty years we'll be laughing about it," Maya says.

"Thirty years?" I slap the table. "Hell, I'm ready to laugh now."

Mom places her hand over mine. "Hon, I think you're experiencing some shock. How about you order a soda? Get some sugar in you."

I shake my head. "I don't want sugar."

"After a morning like yours," Dad says, which is funny, because he has no idea, no idea what this morning really was, "I'd expect nothing less."

I want to laugh, but I almost cry instead.

53

THURSDAY

Thursday night, back behind the trail that borders above my home, even after my eyes had adjusted to the dark, everything was a shadow of a shadow. Saddleback Mountain was dark, the foothills smoldering gray.

Amid the flat space, minimal grass, Brooks dropped his bag and tied a bandana around my eyes.

"Is there a piñata?" I teased.

I couldn't see, could only hear and feel. He kissed me but didn't speak.

"Brooks," I said. "Don't leave."

"Where would I go?" A kiss on my neck.

The zip of a backpack, the clanking of glass, the tap of his Zippo—one, two, three, four, five, ten times. A rustle of fabric. The music of crickets. Another Zippo spark. A strong gust of wind, followed by a *shit-shit-shit,* and then Brooks's lips were on mine again, his tongue opening my mouth.

He untied the bandana, and I blinked at the circle of light. A sleeping bag spread out on the ground, encircled by a ring of mason jars—each slightly dug into the ground, votive candles blinking on the grass. He led me to the blankets. A throw pillow rested in the middle, and I picked it up, the polyester soft against my skin. I ran my hand over the raised fabric, the words. I looked up to Brooks. He watched me, smiling.

"What does it say?"

He flicked his Zippo and held it over the pillow for me to read. A list of epic couples: *Romeo & Juliet, Lancelot & Guinevere, Antony & Cleopatra, Odysseus & Penelope*, but in the middle, in red, two far less extraordinary names.

"Brooks and Audrey," I read.

He shut the Zippo and I clutched the pillow, waited for his lips to meet mine, his gift between us. A moment's kiss, soft, the wind rough.

I pulled back. "Why?" Because a part of me wondered if he knew I knew about his lies, about Cameron. Maybe this was his apology.

He smiled. "I told you. Happy three-month anniversary."

It wasn't an apology. It was a celebration. I had nothing to give him, so I kissed him, wondering if he was counting back to the drive in the canyon, or the date to Balboa Island, or our first kiss in his backyard.

"You've been so patient," he said. "I can't lose you."

I wanted to count the bones in his spine and taste his skin. I wanted to ask him what had really happened, ask him about Cameron, the burning cats and the quaking aspen trees. I wanted to tell him that he scared me when he gripped me. I wanted to tell him what I'd heard his dad say, and that I was beginning to find the pieces, but that I could still see it: two boys on the trail, a boy saving a brother, hitting a wild dog with a stick, and crying for help.

But his fingers pressed gently into my neck, lips whispering across my skin. Thursday night, in the beginning, he was June and July. He was still summer, and my heart swayed. He was still safe.

We fell to the rocky ground, the wind and crickets and coyote howls serenading us. We were together within the circle of flames.

We were only kissing, but then he whispered, "Are you ready?"

The wine was heavy in my limbs. He traced the line of my hip bone with his thumb, and I remembered that I'd once read something about how recovering alcoholics shouldn't date other recovering alcoholics. Doesn't that mean broken people shouldn't date broken people?

He kissed my shoulder and he said, "I brought condoms," and he rolled on top of me. He was heavy, and there was a rock beneath the sleeping bag under my shoulder, digging deep. And I suddenly thought, *I'm not broken. I don't have to be broken.*

"Not now," I said.

"Please."

"No," I said.

"Come on."

It didn't make sense, how all summer he'd been okay to wait, how we'd shared a bed in an empty house on the beach and, even then, it'd mostly been okay. But Thursday night, in this wild and lonely place, he was pushing.

"Audrey," he said. "You're ready for this."

It didn't make sense that all summer he'd lied. His contradictions and stories twisted in my stomach and tasted like the dirt stuck to my lips. And I thought how liars shouldn't date liars.

"Stop," I said. "I don't want to, so please, stop."

So he did.

54

5:12 P.M.

Still at Fashion Island, still waiting on our food. Dad's attempts to soothe me are interrupted by the arrival of the wine. The corkscrew is shiny and sharp enough to cut skin. Beneath the table, I pinch my thighs. I stop crying because Maya is watching and this is a happy moment. The cork pops out of the bottle with no trouble, and Mom and Dad laugh and cheer, because all is well, it's a perfect cork, look at it, the right shade of purple, the right stain line. They even have Maya smell it, it's so darn perfect.

Two glasses are poured and swirled. I should ask for a glass. Something to calm me down. I'm ready to scream. It's too loud on this patio—the clatter of plates and silverware and families yacking and couples whispering and the chew-chew-chew ritual.

There's a fire burning. Homes are melting. At other tables, people check their phones. They crane their necks in search of a TV in the hope of seeing fire on the screen. They smudge their cheeks with blush and gloss their lips only to smudge it back off with tears, then hide their faces with their hands. Deep breaths, deep breaths. I'm not alone in my act of falling apart.

I've been sitting here doing nothing for ten minutes.

The air is thick, becoming suffocating. The smell of fire shouldn't be this strong so close to the ocean—the smoke has closed in since I parked, or maybe I'm losing it, maybe it's the same. But this unfathomable heat, the oven back on broil—nothing is normal. I miss Orange County, the Orange County I know. My home.

I can still feel Brooks's lips on my neck and my cheeks and my hips. The shag rug against my knees. I can feel the wind, the flames glinting like us during those magical July nights. I'm not a virgin. I had sex last night. And there's a fire. And it's my fire too. I did this as much as him.

Dad lifts his wine. "To Maya," he says. "For getting back up after an extraordinary fall."

Maya covers her face with her cloth napkin. "Wow. That's not cheesy at all."

Mom raises her glass as well. "We're so proud of you, sweetie, our prima ballerina."

"Not yet, not even close," she says. "I'll be lucky if I ever dance in a company corps."

And now they all look at me, Mom and Dad with their lifted wine, Maya's cheeks flushed pink. It's my turn to lift my glass with its floating lemon and say something inspiring. And it's like I'm the world-class loser at the table who voluntarily leaped from her audition and never got back up again. But no, that's not true, this isn't about me. It's about Maya, and Maya loves ballet.

I raise my water and say, "To my hero." And I can't meet Maya's gaze as we all clink our glasses because if I do I'll be blubbering again.

A breeze sweeps across the patio and with it comes more smoke. Maybe my phone is accidently switched on Do Not Disturb mode. I pull it out and check, but there are no missed texts or calls. Another eight minutes gone.

"No phones at the table," Mom says.

The food arrives. I want to drown in my risotto.

"I think we can make an exception for phones tonight," Dad says, and, eyes on my phone, he asks, "Any news from Brooks?"

"No." I already went over all of this at the hospital.

"Love woes?" Maya asks.

"His father must be so anxious," Mom says.

"Anxious and proud," Dad amends. "But he hasn't called you?"

I swallow my risotto. "We're probably homeless, and you're asking about my boyfriend?"

Mom and Maya and Dad blink at me.

"Brooks is a firefighter," Mom says. "I think it's a relevant question."

"Homeless," I say.

Maya snaps her fingers. "Hello, drama."

Dad sets his fork on his plate. "Honey, this isn't our first time being evacuated, and it won't be our last. You know it's procedure—they're overly cautious—you should know that from Brooks."

I want to tell him what I learned from Brooks. That I learned how to twist a tale until it resembles the story I want to show and not necessarily the truth. How I learned how to kiss slow and kiss fast. How to start a fire and not so patiently watch it grow.

"You weren't there this morning," I say. "None of you were there."

"You're tired, honey," Mom says.

Maya waves her fork. "Hey, if we're homeless, can we move to Laguna Beach?"

"Say our house does burn." Dad spears a ravioli. "Stressing yourself out isn't going to do a thing. And we wouldn't be *homeless*—we'd only be in search of a new home, temporarily out of place. We're in an extremely fortunate position."

Mom pats my hand. "Take a step back. Try to breathe."

And so I do. I actually lean back in my chair and try to silence this rapid-fire chitchat I've been stuck with all day, since the cops showed up at my house at five in the morning. Maya spins her finger in the remains of her mashed potatoes, waltzing her pinky across the plate. Mom raises her wine glass to her lips, and Dad observes her and Maya and me. He smiles. Yes, they're celebrating, they're somehow happy, but they're also tired.

"I don't know about you geezers," Maya says, nodding at Mom and Dad, breaking the silence, her potato ballet complete. "But if it'd been *me* home alone this morning, I would have passed out."

I smile. "Maya."

"Like, if I ran up and down the stairs enough times, I would've literally passed out," she says, smiling so big. "Medical science can back me up."

Let the house burn, as long as I have her.

55

FRIDAY

When I kissed Hayden on Friday, the fire was still small, still contained. It was after psychology, after I read on my phone that the air quality was rated at a 163. *Unhealthy to everyone.* Panic was setting in, and I couldn't go to my next class—but I couldn't go home either. I had to get off campus, but there's only one road in and out of my school, and you can't get past the parking lot trolls without a slip from the attendance office.

My only option was the hills that run the length of our school.

The bell rang. Hayden followed me out of class. We walked through the courtyard, past the gym and the swimming pool. I texted Grace and told her I didn't feel well, that I wouldn't be meeting everyone at our usual spot for lunch. Hayden walked with me, waving at his basketball buddies as we passed, talking and talking and talking because we needed to make a game plan for our memory project. He wanted to make that game plan ASAP.

"Can we set a time later?" I said, when we reached the athletics fields. "I'll text you."

"You trying to get rid of me?" he asked.

"Sort of," I said.

"Where are you headed?" He glanced toward the football field, the valleys beyond it.

I nodded up. "The T. I'm skipping next period."

The T is just that: a giant T made of cement, set near the ridge of the bank above campus, outlined in white and filled with red. It's nothing special, other than a quiet, non-scratchy place to sit with a view of the school, the Toll Road, and the parched valley below.

Hayden squinted. "You can go up there?"

"It's where most people smoke weed."

"You're skipping class to get high?"

"No," I said. "But so what if I was?"

"So you're going up there now—because?"

"Because I kind of want to scream."

"Well." His smiled wavered. "Can I come? I love a good scream. It's healthy."

I stared at him. Hayden's face was so open. The fresh burn on my hand pulsed. Hayden claiming screaming is healthy—a joke—Hayden who, before this semester, had always been so quiet.

Smoke grew beyond the hills. My chest was tight. "This will be your first time skipping, right?" I said. "Sure you can handle that?"

"Well, senior year—have to rebel at least once." He waved his arms. "Come on, I can't graduate never having gone to the T!"

So together we climbed the dry, scrubby hill.

At the T, Hayden and I sat on the red edge of the concrete, our shoes hanging in the weeds. I was out of breath, sweaty, my side bangs sticking to my forehead. My throat hurt, and I wasn't sure if it was from climbing in the smoke or something more.

"So, we're here," Hayden said. "At the T. Got to admit, I'm slightly underwhelmed."

I pulled my knees to my chest, thinking how silly it was that for so long Hayden had remained only an almost-but-not-really friend. Just my best friend's brother. The guy I avoided running into in the bathroom whenever I slept over.

"Why did you stay away from me?" I asked. "Before, I mean. You only recently started treating me like I'm someone you actually want to be around, only just started to really talk to me."

Hayden squinted. "That's not totally true."

"Sorta true." I nudged his shoulder. "What changed?"

"I don't know. Nothing really." He pushed up his glasses, tried to look at me, only to focus on his shoes instead. "You grew up, and you didn't seem so young anymore. That's all."

I laughed. "I grew up?" I tugged on a weed. "You've always been a year older than me."

He shook his head. "It's more complicated than that."

"What changed?" I asked again. Because something had shifted before the semester started, in the summer, a shift in the way he looked at me, talked to me.

He messed around in his backpack and pulled out a mint. He untwisted the plastic wrapping, plopped it into his mouth, a slight shake in his hands.

"Hayden," I said.

And he replied, "You started dating Brooks."

My skin went numb. "What does Brooks have to do with you and me?"

"It made me realize that you didn't have to be off-limits. That I didn't want you to be only Grace's best friend." Hayden blushed and rubbed his palms against his jeans. "I realized that there was space for more than my usual only-school-and-in-the name-of-school routine. Or, really, that I wanted that space—wanted to hang out—" He glanced at me, stopped, and started again, "But then you had Brooks."

A football scrimmage started down on the field, and shouts echoed across the valley.

"Oh my god," I said. "Jealousy. You're jealous of Brooks?"

He laughed tightly. "Yeah. I guess. I'll own up to that."

It took me a minute to find my voice. "I could've made room, if you'd told me you wanted to hang out."

Hayden finally looked at me. "You honestly think that's true?"

I stared back at him, trying to find my response, wanting to say something, anything, but the hot wind shifted and picked up speed, dirt spiraling around us in a violent gust. And Hayden—so sudden—he leaned in, his arm around me, his hand on my head, protecting my eyes from the dirt and the ash. We braced together against the gust, and it was so odd, how good it felt.

And he was laughing with his arm around me, yelling into the wind, "This was a brilliant idea. Go up to the T on the most hellish of hell days!"

Even over the stench of fire, he smelled like the cool of his mint. He bit into the candy, and the crunch of the sugar—I could feel it. It made me wonder if he could hear my heart, if he could smell my sweat, last night's blood, my scarred skin.

The wind calmed and we separated, sitting up, looking up.

"This is crazy," he said.

"Yeah."

I yanked the green Nalgene from his backpack and chugged. I thought he'd comment on my not asking first, but he only watched me throw back the water.

"I thought you were going to scream," he said when I passed him the bottle. "Was this all a ruse to get me to confess my cardinal teenage sins? I was kind of looking forward to the screaming."

"Oh, right," I said.

And everything bottled up: I screamed like I never had before. I screamed liked I should have some twenty hours earlier. And Hayden joined in, only he pretended to be some kind of animal, a mountain lion, I think. It was strange to hear Hayden's voice in a wild, free way; it was even stranger to scream in front of him. And I wondered if the football players could hear us, if our cries echoed through the courtyard. And it gave me a high, a release too great.

And so when those seconds ended and silence settled, I kissed Hayden.

He kissed me back. Hayden, the second boy I've ever kissed. And it made my heart stall because it was different: slow and tentative. But I pulled him closer, my hand on his neck, a somehow-urgent calm filling me. And then he pushed me away.

"You have a boyfriend," he said, now standing. "Or did you guys break up?"

"It doesn't matter," I said, because I didn't think it did, not with the lies and the fire and the nonexistent photographs from the camping trip. "And you just said you want—"

"Stop," Hayden said. "Just stop."

I sank down off the cement T and into the dirt. That's what I'd said the night before. *Stop.* "I'm sorry," I said.

"God. Audrey. Not like this." He shoved a hand through his curls. "You're my friend," he said. "You're Grace's best friend. Don't hurt yourself through me."

I thought I might be sick. "That's not what I'm doing."

Hayden looked down at the school, down toward the fields. He kicked at the dirt and offered me his hand. But I ignored him, so he asked, "Are you going to be all right?"

"Already am." A lie.

"Let me know when you want to talk or scream again or whatever," he said.

Hayden pushed his way down through the brush, away from me, and then he was gone. I pulled myself back up onto the T and lay across the hot cement. I closed my eyes against the smoke, listening to the crackling of the bristled grass and the howl of the wind and the occasional voices drifting from campus. Guilt pounded in my chest, and the sun burned my skin.

I counted the school bell rings, and I got up at the end of fifth period and texted Hayden.

For the project . . . does Sunday at 8 work?

See you then.

❋ ❋ ❋

I kissed Hayden because I was still thirsty and he smelled like peppermint.

No.

I kissed him because the smoke got into my brain and I was mad at Brooks.

No.

I kissed him because he always smiles with his teeth.

No, I kissed him because I wanted to kiss him and I needed something to feel real, feel good, feel like something other than the asphalt spreading through my limbs.

I kissed him because I like him and I'm selfish.

56

6:35 *P.M.*

At the Ayres Hotel & Spa, Mom tosses her book on the bed. "You're going to study *now?*"

"Not study," I say. "Work on a big-deal, half-my-grade project."

"School's closed, remember," Maya says from the floor, where she's sprawled out with her right leg in the air, foot pointed. "Vacation time."

"But vacation time might only last a day," I say.

Capistrano Unified School District's Robot Lady called all four of our phones with the thrilling news: School is closed tomorrow because of poor air quality. The status of the rest of the week is still pending.

Beat that, snowy states. Wouldn't you love a fire day?

Dad sits on the bed. "Can't it wait until tomorrow?" He takes off his watch, rubs his wrist.

My backpack is hanging from my shoulder, and my freshly charged phone is in my hand, ready with the texts Hayden and I exchanged as evidence.

6:01 P.M.: *I'm at a hotel in Mission Viejo. Where should I meet you?*

6:03 P.M.: *The Ayres?*

6:04 P.M.: *Yes . . .*

6:07 P.M.: *I'll meet you in the lobby?*

6:08 P.M.: *I can come to you!*

And his final reply at 6:10 P.M.: *Want to make it easy for you, see you around 7.*

Neither of us mentioned school being closed, though I bet he knows. I bet we both received Robot Lady calls.

One of the few hotels in the area, the Ayres Hotel & Spa is an oasis for the South OC evacuees who don't want to sleep on cots at Mission Viejo High School. Five minutes and three exits off the Toll Road, it's close enough to home to not feel like we've totally abandoned hope, yet far enough away to ensure we won't be waking to another fateful knock in the morning.

Anyhow, my body wants to collapse, but my mind wants to run. Working on my psychology project seems like fair-enough middle ground.

"We're supposed to present on Wednesday," I say to my parents. "And I promised Hayden. It'd be rude to cancel."

"Honey," Mom says. "I think you should just hang out here. You're exhausted."

They've deflated since dinner. Driving into the ashy parking lot—the smoke too thick to breathe for too long—and then standing in the distraught crowd of the hotel lobby, I think it finally hit them that, maybe, I wasn't being totally overly dramatic at dinner.

"It's for school," I repeat. "And it'll help get my mind off of all of this."

The TV is on and muted. The screen flashes with burning light, and I'm trying not to notice. I move for the door, phone and truck keys grasped tightly in my hand.

"Why don't you two come up here?" Dad asks.

Maya vetoes that idea before I can. "We do *not* need an extra body in this room."

Mom looks around, eyeing the packed space. We're falling over one another as it is. There really isn't room for anyone else in here. "Well," she says.

"So I can go? Seriously," I say, "I feel fine." And oddly it's kind of true. I could dance a full ballet and run from school and back. I can't imagine sitting, chilling out, lying in bed. Who needs sleep when there's smoke to breathe and adrenaline to expend?

Maya pouts. "You're going to leave me? What about our microwave brownies?"

"I'll be back," I say, and I'm going to offer my final argument, but something flashes on the TV and Dad unmutes and I can't not listen.

While over a thousand residents of the gated community Coto de Caza were evacuated, a dramatic shift in the winds sent the fire barreling south, toward the neighboring association, Dove Canyon, while also fanning out west deeper into Caspers Wilderness Park. Over three thousand homes have been evacuated across the communities for this single fire. As of now an official count of ninety-three have been lost—

Ninety-three. Ninety-three homes lost, hundreds more at risk.

I can't breathe.

It's old footage on the TV—daylight—at least three hours old. Canyons and valleys and gulches we've known our entire life engulfed. Neighborhoods we drive by every day. They don't show our bank, our street, our valley. They show a lonely mansion collapsing on a hillside. They show the street that acts as the border between the wild and the civilized, burning bright. Two ruggedly placed estates reduced to blackened frames.

I need to get out of this room before this sinking swarms me.

"If your house burns down, do they call you?" Maya asks.

Mom and Dad look at me. I should be the expert on these things, but I'm not.

The footage cuts to a night scene, live, a reporter on a street, the fire and the hills behind him. He shouts things over the wind that make me want to plug my ears, but Dad's clicking the volume up, up, up so I have no choice but to hear.

It's breaking news. What the stations have been waiting for all day.

A statement has been released by a task force of agencies announcing that Southern California Caspers Fire is officially being declared arson. There will be a press conference this evening when more information is obtained—FBI agents have secured the scene—if you have any information—

No.

—We are told that a potential point of origin has been identified and evidence uncovered near the trail adjacent to Coto De Caza and Cleveland National Forest gate—more information to come—FBI—secured scene—come forward with information—

I have to leave.

"I love you," I say.

But they don't hear me.

I rush to Maya and kiss her hair. She's blinking at the screen. They're blinking at the screen. My hand is on the doorknob now, one foot in the hall. I call over my shoulder, "I'll be back later," and then I'm running to the elevator, but fuck the elevator, that'll take too long. I take the stairs.

Arsonist. Arson. Arsonist. Arson.

57

THURSDAY

O n Thursday night, after Brooks and I'd hiked out beyond the wind-whipped trail, on the sleeping bag spread across the hard ground, after I said *No, stop, don't,* and he did stop, Brooks stayed on top of me for four beats, his weight on his arms. And then, in a breath, he shoved himself away. He said he'd wasted his entire summer in this desert, in this place too dead and artificial to even burn, land not worthy of a fire's warmth and glory.

And I was thinking how he must have been thinking that he'd also wasted his summer on me, those three months, me too stiff and too dry. I can only sit. I can only listen. I can only kiss. The hot wind splitting my skin, I blinked. Brooks held his Seattle-skyline Zippo to his palm. He struck the flame. Didn't flinch. Moved it away. Moved it closer. I leapt forward. Grabbed his arm. He pushed me aside, so easily, and I landed on my back, scraping my elbows.

"Cameron told me that the pain was sharp. Scalding." Brooks laughed, so bitter. "I guess it woke him up. I don't feel a thing."

Dirt kicked up in the wind, sticking to my cheeks. I swallowed past the pulse in my throat. "I know you're lying," I said. "About Cameron. He didn't die last year. He was a kid. When he died, you were both kids."

His green eyes didn't flinch from mine. "You don't know what you're talking about."

This wasn't how I'd planned to confront him, but then again I'd never really had a plan. "How did Cameron die, Brooks?"

Brooks clenched his Zippo. "Like I said."

"Stop lying." I cracked. "He's in every story you've told me about yourself," I said. "All you talk about is you and fire, fire and him. It's how I *know* you. And you've just been lying."

"Stop talking," he said.

"Did you kill Cameron?"

His left eye dripped. "How could you ever ask me that?"

I didn't have an answer. A gust slammed down the canyon. It knocked over jars, whipped our hair into our faces and dust into our eyes. A lit candle fell on dry grass. A tiny spark, an almost start.

"It'd be so much easier for you if I killed him, wouldn't it?" Brooks asked. "I'd finally fit into this broken narrative you've created for me. That'd make you happy. If all along you were dating a cat-burning beast. You'd get to be the hero of this story."

I choked. "You burned Miss Cat?"

He laughed dryly. "Is that what you want to hear?"

Rocks bit into my skin, my head, me. Brooks stood. He was pacing around the circle of mason jar candles, most blown out. His gaze pointed up to the silky, crystalline sky, the blazing stars. His fists were clenched.

But then he was kneeling at his backpack.

"What are you doing?" I asked.

"I want to show you something."

58

6:49 P.M.

"Audrey!" Hayden jogs from the hotel doors. He's backlit from the orange glow of the lobby, making it hard to see his face. "Wow. Déjà vu, right?"

Brooks said it was okay. He said it would be fine. I've stayed quiet and I've stayed low. Has the word *arson* blasted through Luis's bedroom? I'm laughing now, hysteria hot in my throat. Mom was right. What she said at dinner. *Shock*. I am in shock, and a new wave has hit.

Arson. Arsonist. Arson.

I need to do something. What do I do?

And it's ridiculous—the repetition. Hayden drove me home less than twenty-four hours ago. He followed me out of the party when I was almost crying but not yet crying. And then this morning he chased me down to my truck to ask if I needed his help, which I declined. And like a fool, just now,

I charged out of the stairwell and darted through the hotel lobby—almost knocking into people, almost tripping over luggage and toddlers.

"I was going to call you." I hold up my phone in defense, though he wasn't who I was going to call. "Like, just now."

He nods. "Okay."

"Have you heard from Grace?" I ask.

"They're camping in Pismo Beach tonight—with school cancelled, they'll do Big Sur tomorrow—though they're definitely busted. But she's happy, and Quinn is elated."

"Good. That's really, really good to hear."

His eyes are so tired. "Are you okay?"

We might as well be standing on Derek Sanders's driveway. The wind is hot, licked with smoke, dropping ash like rain. "It's kind of," I say, "been a really bad day."

He's messing with the strap on his backpack, unable to stand still. "I would be surprised if you said otherwise." And his exhaustion, his frantic movements—suddenly it hits me.

I press my hands against my eyes, but I already know it. I know it's true. "You were evacuated, weren't you?"

He laughs. "I don't hide emotions well, I guess."

"Grace didn't text me."

"It happened after she left, and she's taking it well, focusing on the road trip." He rubs his neck. "It was a voluntary evacuation. Not mandatory." He winces and closes his eyes for the smallest of moments, as if remembering that mine was mandated at five this morning. "My parents are just playing it safe."

"I'm so sorry," I say.

"You have no reason to apologize."

My breath snags. I have every reason to apologize. "You want to go some-where?" I ask. "Like, somewhere that's not here?" Hayden nods, gestures to his Accord, but I add, "I'm driving."

59

Offense Cycle

When I think of *arson*, I think of firebombs thrown into downtown buildings or gasoline dumped on brittle foothills. I think of middle-aged men and women with decade-old grudges. I think of the act and the aftermath, with no consideration of the before or the motives.

But it turns out that motives are everything, and a high percentage of arsonists are minors.

Friday night, after dinner with Brooks, I found a training manual from the Washington State Department of Social and Health Services online. Supposedly, every year in the U.S., fire kills more people than all other natural disasters combined. And apparently, 40 percent of individuals arrested for arson are under the age of eighteen. And *supposedly*, fire set-ters are typically less assertive, less intelligent, less physically aggressive, and more socially isolated.

I'd like to email the Washington State Department of Social and Health Services on that last one. Ms. Bracket says it's dangerous to generalize. I agree. I demand hard statistics.

Motives are hard to unravel in most cases but typically fall under one of six umbrellas:

- Revenge/Protest: usually anger directed toward a specific entity
- Excitement: a fire setter probably gets a kick out of fires, sometimes sexual
- Mental Health Concern: as in arson is a symptom of another illness
- Concealment: fire setter has another crime to hide
- Vandalism: arson being the result of boredom or revenge
- Profit/Economic Gain: something to do with insurance

But can it really be that simple? As Ms. Bracket says, everything starts at the psyche.

60

Montage

Just last weekend was the second time I encountered Brooks's dad. It was
a work party. Luis's law firm's anniversary or something, held at a ritzy
resort in Laguna Beach, on the edge of a bluff—one wrong step and you're in
the Pacific.

The cloudless night was wrapped in light, the expansive lawn lit by tiki
torches and fire rings and hanging white bulbs and tea candles in mason jars.
Adults interspersed around fire pits perched by the rocks and high tables by
the outdoor bar, clutching cocktails and bacon-wrapped dates. Voices were
slanted, loud, dripping with the September wind—not hot and frantic like at
home, thirty minutes east, but coastal calm and cool.

Brooks and I were the only teenagers in attendance.

It was a late invitation, at least for me. Brooks had called me that morning, frenzied by the opportunity for a fancy night. *Special, something different,*

something nice, you know, and it'd make my dad happy, my dad really wants to see you again, so come, please? I could hear his smile through the phone, feel his lifted mood in the whoosh of his words. Of course I said yes.

When he picked me up, Brooks kissed my cheek. "I've never seen you in white," he said.

I'd borrowed Grace's winter dress from freshmen year—a soft peach number that clung to my waist and fell to my knees. The sheer neckline reminded me of my ballet costumes. I fingered the fabric. "This isn't white."

In slacks and a button-down, his hair not a greasy mess but tousled, cologne ad–worthy, Brooks was freshly shaved, smelling of soap. Standing upright, jaw high. Brooks. *My* Brooks. He held my hand to his mouth, kissed my knuckles.

"I couldn't care less about the dress," he said. "You're beautiful."

At the party he led me to the dance floor—temporary parquet spread out across the lawn. So close, his hands on my waist, mine around his neck. Buffeted by drunken shimmying adults. I'd never danced with a partner before—never made it to that level in ballet—but with Brooks leading me, holding me, it was second nature. It exhilarated me.

We moved from the dance floor to the grass. Brooks circled his arms around my waist, and we swayed across the soft ground. It was better away from the lights, easier to pretend we were alone.

Last Saturday, he looked and felt and smelled like June, like hope and passion, like our date to Balboa Island, the Ferris wheel and the sand, the warm pebble-garden nights in July.

"What would you say if I said I hope we're together forever?" he asked.

He wasn't shaking or fiddling with his Zippo or spitting about how things would soon change. September was ending, so maybe I could set my obsession with Cameron aside. He'd tell me the truth eventually, let me see the quaking aspen photos when his wounds healed. He was everything.

"I'd say forever and ever," I said. But I was dancing on glass, too aware that we were no longer what we'd used to be—that I didn't know if I even still wanted what we'd been.

"You've saved me," he said. Which is funny, because I'd thought he considered himself to be the one doing the saving. That that was what he wanted.

We twirled and Brooks dipped me, held me tight. A camera flashed.

"The stars have arrived!" Luis sang.

He held his phone in one hand, a full wine glass in the other. He was rested and taller than I'd remembered, so far from deflated. Though maybe it was the wine, or his tan cotton shirt, the party glow, or the woman at his arm. Regardless, Luis looked good.

"Hi," Brooks said, flatly, a voice I use with my own dad if don't know what else to say, if I want him to go away.

Luis studied me. "Audrey, you're a knockout," he said. "Isn't she a knockout, Brooks?"

"It's one of her many merits."

Luis looked at the woman. "Did I not tell you, Jena? Are they not great together?"

"Lovely," Jena agreed.

"This place is incredible," I said. "Thank you for having me."

Luis raised his phone in response and, without warning, snapped another photo. "Now don't get mad at me," he said. "Don't freak out, Brooks, but can I just tell you, Audrey, can I just tell you how grateful I am for you, how happy I am—"

Brooks moaned. "Dad, *don't*."

"No, no, don't *don't* me," Luis said, his lips wine-stained. "She ought to know how glad I am she's around. What she did for you. Never thought you'd get past everything—what with Cameron—poor dear Cameron—" Brooks was sweating, clenching my hand in his. "But you're like a different guy now. And it's kind of cool. Jena, isn't my son cool?"

"Great," Brooks said. "Got it. I'm cool."

Luis stepped closer, teetering drunk, and said, "Cheers to you, Audrey."

He raised his glass just as Brooks shifted abruptly—as if to step between his dad and me, as if to turn me away—and knocked Luis's wine from his hand. A sticky cool splash across my chest. A sour sweetness on my lips.

Brooks said *shit* and Luis said *shit* and I rubbed at the fabric, because that was my first reaction. Luis said sorry, and Brooks snapped and told him to let us be, and Luis said he'd show me the way to the bathroom. Jena took my hand and announced *she'd* take me to the ladies' room and ordered Brooks and Luis to the bar for club soda.

And that settled that.

It was one of those fancy bathrooms with cloth towels and marble floors and shutter stalls. I was shaking. *What would you say if I said I hope we're together forever?* I rubbed the toe of my shoe on the tile, and Jena worked to calm the bloodlike stain on my chest. Gentle pats with damp towels. *Forever and ever and ever.* My throat was threatening to close. *You saved me.* The wine and Luis's drunken toast and Brooks so eager, Brooks so angry, Brooks so everything. *Never thought you'd get past everything—what with Cameron—poor dear Cameron.* I was heavy and damp.

"You go ahead and cry it out," Jena said. "You're certainly not the first to lose it over a stained dress."

"It's not the dress."

A knock on the door. The club soda.

Jena cracked the can and dampened a new towel. "Don't let Luis get to you," she said. I was shivering, my skin cold where the wine had hit. "You okay?" she asked.

I forced a smile. "I'm fine."

Nodding, she turned and swished out of the bathroom, her heels clicking on the tiles. "I'll tell Brooks you'll be out soon."

I counted to one hundred before I left the bathroom, heading for the lighted walkway. But I froze when I heard Luis snarl his name. *Cameron—*

They were arguing, Brooks's dad and Jena.

I pressed my body against the wall and listened.

Brooks is fine—I know what I can and cannot say—not something you can step into—

He was drunk. I stood there, straining to hear.

Cameron, I heard him say. *Cameron.*

61

7:11 P.M.

I 've spent far too much of today in this truck.

But here I am, with Hayden, speeding on the Toll Road, headed toward the smoke, headed to the only place in town that stays open late. Corky's Diner, which happens to be closer to our school, to our homes, to the fire than the hotel.

I swear it really is our only option, at least out of places that are familiar.

Hayden is messing with his seat belt and chewing his thumbnail. It's like last night. Only we're in my truck, and our roles are reversed. And it's not like last night because I'm not running away. I'm moving forward.

"Thanks again for the ride last night," I say. "It wasn't my finest moment."

"Honestly?" Hayden says. "It was the highlight of the past twenty-four hours."

My windshield wipers occasionally swipe back and forth, clearing the accumulating ash from my view. I drive and follow the white lines of the road, pretending that the thickening ash is a winter storm. We're not here, Hayden and I. We're not driving through a fire in Orange County, but a blizzard in the Rocky Mountains.

"We should have just gone somewhere near the hotel, the Spectrum even," Hayden says. "It feels like we're driving into the fire."

He's right. This ash isn't a good sign, but I say, "And miss out on Corky's ambiance? No way." He doesn't respond, only stares straight ahead. "I'm sorry about Friday," I say. "The T."

"I'm not the only one you should be apologizing to," he says.

I grip the wheel. "I wasn't thinking. It was just, you know, one of those stupid things you do when you're not thinking."

"Ouch."

"That's not—" I shake my head.

Hayden doesn't respond. When I glance over, he's leaning against the door, leaning as far from me as possible as if to get a fuller view of me. He's watching me, like I watched him last night. I wonder what he sees in my profile in the little bit of light.

"Okay," he says.

And I'm going to say something more, but my phone starts buzzing in the front pocket of Grace's shorts.

62

Biting My Knees

Last Saturday in Laguna Beach, Jena asked Luis to lay it out for her, to
help her comprehend. It was hard to hear because the jazz band started
back up again, but I stayed and strained to catch every word. It felt like darts
shot straight into my ears.

An accident—

Kids, so young—

It was too fast—

Cameron—

It broke him—

Losing Cameron—

Only a boy—

Cameron—

And last Saturday night, their voices drifted further as they headed back
to the party, and I moved from the wall and watched Brooks's dad and his

girlfriend walk the lighted path, arm in arm. The words echoed in the wind. *Accident. Only a boy.* The fragments split my skin. *Kids, so young.* Seventeen and twenty does not equate with *young kids.*

Shivering in Grace's wine-stained dress, this is what I did:

I pulled my hair over my shoulder so it concealed the stain, and I crossed my arms against my chest for good measure and walked through the party until I found Brooks sitting on a bench, playing with his Zippo. He looked out to the black ocean. I kissed him on the lips, even though I wanted to ask why he'd lied, and I wanted to hold him because his grief felt too great, even greater than before, and I wanted to scream because he didn't trust me, because—one way or another—he hadn't told me the truth.

Brooks asked me what was wrong, and I said nothing.

This is what happened after:

Brooks drove me home, and we made out in the Audi parked on my street, and he tried to put his hand under my dress. But I needed one thing to stay the same, and I still felt sick. So I said goodnight, and then it was over and Sunday passed and the week carried on, except I had Luis's broken explanation scattered in my mind. Then Thursday, our anniversary—I finally said something.

On Friday, there were only sparks and heat, because Friday I was numb and terrified, so I played pretend. Except Hayden, he wasn't pretend. And last night was a new Saturday at Derek Sanders's house and it was something, because I wanted it to be something. And now there's today, another Sunday, and today—tonight—is shit. *Shit shit shit.*

63

7:18 P.M.

"It's Grace," I say.

I know it's illegal and terrible to text and drive, and I know Hayden is probably judging me or maybe fearing for his life, but once I start I can't stop, because this is what Grace has to say:

I found service and CNN reported that a firefighter died . . . Any word from Brooks? They didn't say a name. I'm freaking out. But they totally would have called you, right?

Like, I'm sure he's fine. He's Brooks. (And oh my gosh YAY for Maya! So happy and relieved and ahhhhhh she's a star!)

Also Hayden and I were evacuated too!

I can't believe someone's dead.

"Audrey," Hayden says.

Hayden's hand is on mine as I clench the steering wheel because I'm still driving, but I dropped the phone, and it's now lit up on the floor of the cab.

Maybe Brooks is fine, maybe he's alive, maybe he's drinking a beer or spraying water on the fire, but that doesn't change the fact that someone's dead.

Guilt like that.

It takes you places.

"Audrey, pull over," Hayden is saying. "You should pull over."

For the second time today, I pull onto the shoulder of the Toll Road, an isolated stretch of concrete in untouched foothills. I roll off gently and click on the hazards.

"What's going on?" Hayden asks.

No cars pass. We're too close to the fire. Those evacuated are long gone, and those allowed to remain home have sealed their doors and windows.

"A firefighter died," I say. "Grace read it on the news."

"Oh." He exhales. "Are you okay?"

"No," I say, my most honest answer of the day.

I wait for him to ask me what happened, but instead he says, "Close your eyes."

"What?"

"I have an idea," he says, "for our project, and I think right now is a prime moment to give it a try, so close your eyes." He touches my hand. "Think about anything other than what you just read, but don't leave the truck. Stay right here, but remember something."

My legs are shaking and my nose is stuffed up and I don't have a tissue and it's too damn quiet. Hayden's breath. My own. The clicking of the truck's hazards. The whoosh of the wind against the cab. A helicopter overhead. With my eyes closed, I see white stars on black. I see the fire. The smoke curdling into the morning sky. I think of what Luis said the last time I was parked on the side of the Toll Road, and I think of what Brooks said in Balboa after he lit those matches.

I think about what was said on TV. Arson. Someone is dead.

Hayden touches my hand again.

Remember something, he said. *Don't leave the truck.*

So much of my time with Brooks has been spent in his Audi—in motion, in between, like today. Brooks has never been in my truck, my grandma's old truck. I only got my license two weeks ago, plus it's habitual: Brooks has always picked me up in the Audi. He drives and we kiss. He said it was okay; it was okay that I didn't feel ready yet, that he'd wait forever if that's what I wanted. He said we were like the aspen trees that he and his brother used to hike to see. That's what I remember: not my truck but the quiet moments between him and me, the warm moments when we were weaving through the canyons, as if moving toward a dream.

I can feel Hayden watching me when he asks, "Do you have a memory?"

I nod.

"Okay. Let's go outside."

Hayden opens his door, and we tumble out onto the weed-choked shoulder. He looks around. "Crap," he says.

Which is an understatement.

I've traveled up this Toll Road dozens of times, but now it's another world. The stench of smoke is consuming, as thick as it was in my house this morning, only stretched out, relentless, like we're in a dome. I'm coughing. A helicopter bounces in the dark. I can't see the stars. My eyes sting.

We're in the wrong canyon to see flames, but I know the fire is close. Closer than I originally thought. It's near, being fed by this wind. My heart batters. No nighttime reprieve for the firefighters.

"This is bad," Hayden says.

My phone vibrates. A call. I know the number now: Luis. I silence it. I can't. Not now.

Every inhale hurts. "Why are we out here again?"

"My idea." He scrunches his face, looks at me. "Okay. Try to think of another memory now that you're outside."

"You're not going to make me dance at the end of this, are you?"

"Only if you want to."

I lean against the truck and let the wind strike my skin. I close my eyes. Last night, on Derek Sanders's parents' balcony, the flames like the guiding beams for an airplane's landing—and Brooks and me, losing it, all the while, refusing to let the other go. Us on the floor, the smoke smelled close, the wind was so strong, but in comparison to this moment, the fire was merely background noise.

Right now the fire is everything.

I open my eyes. Hayden isn't facing me but looking down at the tract homes across the valley. The stucco houses in the square yards are safe—not in the fire's path. It's after 7 p.m., but only a few lights are on. Families are inside, continuing their lives. How many heard the news of a dead firefighter on CNN?

My phone vibrates again. Maya. I answer.

"Audrey," Maya cries. "A firefighter died. Is Brooks—"

"He's okay. He's going to be okay."

"You can't know that. I don't understand how you can be so calm. How can you—I don't get it—" I hear Mom shushing her, trying to calm her down. I hear the TV in the background. The word again. *Arson.* And Maya is telling Mom it's a sister thing, and a door slams, and then silence.

"Maya?"

A pause. "*Where are you?*" she asks.

"What?"

"You're outside," Maya says. "I can hear the wind. I thought you were studying."

"We're taking a breather."

She gasps. "You're going to look for Brooks."

"I'm not!"

"What are you doing? Audrey, *what are you doing?*" Her voice breaks. "I know something is up. I know it. You're acting as if Brooks is nothing to you. You can trust me. I'm your *sister.*"

I'm crying. "I love him, Maya."

"I know."

We both cry. We waste a minute crying together on the phone, and it helps—simply being on the phone with my sister—it relieves a swell of pressure in my chest.

"When are you coming back?" she asks.

"I don't know," I say. "As soon as I can."

Silence. And then, "Do you think there's hope for Shadow?"

"I do." And I have to believe it. "We'll call all the shelters," I say. "Tomorrow, Tuesday, all week."

"Please be safe."

"I love you," I say, and she says, "I love you too," and I somehow don't cry again.

When I hang up, I make my way to Hayden, to the crest of the canyon. We look out over the maze of homes below us.

"Maya," I say. "She's not taking the evacuation well."

Hayden squints. "How are you taking it?"

I laugh. "I'm falling apart," I say. And it's a foolish hope, given all that I know, what I saw this morning, but I need this hope, so I hiccup and say, "But maybe our house will be okay."

Hayden stares at me like we're in class and I asked about the date of an exam we're scheduled to take that day. He shakes his head. "Oh," he says, "Audrey."

"What?" But I see it in his eyes, his hunched shoulders. He scrubs his hand behind his neck. "I mean, your neighborhood, the ones surrounding it—"

My grandmother's paintings. The photo albums I left on the living room bookshelves. Maya's journals. Shadow, maybe Shadow, despite what I just said. My sister's beloved first cat. She might be okay, but I can't know that. Our home. Where Maya and I grew up. Where we pretended to be royal mermaids. The home my parents built and loved in.

"Oh." It's all I can I say too.

"I'm so sorry," he says.

I knew there was a high probability of my house burning. I was there. It was so close. But I never really thought—how could I think—I don't want to go anywhere. I have nowhere. I'm gutted. My home gone.

"There's a site online," Hayden's saying, "where they update the evacuations and list the hit neighborhoods. I thought you knew."

I shake my head. I'm shivering in the heat. His and Grace's house might burn down too. Neighborhoods destroyed. How many families without homes, without the financial ability to simply build again like my parents? It's hard not to hate myself, hard not to let my anger with myself take over, my guilt too—it's hard to breathe normally, and I need to do something, anything—

When I hug Hayden, he doesn't act surprised, though I am. Surprised by my want to hold and be held, surprised by how it feels. It's strange because all my life I've flinched away from touch, afraid of my family's embrace, of them being too close, of exposing too much of myself. And all my life I've panicked at the idea of what it means for someone to feel my body, to be so close to me.

And gradually, Brooks tangled so near, and I was numb and ecstatic and afraid and confused. I thought I'd give myself to him—thinking I could mend his scars, make him okay, telling myself I needed him too because he was my thing. Thinking that I owed him because his brother was dead, and I was the only one who could really help ease his pain. But none of that was true. It was never my job, never my obligation.

And hugging Hayden isn't anything like hugging Brooks, and it isn't like Friday when I caught Hayden off guard with my lips. Hugging Hayden is steady and simple and assuring.

He holds me until I back away, and I say, "Thank you."

"For what?"

"Everything. Being a friend. Being an awesome brother to Grace. Being a great psych partner and pushing me," I say, and I laugh and add, "For taking me home last night. For making me pull over."

"It was kind of self-preservation. My making you stop the car—I didn't want to die."

"Your idea though," I say. "What was the point?"

"I read something when researching for our project, how context influences how we remember things—where you are, who you're with, what you're feeling." He kicks at the gravel. "That every time we remember an event, we change it based on our immediate surroundings, and particular scenarios can salvage what's been repressed."

I stare at him. "And you decided to play with this theory while driving through a smoke storm because?"

"It was an on the fly decision," he says, a tense laugh. "I thought it might help your anxiety if you paused, focused on something other than the fire. Like a weird meditation. It helps me sometimes."

I want to laugh at the word *anxiety*—if only that was all I was feeling—and tell him that the experiment failed, that the fire still consumed my thoughts. But I *am* calmer, as calm as I could be right now. And that probably has more to do with my talking to Maya, but the focused thinking surely helped.

And so all I say is, "Huh. Well, thank you."

My lips are chapped, the wind so hot. I'm trying to digest what Hayden said, the hypothesis—I can't help but wonder if, after the last three days, every memory with Brooks has become tainted. How differently would I remember the past three months if Thursday night had never happened?

"Last night, at the party," Hayden says. "Why were you running?"

But I don't have to answer because my phone is buzzing and buzzing in the pocket of Grace's shorts. Not texts but a call. And it's not Grace.

It's Brooks. He's calling me.

He's alive.

64

SATURDAY

Saturday night, still at the party, after Brooks and I moved inside from the balcony, the torchlights and pool lights and back porch lights illuminated Derek Sanders's parents' chandelier suspended above the bed. The crystal leaves hanging from the iron arms clinked in the wind.

Brooks was sweet—sweeter and gentler and more vulnerable than June and July combined. He kissed my eyes and told me how beautiful I was. How much he loved me. How I had saved him. He cried about Cameron and told me how much it hurt not to have his brother anymore. He apologized for everything, all the vicious things he'd ever said or done. He apologized for Thursday night, for the fire. *Can you forgive me?* His shoulders shook in the dark.

And then we were kissing. My hands were under his shirt, grazing his stomach. His hands were under mine, gliding around my waist, beneath my bra. I stood up to check the door. It was locked.

Really? he asked.

I nodded yes.

And I don't know why, after saying no for so long, after not having the desire, it then felt somewhat okay. We were moving fast and slow and fast. I was still unsure, still shaking, but it didn't seem to matter anymore. We were past waiting, and his want outweighed my hesitation, my uncertainty. I was numb from Thursday. The fire was building, and I was drunk and needed tangible control over one thing in my life.

I also wanted to believe that Brooks was still good and sweet, that *we* were still good and sweet—that he loved me and I loved him, and that nothing else mattered.

And maybe I am actually finally starting to feel comfortable with myself.

I let him pull off my shirt. I pulled off his. He unbuttoned my jeans, eased them from my legs. We fell down to the floor together. And it didn't make everything okay, but it was okay.

But afterward, still lying on the rug, Brooks trying to catch his breath, I asked, *Why did you lie about Cameron?* He didn't answer, and another whisper slipped from my lips. *Why did you start the fire?*

And eyes wet, he said, "I knew you'd finally want me if we had a fire."

My chest throbbed. "You think that's what this was?" The question came out as a sob. I stared at him, his vacant eyes. "You're sick."

And Brooks said, "Not as sick as Cameron. Not sick enough to pour gasoline on myself."

I got dressed, realizing how disgusting it was for him to think up such a story. And I told him that, said it out loud. And, last night, I left him crying on the shag rug in Derek Sanders's parents' bedroom.

65

7:45 P.M.

My phone is pressed to my ear and Brooks says hi, as if it's any day, just a normal Sunday, and he's calling to see if I want to go for ice cream at the lake.

I walk away from Hayden. "You're alive," I say.

"Barely," he says. "You have no idea."

I can hear the wind through the phone. And I think it's funny because it pulses there when it doesn't pulse here, like an exchange, like it's on the same path and there's a delay for the time it takes for the wind to get from there to here. And, you know, I've been waiting for his call all day, and I'm shaking because he's not dead, it wasn't him who died. But someone did die, someone entirely innocent, a life gone. I can't swallow the thought.

"My dad," he says. "He shouldn't have called you. He shouldn't have." Brooks doesn't sound like he did this morning, excited, ready to fight. He is terrified. "Audrey, you there?"

"I'm here."

I thought I would cry when he finally called, but I am not crying. I am numb, and Hayden is biting his thumbnail, pretending not to be watching me as I pull up thorns from the ground.

"I'm going away," Brooks says. "I'm leaving."

"What?"

"Alaska, remember, we can go and they'll never—"

"We need to go to the cops," I say.

"I can't," he says. "My dad, my mom—this will ruin them. *This*, I can't do this to them." His words tumble, and I want to tell him he already did—he already did this.

"Where are you?" I ask, and Hayden stares at me, and I don't care. I'm ready to keep talking even with him listening, but he nods toward the truck and retreats into the cab for cleaner air, maybe my privacy, and I say to Brooks, "I'm going to find you, and we're going to make this right."

"I only called to say goodbye," he says as he did this morning.

"This is not goodbye."

"Audie."

"If you won't go with me, I'll do it alone," I say.

My throat is sticky, and my eyes burn from the smoke and ash that falls so similarly to snow. I think of Colorado, a dream school, a hope—I still have time to find my thing, and maybe I never needed a thing but rather an acceptance that this is my life, *my* life, and that alone is a thing. My confessing to my part in this fire won't destroy me—it'll save me.

"We'll be okay," I say.

"*Wait*," Brooks says. "Wait. *You* can make it okay. You're only sixteen. You're a minor." He speaks too fast. "And it was an accident."

But it wasn't an accident.

I'm cold. "What are you saying?"

And he talks, a frantic sound. "A brokenhearted teenager with a history of depression, obsession, a pyromaniac since she bombed ballet. You fell for an older guy, a volunteer firefighter, a protector, you loved me so deeply that I became your life—and we can tell them, we can lie—Audrey, listen, I broke up with you at your romantic anniversary surprise."

I'm no longer cold. My blood boils. I push myself up to standing.

"My leaving broke you so bad that you started a wildfire to win me back," he says, "and you lost control—"

"Brooks." It doesn't make sense, what he's asking, the mass of his request.

"It's the only way. I need you to do this. You're a minor, and it won't be so bad, but *me*, I'll be locked up the rest of my life." His voice isn't malicious, isn't demanding—he's begging, a heartbreaking plea—and he says, "After your time is over, we can go. We can go. You and me, we're like those aspens, remember?"

After your time is over.

It's a knife to my heart.

"You're asking me to take all the blame," I say.

"I'll go now—I'll do it for you—" I think he's crying. "If you won't run away with me, if you won't let me go—" A pause, and I hear him suck in a breath, and his tone changes, taking control. "For my dad, my mom, us. You have to do this. Otherwise I'll be locked up, and we'll never *be*. If you want to tell the truth, this is the only way."

"But it isn't the truth," I say.

"It can be."

Ash sticks to my lips. I stare at the homes in the canyons, and I unclench my fist and look down at the silver of the Zippo. I imagine it. Going forward, giving a false confession. I'm a minor. It won't ruin me, not entirely. But confessing will destroy him.

And I *am* to blame. I am. I didn't report the fire when it first started, and if I had, no one would have lost their home, a firefighter would still be alive, only a patch of valley and hillside would be charred. I built this wildfire too—fanning the flames with my silence.

Thinking I could save him by protecting his fire.

Thinking I could save us by protecting our fire.

"Audrey?"

I hear myself saying it. Telling the lie. *My heart was broken. I started the Caspers Fire, a gift to him. It was me. I'm so sorry. It was me.*

"No," I say.

"I'll go now." A threat. "Your hair. You skin. The forensics team—they'll trace it."

He doesn't mention his jars, the sleeping bag he brought, but he doesn't need to: He's set on his plan. And who would they believe—a sixteen-year-old with a history of instability or a diligent firefighter?

"Where are you?" I ask.

"I can't do this to my dad."

"Tell me where you are," I say, because I've already walked back to the truck, already opened the door. From the passenger seat, Hayden gapes at me because I've already peeled back onto the road.

There's a pause, but finally Brooks says, "Tesoro."

"What?"

"The school, Audrey," he says. "I'm at the school."

66

———

THURSDAY

There's a Hail Mary method in firefighting. If you can't outrun a fire, you give in. In the 1940s, when Idaho's Mann Gulch Fire was closing in on the firefighters, chasing them uphill, gaining, the crew's foreman finally stopped running and set fire to the ground at his feet—blackening a circle of grass so he could lie face-down on the smoldering embers as the fire spread. Wagner Dodge, that was his name. He lived. The others who continued to run didn't.

A burn circle, that's the Hail Mary. Collapse inside and dig past the ash for oxygen, a gasping breath. Soil for air. Fire can't burn what it has already touched. That's the idea. Retreat into the burn and wait it out, don't look up, keep your head down. Let the fire skirt over your back. And live.

That's what Brooks told me on Thursday night, as he pulled a school notebook from his pack. He lit the pages with his Zippo and held it down to the grass, lowered the flame, walking in an outward loop. A wash of light. Sizzling weeds. He wasn't saving us, wasn't saving the valley, but feeding the dry land.

"It's beautiful," he said.

"Brooks," I said. "Brooks."

The heat was consuming. I didn't think. I jumped on him, made a grab for the torch of papers, reaching for it with my bare hand. An instinctive reaction—thinking maybe I could stop it, stop him. I dropped back, howling. My skin being ripped. That's what it felt like.

His arms were around me in an instant as he pulled me into him. We hit the ground, tumbling away from the heat, the fire. And then we were sitting cocooned, my hand in agony. I gripped the ampersand pillow to my chest. *I miss you*, I thought he said, holding my knuckles to his lips. *I miss Cameron so much.* The flames were growing.

I remember raising my head and thinking how for a moment it looked like fireflies were flickering through the brush. And I remember thinking, *No, more like Fourth of July sparklers.* My breath held, skin searing. Brooks still holding me, not moving, both of us watching the flames. The sparklers didn't fizzle out like they were supposed to—they grew and thickened into a dozen pockets of light. The wind ripped the grass, feeding the flames. Not a burn circle. Not a contained Hail Mary, but the beginning of something vast and terrifying.

"Brooks," I said. He was transfixed, staring at the light. And I noticed his Zippo on the ground then, a shining glint. I fisted it with my burned hand, let the throb rock through my gut. "*Brooks,*" I said again.

But then he was pulling at my arm, pulling me away.

"We need to run," he said. "Can you run?"

But he was already on his feet, his pack swung onto his shoulder. He tugged at my unburned hand before letting go, and then he was running and I was running after him, pillow and Zippo in hand, the heat on my back.

67

7:56 P.M.

Need to get to Tesoro High School?

The Toll Road is the most direct route. A total rip-off, but hey, you're in Orange County. Join the overspending club and take the 241 South until it spits you out onto Oso Parkway. The road will end, and you'll be forced to exit. Smile for the Toll Booth cameras. You'll be billed later.

Turn right on Oso Parkway. Make an immediate left at the stoplight and follow the steep hill down into the valley. Welcome! You're at Tesoro High School.

Bonus points if your Psychology partner is in the passenger seat saying, *What happened what's going on what are you doing why aren't you answering me for once answer me.* If he's nearly hyperventilating, even more bonus points, because it adds an extra layer of excitement.

Is it nighttime? Are you lost? Confused? Well, usually, the only marker for the entrance is a gaudy red sign with a cartoon Titan, but tonight you're in luck.

You'll know you're in the right place if you see red and blue and white flashing lights; a barricade blocking the left turn, the only road in and out of the school, because—duh—authorized vehicles only; vans from every news station in the county and newscasters touching up their lipstick, smoothing their hair, pointing at my school, at the glow beyond, along with their cameras and microphones and sound sheets and floodlights because this is it, this is happening, we're on live TV; brave South Orange County citizens standing on the sidewalk, as close as they can get, observing the chaos, waving their hands for the TV, holding handmade signs for the firefighters camped out down below on the sport fields, declaring their support and appreciation.

Oh, and the final indication of your location? Down and out—past the stucco single-story buildings and courtyards, past the blacktop and portables, past the football, baseball, and track fields, past the stadium bleachers—take a good look, because there's Caspers Fire swarming bright and hot, spilling out from the hills into the valley.

At this point your Psychology partner will be shocked into silence.

At this point you're obviously well aware of your location.

Welcome to Tesoro High School. Home of the Titans.

Every semester, the school holds a fire drill. We line up with our homerooms on the football field and wait for the okay under the splintering sun. It's idiotic. There's always been a running joke that if there were a fire on campus, we'd be toast. Nowhere to escape. All of us trapped in the valley with only one road out, twirling our thumbs like dimwits on the parched grass.

Because here's the thing: If there *were* a fire during the school day, chances are it wouldn't be the school alight, but the land—flame sizzling across the valley brush, racing toward us. Like I said, there's only one street down into the school, only one street out. An endangered beetle prevents the district from pouring more concrete on the surrounding hills. As it is, there's only enough room for faculty and seniors to park on campus. Juniors like me resort to parking on residential streets a twenty-minute walk away.

That's where I park my truck now.

68

8:02 P.M.

I park the truck, keeping my hands on the wheel for five too many seconds.

"What are we doing?" Hayden asks.

"Nothing I can't handle," I say, for me, not for him.

Mom texts me, asking for an update. She tells me Maya is watching a show on her laptop. Mom doesn't mention our house burning, but she asks if I'm okay, and I'm not lying when I write back and say:

Running on adrenaline . . . maybe another hour or so?

"Audrey, look at me," Hayden says. "What is going on?"

I already announced the change of plans during the short drive over—that I'm officially not up to completing any schoolwork tonight—but I'm not entirely sure where to start, so I push my door open against the wind and climb out. Hayden follows my lead.

"Let's go to the cops," he says. "I heard you say something about going to the cops. That's *definitely* a better option than whatever you're thinking."

I could beat Brooks to the punch. Indict him. But I won't. That's his job.

"I need to get to school first," I say.

Hayden laughs. "You're joking, right? It's blocked off. Audrey, *it's on fire*—"

"The school isn't on fire. The firefighters are camped out there, so clearly it's not on fire."

"Well, the fire is *close*," he says. "Who do you know who is at the school right now?"

"Brooks."

"Great," Hayden says. "That's just great."

"He's a firefighter, remember."

"A volunteer firefighter," Hayden says.

"I can drop you off at the Jack in the Box," I say, nodding to the truck. But then I shake my head. I'm running out of time and the smoke is tight in my lungs. "Or can you walk? It's fifteen minutes, tops."

Hayden stares at me. "What the hell is wrong with you?" he asks.

"What?" My already-winded pulse takes race.

"I am an idiot," he says.

"What?"

"How many times do I have to tell you?" he asks. "You're more than my sister's friend. But you're so obsessed with trying to fix Brooks. You act like he's all you have."

I wrap my arms around myself and watch Hayden rub his glasses on his shirt. The sycamore trees that line this street are bending, nearly snapping, in the gusts.

"I'm sorry," he says, always too quick to apologize.

But it's too late because I say, "Well, for the record, you're selfish. You didn't even attempt to be my friend until I had a boyfriend. That sucks. That really sucks."

"I know," he says.

I close my eyes against the smoke, needing a break, needing this day to end. I don't want to think or feel for another second, but there's still so much to face. And I don't know what happens next. The fire could move too swiftly for us to outrun it. I could be handcuffed. And so I know I need to be honest with Hayden. He deserves the truth, and this might be my last chance.

So I say, "Friday. I tried to open up to you on Friday."

He laughs. "That's not what you were doing."

"You're wrong."

Hayden looks up to the smoke. "Audrey." His voice is strained. "It's fine. Let's just forget it. I don't need to be placated. I get it. We're cool, okay?"

And maybe I'm wrong and what I'm feeling *is* the fire: this inexplicable flurry in my heart amid my grief, this subtle want for Hayden. Maybe it's even the Santa Ana winds. They trigger passion, restlessness, stolen kisses on hills above high schools. Murder rates rise. Infidelity and shouts of anger are the norm. It's why arson is so common during California's driest season.

But, nonetheless, I say, "I don't want to forget it."

Because I know it in my heart, Hayden and me: We aren't just the October wind, not merely desire and action fueled by the fire. And, in a perfect world, we'd have the chance to see what *we* can mean when the deserts cool and the air stills, when the fire is only blackened land, when I've learned how to stand on my own two feet. But that opportunity isn't guaranteed.

"You don't want to forget it for my sake or yours?" Hayden asks.

I level my gaze "Both."

I need to run. I need to get to Brooks and makes things right. I want to save this conversation for when things are simpler, but this might be my last chance with Hayden. My last chance to show him that our kiss wasn't only an action aggravated by the fire, the wind, and what he'll soon learn I did.

"On Friday," I say. "My kissing you wasn't me trying to hurt myself. On some level, maybe, yeah, but it was also so much more. You mean so much more to me than you think, and I was trying to understand that space, understand *my* want."

Hayden fumbles with his glasses, still struggling to clean the lenses. I take them from him and meet his eyes. He's nearsighted. He can see me just fine.

"I kissed you because I like you," I say.

He doesn't nod, only meets my gaze with a slight smile that feels so out of place given the night's circumstances, but then I guess everything is out of place.

"Okay," Hayden says.

And he finally stills, and I tug on his shirt and press my lips to his cheek. He wraps his arms around me and holds me even tighter than when we hugged earlier. This is the best of hugs, his hand on the back of my head. And even if we simmer into nothing—even if all of this is simply a symptom of the Devil's Winds—this moment will be enough.

"I'm *not* trying to hurt myself through you," I say again.

"I believe you."

I nudge out of Hayden's embrace and hand his glasses back to him, but there's one last thing to say. I have to tell him even though I know he'll never look at me the same.

"I started the fire."

He recoils. "What?"

But that's not true. "Brooks and I started the fire."

"You're confused," Hayden says.

"We did this."

"You did this?"

"I'm sorry," I say, though it's so far from enough.

"Audrey." He looks to the bright smoke beyond the hills. "Audrey, what the *fuck*?"

"It's why I have to find him."

His face shows sorrow, not rage. "*How*? And why the hell didn't you tell someone?"

"I'll explain," I say. "I'll tell you everything. I promise."

But I was wrong. Hayden isn't looking at me like I've changed. He looks at me like I'm still the girl he knows, who was once only his sister's best friend but now could be something more. He looks at me like I'm someone he cares about who just told him the devastating truth.

"I have to find Brooks," I say, because Brooks wants to give this fire solely to me and I won't take it. "Before he—I don't know. Makes a bigger mistake."

"I'm coming with you," Hayden says.

So I ask, "How are your shoes?"

Hayden raises his leg, shows off his green Pumas. "Prime for an evening trek."

69

8:17 P.M.

We abandon the truck.

I walk fast, but Hayden keeps up. We pass evacuated neighborhoods, where the absence of noise—kids playing in the streets, car engines and alarms, TVs echoing from homes—is louder than the wind. The stretch of the evacuation zones, how far this fire now threatens to reach, makes it even harder to breathe. Once we reach Oso Parkway, the main road, we sprint. The glare of the barricade comes into view. We keep to the shadows, away from the sirens and newscasters and onlookers. We cut through a border of succulents and into the tall weeds and shrubs of the bank that curves above our school.

We can see everything.

Our school is lit up. It's like it's a game night—the bright lights glowing over the football field—only instead of a stadium full of athletes and crowds of students in the stands, the field is a city of white tents and white trailers. It makes sense that they chose Tesoro, our concrete island in the middle of an isolated gulf, just a short drive away from the roaring inferno.

An inferno that looks too close for comfort. It's enough to send me to my knees, how fast the fire grew, how far it's traveled. The raging orange swell is even more fixating at night, against the black sky and smoke. It's hard to focus. I don't want to look away.

"And I thought Friday was hell," Hayden says.

I always wondered what that blocked-off road was for—the road that starts at the side of the school and snakes behind, past the barbed-wire fences, the road I assumed led to nowhere. What do you know? Nowhere Road leads to fire—a pulsing gold snake that ravels along the black ridge of the hills beyond campus. The sky throbs orange so bright, the ash falls white like thick pelts of snow. It's so close. Is it supposed to be so close?

"Audrey, Audrey, Audrey, Audr—"

I spin to Hayden. "*What?*"

His face is blanched. "This is very bad."

I shove my hand through my hair, and my palm is caked in dirt and ash. "Using my name as a curse word is not going to make it better."

Hayden and I walk single file, following the chain fence that divides what the school owns and what the government has saved. The glare of the fire and the glare of the school and the glare of the camp are so bright, it makes the hillsides gray. It's so strange. It's so grotesquely strange to see my school crawling with firefighters, echoing with the sputter of radios and orders shouted and the buzzing of the media up on the hill. My campus bucketed with smoke.

I didn't think I cared that much about my school, but now I realize I do.

"If Brooks is a firefighter, why are we sneaking around to meet him?" Hayden asks.

"He ran away."

"Well," Hayden says. "That's great." I hear him trip on a branch or a rock behind me. "A runaway firefighter who committed arson," he says. When I say nothing, Hayden asks, "Are you going to tell him we kissed?"

"Not the best time for that," I say.

Hayden fumbles behind me, tripping over debris again. I peel off Grace's hoodie. It's damp with sweat. I tie it around my mouth, breathe in my own dirt and smell, like I did this morning.

"This is illegal," Hayden now says. "How much did you even sleep last night? You need sleep. There was a mountain lion sighting in Coto last week. If there was a mountain lion over there, there's probably a mountain lion over here."

A helicopter is above us, beaming lights on the hillside. We're on the wrong side of the fence, the side with a sign that says NO TRESPASSING. The helicopter—the shock of it, the shared fear of being spotted—sends Hayden and me to our knees. We're facing each other.

For a fleeting second, the light finds Hayden's face.

"Did they see us?" he whispers.

"No."

The helicopter isn't looking for us. It leaves us in the shadows, swings toward the fire and then back around, lands on a makeshift helipad in the valley. I look at my phone. 8:41 P.M.

I stand up, offer Hayden my hand. We start walking again.

We hike until we're above the athletics fields, where the main portion of the fire camp is set. White rusted trailers. Tents. Trucks on our beloved football field. It smells like a distorted summer. Hot dogs. Chili. The scent of burning land.

I figured firefighters would be fighting the fire, but so many are milling around. There are too many of them, and I know from Brooks that this means the winds are making it too dangerous for them to work. And then I realize—I look closer—they're not lining up for hot dogs. They're deconstructing the camp, orders shouted, tents broken down.

I've become nearly immune to it. The wind. The smoke and the ash. The heat. All day, I've been pushing my body through the conditions, and I have to stop to realize that this is the worst it's been yet. The gusts pull up roots from the hillside, yank at the nylon covers of the tents below, push down newly planted sycamores in the parking lot with greater ease than Grace in her mom's Land Rover. The fire is raging closer as the winds change, and the carefully chosen fire camp is at risk of being engulfed.

The fire is on its way, swarming toward us like a dust storm of blaze.

Is that what's happening?

"Audrey," Hayden says. "Audrey, we need to get out of here. They're leaving. You see that, right? The *firefighters* are leaving."

I glance at him. "I have to do this." I point to a truck headed toward the fire, filled with people in uniform. "And *they're* not leaving. It's fine. It's totally fine." But I know that the crew is speeding to complete a last-minute trench, a throw-out hope to save the school, to delay what is seemingly inevitable.

"This isn't safe," Hayden says. "I'm freaking out. How are you not freaking out?"

"I don't have the time to freak out." And I think that's the truth.

I focus on finding a route across campus. It's easy. There's an alley between the portables on the blacktop and the athletics fields—this is how we'll get to the other side, to the T, to Brooks.

First we have to jump the fence. The metal is cool in my hands. I'd expected it to be warm. I climb, coil by coil, and swing myself over to the other side and land on my feet.

"How did you do that?" Hayden asks.

"Ballet," I say. "I didn't think I could do it, but I figured I'd try. That's how I used to approach ballet choreography."

He tosses his backpack over, wipes his hands on his jeans, and climbs. He isn't as graceful as me. He makes it halfway and then slips off and falls back, swearing a lot. He tries again and this time pulls himself over the wire, snags his T-shirt, and falls face-first on the slope.

"Can you erase that from your memory, please?"

Somehow, despite what we're doing, I laugh. "Are you hurt?"

"Don't think so."

I help him up. "We have to run, Hayden."

We need to run. Can you run?

We run from one end of campus to the other. The wind tunnels in between buildings, trash spiraling, trees threatening to snap, forgotten graded papers crunched under lockers. We hear shouting and radio orders, and we hide behind a dumpster when a truck rumbles by, but otherwise, this is way too easy.

And it's weird because it feels like it's a Friday night and a football game is still in progress and we're on some bizarre scavenger hunt with friends. We pass the skinny palm trees that line the entrance of the stadium, and I don't let myself turn for a closer look of the fire camp because if I can see them they can see me—that's the rational explanation. We cross the utility road that leads to the fire, and—so quickly—we're back on brittle wild land, back in the shadows, and I know we've made it.

There's no fence on this side.

"Now what?" Hayden asks.

"I'm going to the T," I say.

He's leaning over, hands on his knees. "Grace isn't going to believe any of this."

I take a deep breath. "You need to stay here."

"You're serious?" He looks up at me. "What if you need help?"

"I won't." I need to do this alone. "Wait here," I say.

"No—"

"Trust me, Hayden. Please?"

Hayden shakes his head, curses under his breath, but finally says, "If you're not down here after thirty minutes, I'm coming up."

Fine. "Okay."

So I climb. It's not far, maybe a twenty-minute ascent. The hill is dry, hard packed and rocky, but the path through the brush is well worn with loose gravel. Smoke has made a home in my body. I'm almost there when I freeze at the sound of coughing. It's him.

I walk the trail to Brooks.

70

9:09 P.M.

I see him now, up ahead.

First the reflective strips of his jacket and pants and boots, then the glare of his helmet, which he holds against his chest. A fist of air leaves my lungs. He's streaked with soot—soiled and burnt and beat. He's been working all day. He's been running all day, all night. This isn't a costume. It's real. There's a soiled red bandana tied around his neck, goggles at his feet.

Brooks is a firefighter. That wasn't a lie.

He's sitting in the dirt, his back against the ledge of the T where I kissed Hayden on Friday. His shoulders are hunched over. He's struggling to flick a white lighter against the yellow toe of his boot. The small glints light his face. My chest aches.

He looks up. "Audie."

I can't move, because I want to go to him and hold him, and I want to kick him and make him bleed. I hate him for what he's done. And what I've done because of him, for what he's asked of me: lying or running. I hold my elbows.

He looks to the fire and waves to the burning hills. "It's beautiful."

A searing bruise spreads through my body. "I won't do it," I say. "Take the fall for you."

His gaze meets mine. "You have to."

My eyes sting. "You're breaking my heart."

"Audie," he says, and he rushes to me, and now he's holding me and kissing my hair. He smells like campfire and sweat and mud. He says he fucked up, he fucked up so bad. "This is the only way. It being your fire," he says. "It has to be."

He's not letting it go. It's the story he's warped into his new truth.

"Come with me," I beg. "Tell the truth."

I let him hold me. Minutes pass, and I think he's ready to leave with me. Ready to head down the hill to the lights at the front of the school. Ready to face what we did.

But then he releases me and he says, "I killed him." And I'm not sure if he's referring to Cameron or the firefighter lost in the flames. "Do you hear me?" Brooks asks, his eyes wild. "Someone is dead. Do you get it yet?"

And I do. I do get it. "Murder," I say. "We'll be tried for homicide."

"We? There is no *we*," he says. "You. As a minor—you'll be charged with homicide."

71

9:18 P.M.

Brooks nudges me to view the fire, his grip on my shoulders tight.

"You made this," he says.

"No."

"It's the only way for me to stay."

"It's *not*," I say.

But he's right. If we confess the truth, he'll be locked up for most of his life.

Brooks spins me around to face him. His eyes are bright, frantic, like the first night I met him—everything a possibility. "You even have the Zippo," he says. "It'll make the final touch. You can show it, the Zippo, how you started the fire using what you stole when I left you. They'll never doubt the story."

"I don't know where the Zippo is," I say.

"Come on, Audie." The softest laugh.

"I was silent. I didn't stop you or the fire from growing. I didn't call it in. I'm responsible," I say. "But not like you."

His left eyes drips, and both eyes are swollen, like he's been fighting tears all day, like he's been splintering piece by piece, hour by hour.

"You set fire to dried ground—earth you've always known would easily burn," I say. "Rather than tell me the truth about Cameron, you made a new fire."

He breathes fast. "I know. I *know*."

"Arson. That's what you did. I won't take the blame to protect you." I wipe away tears and soot from my face. "And if you love me, you won't ask me to again."

He's nodding, he's actually nodding. Turning away, he paces—paces to the T and back, as if caged, as if there's a gun to his head. But then he stops. He sweeps to me. A smile. That smile so wide, sincere. "Then Alaska." He breathes. "The northern lights. You and me."

The dream of it flickers, the possibility, the wildness of the adventure. Snow and ice, the dark winters, the endless days of summer—the world a mystery. But the vision isn't mine.

"I'm confessing with or without you," I say.

He holds my shoulders, leans on me with too much weight. "I was going to stop it," he says. "I thought I'd stop it. That it'd be different. I'd make my dad proud, maybe even my mom—that she could stand to look at me again."

I'm too heavy. I'm too heavy with his grief, his guilt, his dream of being a hero. The story he created, the story he built his identity on—it's collapsed. I'm tired of grasping at the seams of his lie. We're wasting time. Fifteen minutes. At least fifteen minutes have passed since I climbed.

"Tell me what happened with Cameron."

He backs away from me, lets out a choked laugh. "God," he says. "That's the only reason you're here, isn't it?" He tilts his head up, his mouth wide as if to catch ash on his tongue. "You only want to confirm I'm this beast you've set out to slay."

I pull the Zippo from my pocket and hold it out in my palm. An offering. "Tell me and I'll give it back." I shake so bad it's hard to stand. "I need to know."

He eyes the Zippo wearily. "You know enough about Cameron's death to know that that trash is meaningless." Brooks walks to the T and sits at its edge. "And the truth—it's meaningless too. My brother is dead either way. I told you a new version. What difference does it make?"

"Understanding," I say. "I want to understand."

He stares up at me. "It was such a relief for someone I love to look at me and not see a killer. It was a lie, fine, but I changed the story *for* you," he says. "And you loved me for it."

I shake my head. "I love you for you."

"Cameron died when I was eight," Brooks says. "He died in a fire I set."

"An accident," I say.

"I killed him. There was no dog. No fancy settlement. My dad bought the Audi." He gestures to his bad eye. "This came from fire. From the fire *I* set. It's a *burn*, not a dog scratch."

I press my hand to my chest and breathe through the smoke, this pain.

"Cameron left me to play with his friends while our parents were gone. He was supposed to be watching me, hanging out with *me*, but he hid my bike so I wouldn't follow him."

I squeeze the Zippo.

"I was bored, angry, so I crawled under the deck and started a fire. I used Doritos for kindling like he'd shown me, and his comic books for revenge. It blew up so fast. I was happy, you know, because it was *my* fire and I wouldn't have to share it. Then it got big quick. I tried kicking dirt on it." He kicks at the ground, as if to demonstrate. "But the dirt was full of pine needles, dried branches, so it only grew, and a lit splinter hit my eye. I crawled out, howling, the pain, you know, and I ran into the woods behind our yard. When I looked back, the house was a torch."

"You were a kid," I say. "A child."

Brooks laughs, the sound shattered by a sob. "I loved it. I loved that Cameron would be pissed because he missed it. *He* was the one obsessed with fire. Always messing with cherry bombs and fireworks. I loved that I'd created something bigger than he had. I stood there and watched my house burn, and I didn't do a thing."

"You're not remembering what you felt right," I say. "You can't be."

"I am," he says. "Every detail is seared in." His voice cracks. "They found his charred remains in my room. He'd come back for me and got trapped." Brooks's eyes meet mine. "I guess he decided I was old enough, good enough to play with him after all."

I can't move. "What could you have done to stop it? You were eight."

"I didn't want to stop it," he says. And then, "It was easier to let you love me if you didn't know why I am who I am."

"Who burned cats then?" I ask. "If Cameron died when he was eleven, then who burned—"

He stares at me. "Who do you think?"

"You're not a monster," I say.

"No?" He's no longer laughing. "Well, it doesn't take much. It doesn't take much to keep something down." But he dips his head. "Miss Cat ran away, that's the truth."

My heart beats too fast. The wind shifts again and—for a moment—embers fall, small hot shocks with the potential to start a new blaze where we stand. We have to leave. We have to go.

"I'm so sorry for what happened with Cameron," I say. "I can't imagine. I can't. But it wasn't your fault, and it doesn't change you, it doesn't change how I see you." And I am sorry. I am. "But *this*," I say. "The fire. What we did. Someone is dead. We did that. You did it."

"Audrey," he says. "It's your turn. Your turn to tell a story."

I toss the Zippo to his feet. "I won't lie for you."

I turn and start for the rocky path that heads back down to campus. But a snap of twigs. A tumble of rocks. I'm on my stomach. Brooks is on top of me. I taste dirt. And it's like Thursday night, only this time he doesn't go sweet and sad. I reel onto my back and try to push him off but it hurts, hurts so bad, the day long overdone.

"You have to come with me," he says. "I won't let you go."

He has me pinned. I hit. Scratch. Scream. Thinking maybe I need Hayden's help after all. But Brooks shifts and loosens his grip for a moment. Space opens, and I thrust my knee into his groin, hard. He grunts and curves into himself, moaning.

I roll away and push myself to standing.

"This isn't you," I say. "*Brooks, this isn't you.*"

He sits, hunched into himself. It feels as if it takes minutes to speak. He runs his hands across his face, his fingers clenching. And then, finally, he says, "Come with me."

"I can't." Because after this day—all of its pressure and pain, and my moving through it without him, on my own—I know why I have to stay.

"I love you, Brooks, but I don't need you. I don't need *this*."

315

He pauses at my words. His head down. His shoulders loosening. When he stands, he does so with care, and I see the glint back in his palm. The Zippo. He gave it meaning with his story, his desperation to see himself as something different than a boy who caused his brother's death. He runs his finger over the silver Seattle skyline. He looks at me—suddenly so calm.

And he asks, gently, "Do you regret last night?"

"No." The truth.

He looks down at the Zippo. "It never should have been suicide," he murmurs, slipping it into a pocket. "An accident with his friends, on a sailboat, something—that lie would have hurt less. Not as grotesque. It still hurt so bad to believe it, to tell it."

"Your guilt," I say. "Get rid of it. You were just a kid."

Brooks smiles. "I miss him every day, who he was, who he didn't have the chance to be."

We stand close. The wind howls and ash swirls. Brooks watches it, the fire—seemingly closer since I climbed. His breath is tattered but soft. I reach for his hand. He squeezes mine and a quiet washes over him. His expression almost serene, looking to the hills yet to burn and the land already ravaged.

"Okay," he finally says, still holding my hand. "Okay. This is okay."

He's relenting. We're doing this. My heart is loud in my ears. The air is blistering dry. Brooks kisses my hand, like on our first night.

And then he lets go.

His absence is an immediate throb. He turns away. Not toward the school or the light on the hills above.

He turns to the fire.

I grab his arm. "Brooks."

He smiles. "I'll meet you there."

"What?"

His burned eye drips. "This is it."

I'm trembling. *"No.* I won't let you." I grip his arm tight. "I'll do it," I say, before I can think. "I'll take the blame, stay quiet—" Because I know if he runs, if he leaves, I won't be able to keep up. And it can't end this way. He can still have hope, even with a charge of arson and second-degree homicide. There is still hope.

"I never should have asked you to lie," he says.

His stillness makes me sob. "Killing yourself won't make you a hero."

Brooks eyes are like sparks, like it's July and he's falling in love with me all over again, falling in love with his new past. "That's not what I'm doing. I wouldn't do that to you. To my dad." He shakes his head. "I'm going north, alone. And *you.* You can tell the truth. All of it."

I stare at him. His expression holds more courage than I've seen in weeks. The passion that initially swept me away, he's found a new flame in a new place—a thing to grasp on to for hope.

"I'll hike back, past the fire, around it. I have cash in my car, and maybe I can beat the cops to it, maybe not, but even still—I'll try to get a train ticket to Washington. And from there, hitchhike up, get past the borders somehow— take the ferry." He pulls off his reflective jacket, drops it to the ground. He'll hike in only his black shirt and turnout pants. "I can do this. It's possible. Another chance. I have to try."

My mouth won't work. *I love you. Don't go. Don't run. Stay. It'll be okay.* But I'm choking on smoke, choking on my heartbreak.

"It's still cold in Alaska," he says. "And I think I need that change."

I look to the fire, its irrational swarm. "It's too dangerous. Brooks, you *know* it's too dangerous. It'll take you all night to walk to a main road, to get to your car. The fire—you'll get caught in it. You could die. And Alaska—how will you—? *Please.*" I break off. "Don't go."

He cups my chin in his hand. "My Audie, always an open heart." His voice a tremble. He's scared too. "Keeping this lie would kill you. And me?" He's smiling so sincere, so big I can see his sharp back tooth. "I have to try again," he says. "Tell my dad I'm okay, that I love him and Mom, that I'm so sorry. That I'll try to be better."

"Give the truth a try."

He holds me close. "I'm sorry," he says.

"What if I can't do it?" I ask. "Confess alone. I'm scared."

"You'll blow them away."

He kisses my forehead. "We'll always be entwined, like those aspen trees. You and me," he says. "Don't forget."

And in one swoop, he shoves me away, gentle enough not to hurt me again, but strong enough to send me stumbling back.

"Brooks."

He looks up to the media and police on the ridge and says, "Go."

And then he's securing the bandana over his mouth. He's walking away, running into the brush, to the blooming red. I'm running too. I'm screaming for him, shouting his name, begging him to stop. But I stumble over high brush. The smoke is too thick. The fire a massive fury of red and orange and light. His expansive fire so bright it feels like it could blind like the sun. How will he skirt it? Get around it? It's impossible. Hayden is shouting my name, and Brooks is moving too fast. His body is used to the smoke. He's trained for these conditions. I can't follow him. I can't stop him. He's a dark shadow against the flames. But then I can't see him anymore, I can only see fire. I can only feel the strong, erratic winds.

A burning leaf floats down above me. A single firefly. *I'll meet you there.* I can't save him. I never could. But maybe there is still hope. Maybe I get stronger, and he gets a new story. He gets Alaska.

But the winds—the fire—his dehydration. His living on lies. I can see him trapped by fire, burning alive, unable to complete a Hail Mary fire circle. Brooks walking into a fire. The risk is so high.

I turn, and I run toward the lights above the school.

"Audrey!" Hayden's calling for me, the thirty minutes past, my earlier screams an echo.

"I'm here," I yell. "I'm right here."

72

10:04 P.M.

I run so fast the earth burns in my shins and knees. Hayden barely keeps up. I slide down the steepest part of the hillside, falling with the rocks and brush that break my skin, until I can stand again.

Brooks is walking to the fire. He's walking around the fire. He's running to Alaska. The campus is emptied, the fire camp mostly broken down. But the media is still up there, utilizing the epic bright view. When I hit the pavement of the parking lot, I hurdle toward their lights. I pound up the steep street, the one entrance and exit for my school. The asphalt rings through my knees.

I'm wheezing when I reach the top—where the media is set up, surrounding the illuminated entry. And I see everything: the black hills I've climbed, the concrete T in the high shadows, the vacated school below, the tents and trailers left behind, the cops behind me and the cops in front of me, the onlookers, the dim Toll Road I sped down tonight, and the raging zigzagging blaze I've watched from the very beginning. I see Hayden, and my heart throbs because he didn't wait in the truck. He didn't run away. He's still here.

I try to speak to those I pass, but my voice is locked in my throat. My lungs still burn. They stare. Step back. What do they see? A girl with scraped, bleeding legs, hair tangled with ash and dirt, a soot-stained face. My vision blurs, but I see the cameras, those blinding lights, the parked vans blocking two lanes of Oso Parkway, the newscasters and their bright lips and their hair that whips in the wind.

I see a woman in a uniform decorated with badges. Authority. She's standing in front of the cameras, a swarm of microphones horseshoed around her. The 10 o'clock news. The official press conference. She's explaining the extreme changes—the fire's erratic movement toward the school and neighborhoods in the local proximity. She's announcing the fire as arson.

"Audrey," Hayden says, catching up to me. "Audrey, we need to get you help."

I think of Mom and Dad in the hotel bed. Did they go to sleep or are they still watching the news? Do they know we don't have a home? I think of Luis. Alone in that empty house, brokenhearted. Does Brooks's mom know? Is she watching the fire from Seattle? This morning, our hike, I should have told Grace. I should have told her then. Are she and Quinn swimming in the moonlit Pacific? I think of Maya, hopefully asleep so deeply, waiting to share a brownie with me.

And I think of Brooks. I see him sitting high up in a quaking aspen tree. He's flicking his Seattle-skyline Zippo. He's saying, *Let's go, let's go to Alaska. I love you. Don't you see?* I do. I see Brooks. On the beach, in the Audi, on the stones of the pebble garden. I see him heading off into the fire. I see him in Alaska, breathing frozen air, living on ice.

I only came to say goodbye.

I step into the lights. My legs tremble. My ears ring until the ringing is replaced with a dull hum of whispered chatter. I walk to the woman, the firefighter lieutenant speaking into the microphones. She sees me, stops talking, and starts again. She stutters at my approach. I feel the wind and the heat on my blistered skin. I stand beside her now. I'm nudging her aside. I'm in front of the microphones.

I'm here.

Did you know that silence has a feeling? The silence before words, your own words—that silence. I feel it, and I feel how all eyes are on me, waiting for me to speak. I still shake, but I'm not crying anymore. A sparkler lights in my chest. Burning, burning, burning.

I look into the pounding lights. "My name is Audrey Harper," I say, "and I know who started the Caspers Fire."

All at once, questions come from every direction.

"Are you hurt?"

"Are you okay?"

"Do you need help?"

The sparkler sizzles hotter, and I say, "Yes."

Acknowledgments

I wrote the first version of the novel that would eventually transform into *Nothing Left to Burn* when I was fourteen, and over the twelve years of both the novel's development and my own as a writer, I have received endless support. All of this is to say, prepare yourself for grand but genuine dramatics.

Thank you to my agent, Sarah Davies, who held a stethoscope to my manuscript and challenged me to clear out the muck and find its smothered beating heart. I'm utterly grateful for your fearlessness and your critical role in making my dream come true. Endless cups of tea lifted in gratitude. I feel ruthless with you at my side.

Thank you to my editor, Marissa Grossman. I sobbed after our first phone call and I sobbed when I read your first edit letter: no one has understood this novel and what I've attempted to do as much as you. Ben Schrank, thank you, thank you, thank you. To my cover designer, Corina Lupp, after all the ruckus I made, there is no way you don't already know how much I love this cover. Thanks to my publicist, Lizzie Goodell, my copyeditor, Ivan Anderson, and proofreaders, Krista Ahlberg and Samantha Hoback, and the entire team at Razorbill: you have made this dream-becoming-reality thing such a pleasure, and I firmly believe that there is no better home for this story than with you.

Maureen McHugh. You told me to take Audrey to the flames, to not flinch, and, within two weeks, the present of this novel didn't span six months but rather a single day, and Brooks—*boom*—he became a firefighter. I hope I did you proud. Peter Behrens, well, I can't say what you told me *exactly* because it'd spoil any reader who's skipped ahead, but when you dropped my manuscript on your desk and said, "I don't buy Brooks," you helped open the door that finally clicked him into place.

Steven Hayward, oy, how to say thank you? Because, dang, we worked together *a lot* from fiction to Shakespeare to general wonky life wisdom. Your mentorship made my experience (and my writing) at Colorado College all the richer.

Continuing the CC love: I owe so much to so many but most especially to Re Evitt, Jan Edwards, Tracy Santa, and my fellow 2014 fictioneers. Let's take another photo in front of a tree soon.

Elizabeth Law, who pulled at the weeds, and then at the story's largest invasive root that I'd overlooked for years, thank you so much.

I'm indebted to Stephenie Meyer for the guidance and support she offered when I was fourteen. I am not entirely sure how I convinced you to read the first book I ever wrote, but thank you for that and more.

Sending warmth to all of the friends I was lucky to have in Alaska and while on submission, who kept me alive during (literally) the darkest and sunniest days. August Johnson and Elle Fournier, thank you for keeping me so deliciously well fed and soothing me when I was at my worst. Those midnight chicken and waffles saved my life. Micah Allen, thanks for the pints and the madcap conversations, as well as your love. And thank you to Daryl Farmer, for being a pillar of support during my time at UAF.

Also up in the far reaches of Alaska, thank you to the composition students I had the pleasure of teaching while I was revising and on submission.

A million thank-yous and a million tacos to Rachel Lynn Solomon. You're the best guru a girl could ask for and now one of my dearest friends. It's a surreal honor to be debuting in 2018 with you.

Thank you to Leonardo C. Maniscalco, captain of the Escondido Fire Department (retired) for the generous, enlightening phone call and answering even my most off-the-wall questions with such kindness. I know I skewed some logistics and rules for the sake of story, especially when it comes to volunteer firefighters. Forgive me!

Thank you to the Orange County Fire Authority—particularly Station 18 (Trabuco Canyon), Station 14 (Silverado Canyon), and Station 40 (Coto de Caza). I hold the greatest level of respect and awe for you.

To every agent I queried from 2006 to 2013. Obviously all of you rejected me. Thank you for that. I'm serious. I was not ready, and every rejection only made me work harder until I was.

To those who read my many messy manuscripts over the past decade and pushed me to be a better person, particularly Christina Hayden (fight club in steakhouse bathrooms forever), Kady Weatherford, Bree Painter, Karli Golightly, Elle Cosimano, Tessa Elwood, Rachel Griffin, Fayie Nuss, Jessie McMullin, Shola Gordon, Erin Sullivan, John Konugres (you said you better get a shout-out for moving my one-hundred-pound desk back in 2010, but you're here for more reasons than that), Jamie Pang, Ali Abraham, Jane Humen, Kenny Skiba, Hannah Jornacion, Nikki Roberti, Anna Brittain, Sonia Hart, and so many more.

Regan Campbell, thank you for your immeasurable love, for your ridiculous Midwestern patience, for reminding me to take breaks, and for going along with my outrageous plan to drive a Mini Cooper round-trip from Southern California to Interior Alaska. Thank you for writing *burns cats???* on the Greuning conference room white board when I was on the floor, muttering about my horrific nightmare. Thank you for all of this and so, so much more.

To my late aunt Carol, who asked, "Why not?" when I hesitated on pursuing outlandish dreams.

My entire giant family tree from Utah to California and afar: I love you. I am so lucky.

A shout-out to my black lab, my pup, my baby, my brother's dog, Bellatrix. She already has a whole blog post to her name, so no need to elaborate.

To my parents—I'm baffled by how two people can be so supportive and carry such love. Neither one of you once questioned my writing but rather fanned the obsession. I love you.

Finally, to my siblings: Amber, Madeline, and Grant. I can't write too much because if I write too much I'll start crying and won't stop typing and I'll refuse to edit it down and then there will be no acknowledgments in this book. You guys put up with me when I was a camera-hogging child, a snarling teenager, and now a still very loud me. I've thrown fake trees at your friends, slammed doors, kidnapped the family dog, and somehow you still all treat me with unfathomable love. You three are my best friends and I'm the luckiest girl because of it.